A SILVER BELLES

Christmas

REBECCA SAMS WILLIS

For my mother, Linda, and my sister, Jacki,
two of the most adventurous, kind-hearted and generous
people I know.

I love you both to infinity.

A Note from the Author

Dear Friends,

With millions of books to choose from, I'm so honored that you chose my debut novel, "A Silver Belles Christmas." I absolutely loved creating the little town of Laurel Valley and its quirky, yet adorable characters. It was difficult to say goodby to them at the end, so there might be a sequel in the future! Please consider staying in touch by subscribing to my newsletter at www.RebeccaSamsWillis.com.

Hugs,

Rebecca

Chapter One

We need to talk about our relationship. Rachel Noelle read the text message from her boyfriend three more times. The words had followed a dinner invitation, and one thing her voracious appetite for romance novels taught her was this statement usually foreshadowed an impending breakup. Grant Kensington was never spontaneous, especially on a weeknight, and her mind was swimming with possible scenarios.

Rachel's eyes anxiously darted around the office as she deliberated her response, finally landing on the window adjacent to her desk. She could see the branches of the trees encased in a fine layer of ice waving gently in the wind. The rain tapped a soothing white noise against the glass, but did nothing to quell the angst brewing in her chest.

She stared at his words, hoping to gain some telepathic insight to their meaning. How could she give an appropriate response if she didn't know what his intentions were? Although they'd been spending less and less time together due to his new business, it just didn't seem plausible that he would suddenly call it quits.

Besides, plans were underway for her to move to St. Louis where he lived. Rachel wanted to open an art school for children, and he was the one to convince her that it would do better in a larger city. But doubt continued to cloud her brain as her fingers tapped out a quick reply.

Sounds good. Does six o'clock work? Flutters danced in her chest, matching the three dots bobbing on her screen.

Conference call at 3. I might run a little late. He ended the reply with a heart emoji. Her brow furrowed with confusion. No one would send a pre-breakup text ending with a heart emoji. A thought began wedging its way through the emotional flurry, and a burst of elation swept through her. He's going to propose!

Rachel's brain quickly switched gears and envisioned a romantic scene with Grant down on one knee, offering her a gigantic diamond ring. The thought wrapped around her like a warm hug, and she settled back into her chair with a relaxing sigh.

Although an enormous pile of file folders brimming with paperwork teetered on the edge of her desk, Grant's text had drained her motivation to work, so she decided to do a little reconnaissance online instead.

A quick internet search for wedding venues in St. Louis produced vibrant images of romantic settings. Inching farther to the edge of her seat, she gazed at the computer screen with her chin resting on one hand while the other scrolled through the list. An image of The Grand Hall in the St. Louis Union Station Hotel caught her attention, and she let out a small gasp at its mesmerizing beauty. Soaring, sixty-five-foot arched ceilings, gold leaf accents, art glass windows, and mosaics created an incredible canopy over the rows of tables adorned with silver vases overflowing with pink and cream-colored roses. It was the fairytale wedding venue she'd been dreaming of since childhood.

Her eyes cast down to the text on her phone, and she read the conversation again. Something about the urgency of his words continued to tug at the back of her mind, warning her to put the brakes on her excitement.

"Hey Rachel, can you come in here for a sec?" Judy Sullivan's perky voice rattled through the speaker, startling Rachel from her daydream. Without taking her eyes off the monitor, she reached for the intercom button to respond, sending the files crashing to the floor. Papers, sticky notes, and tiny phone messages fluttered in all directions. Frustrated the office still had not fully embraced the digital age, she groaned heavily then punched the intercom button.

"Sure! Give me two minutes," she said, hoping there were no hints of exasperation in her tone.

As Judy's personal assistant, Rachel had the pleasure of fielding irate clients demanding to speak with their lawyer to discuss the petty grumblings that could only happen in a small town. A particularly bothersome phone call from Mr. Merriweather had set a grim tone to Rachel's morning, mirroring the gloomy weather outside. He was sure the flashing twinkly lights surrounding the window of The Curio Shop were the reason he got distracted while driving to his hardware store, resulting in a minor fender bender. "Her gaudy Christmas display is a dad-gum safety hazard!" he'd shouted through the phone. He was now seeking restitution from the benevolent antique toy and collectible store owner, Ellen Perry.

After shoving thousands of papers into random folders, Rachel plopped the whole mess back onto her desk with an exaggerated sigh, then ducked around the corner to Judy's office. Judy was sitting at her desk studying a packet of legal-size papers through bright red, thick-rimmed glasses. An elegant bun held her ash-blond hair away from her face.

"This lawsuit Mr. Merriweather had me draw up is ridiculous," she said through gritted teeth. "When will that crazy old goat retire and move to Florida?"

Rachel stifled a laugh. Very few things could rattle Judy's even composure, and Mr. Merriweather, the town's most eccentric, albeit beloved, resident was one of them. For the most part, he was a kind and gentle old fellow, but occasionally he'd get a bee in his bonnet about something. There was no rest until the alleged issue was resolved, and unfortunately, the Sullivan Law Firm was number one on his speed dial.

"Are you ready for lunch? Reservation's in fifteen minutes," Rachel said, tapping her watch for emphasis.

Judy let out a deflated sigh. "Would you mind going without me?" she pleaded. "I'm right in the middle of this mess." She spread her arms across her desk, showcasing the jumble of files and legal pads like a game show hostess. Their weekly lunch meetings had become a pleasant escape from the grind of the office, giving them a chance to discuss Judy's client list uninterrupted. This time, Judy had invited her nephew, Tyler Patterson, to join them. He had moved to town two weeks ago with his father, and Rachel was looking forward to meeting their newest resident, although she secretly wondered why anyone would move to a sleepy town like Laurel Valley.

"Um," Rachel hesitated, feeling the lunch might be a bit awkward without Judy there, especially after receiving a cryptic text from Grant. "No problem," she finally replied, tugging her lips into an awkward smile.

"Great!" Judy began rummaging around her desk and found a stack of three yellow envelopes. "Could you also deliver a couple of things for me? The top one is for Tyler, and the other two are for Mrs. Perry and Mr. Merriweather."

"Sure, I'll deliver them after lunch."

"Thanks. And tell Tyler we're still on for dinner Wednesday night."

"You got it," Rachel replied, turning to leave.

"One more *tiny* thing," Judy said, catching Rachel's attention. A Cheshire Cat-like grin appeared on Judy's face that Rachel knew all too well. It was only produced when the task at hand was an unfavorable one. Rachel held her breath, awaiting the bomb to drop. Judy placed her hands palms down on her desk as if bracing herself for Rachel's reaction. "I need you to take over planning the Christmas Potluck."

Rachel blinked quickly, attempting to keep her nose from scrunching up. She would rather scrub the dumpsters behind the building than get involved with any holiday hoopla. Judy knew this about her and winced at the expression on Rachel's face.

"I know you're not into holiday stuff, and I wouldn't ask, but I've got this massive report I need to get done before the end of the year, and Mr. Merriweather's latest complaint has put me behind." She waved the packet of papers in the air. "It's literally killing me. I can't put another thing on my plate."

Rachel's eyes scanned the chaos on her boss's desk. Planning a Christmas potluck was going to be about as enjoyable as scraping off old wallpaper. December brought up bad memories and she did everything possible to dodge the holiday shenanigans altogether. But a personal plea from Judy was the one thing that could coax her from her protective cocoon.

"Okay," she said, trying to hide the reluctance in her voice. "I'll handle it."

"Thank you, thank you, thank you!" Judy pumped her fits in the air with exhilaration. "It'll help me out so much. Oh! I already asked Tyler if he could give you a hand, so it really won't be much work at all."

Rachel narrowed her eyes, slightly annoyed with Judy's presumptions.

"Well, I knew you'd give in if I begged," Judy said with a sheepish grin. "You two will get along great."

Rachel laughed and shook her head as she headed back to her desk. "I'm sure he'll be a big help," she shouted back with a hint of sarcasm. Her mood this morning had gone from bad to good and back to bad in a matter of fifteen minutes. She wasn't even planning to *attend* the potluck this year, much less plan the whole thing. Last year, the heat in the VFW building went out, and everyone struggled to hold on to their paper cups with fluffy mitten hands. The floor was a sticky mess by the end of the evening. The year before that, Shop Smart had a surplus of canned sweet potatoes, so they ran a big sale: buy one, get three free. This resulted in thirty-six variations of sweet potato pie at the potluck, and no one brought a main dish. Lesson learned. They now had a spreadsheet to keep track of who was bringing what.

Back at her desk, Rachel took a deep breath in an attempt to keep herself calm, then thrust her arms into her coat, pulled a woolen cap on her head, and headed out to meet Tyler. The frigid air was accompanied by a relentless drizzle of rain pecking at her face, so she decided to drive the three blocks to the restaurant. She eased into her little economy car and headed towards the north end of Laurel Valley. The late-night snow had turned to slush in the drizzle, making a rhythmic splattering sound against the undercarriage.

She approached a traffic light signifying the center of town and came to a halt, waiting for shoppers to cross her path. Quaint artisanal shops selling gourmet spices, hand-blown glass art, antiques, and delectable cupcakes dotted the drive along Main Street. This corner was the hub of downtown and had the most foot traffic.

Glitter & Gold, the local jewelry store, occupied the intersection's southwest corner. She had browsed through it recently, admiring engagement rings under the guise of having her watch repaired. The local coffeehouse, Valley Brews, occupied the upper left corner. Rachel could

7

almost smell the aromas of woodsy vanilla and orange zest beckoning the shoppers in for their mid-day caffeine fix. To her right was the infamous Curio Shop Mr. Merriweather had been up-in-arms about.

"Wow!" she said out loud, catching sight of Mrs. Perry's window display. Maybe Mr. Merriweather was right. The large glass window was framed in lighted garland and red velvet bows. This year, she had twice the multi-colored lights blinking to the beat of the Christmas music playing from a small speaker. Rachel laughed to herself. Mrs. Perry was known for going overboard during the holidays and even wore a different ugly sweater each day of December, but this display was a bit over the top, even for her.

From her car, Rachel could see the beautiful miniature Christmas village with illuminated Victorian buildings glistening in the window. A tiny green train made its way around the town, and a bittersweet memory flooded her mind's eye. She could still feel the warmth of her grandmother's hand wrapping around hers as they eagerly awaited the train to emerge from the tunnel, then squealed with joy as the plumes of steam escaped the engine. That night should have become one of her fondest childhood memories. Instead, it became one of her darkest.

A car horn startled her from her thoughts. The light had turned green, so she proceeded through the intersection, then continued to the next block towards her favorite restaurant. Housed in Laurel Valley's former Starstruck Theater, Sawyer's kept its theatrical heritage throughout the decor, blending modern elements with its former art déco design. The entrance displayed a beautiful, curved staircase leading to a balcony, now used for second-level seating. Old cinematic posters hung on the exposed brick walls.

Rachel knew Dave Sawyer, the owner, and after chatting briefly with him, he escorted her through the restaurant. A tiny hint of sunlight broke through the dark clouds and shone through the large, wavy glass windows, creating a kaleidoscope of color through the crystal glassware. They weaved between vintage marble-topped tables, each dressed with a delicate vase of fresh flowers, then stopped at a small table where a man sat looking down at the menu in his hands.

"Here we are," Dave said, pulling out a chair for her. As Tyler Patterson rose from his seat and extended his hand, Rachel's breath caught in her chest.

"Hey, Rachel, it's so nice to meet you."

Chapter Two

H is eyes were the first thing that struck her.
They were a warm, milk chocolate brown with
caramel-colored rings encircling the center, reminding her
of a chocolate sundae. His lips were parted in a friendly
smile, framing perfect white teeth, and his wavy dark
brown hair was slicked back and curled out at the ends,
giving him a casual yet polished appearance.

Surprised by his exceptional good looks, Rachel's
cheeks tingled as she raised her hand to shake his, gripping
it harder than she intended. "Hi, I'm Rachel," she said,
then gave herself a mental kick, realizing he already knew
her name. She shook her head and laughed. "I mean, it's
nice to meet you, too." He gave her a pardoning wink and
sat back down.

After shrugging out of her coat, she hung it on the back
of her chair, then slid the hat from her head. She glanced
at Tyler, whose eyes had become wide. She could tell he
was stifling a laugh, but he politely returned his eyes to
his menu. Rachel squinted at him, wondering what was
so funny. Looking back up at her, he took one hand and

smoothed down his hair, giving her the impression she should do the same. She slowly raised a hand to her head, trying to appear casual, then instantly felt her hair sticking out in all directions from the static electricity. Heat rushed to her cheeks, and she rolled her eyes with embarrassment, then hastily grabbed her menu.

The server approached the table with a pitcher of water and filled their glasses. Rachel's mouth had suddenly become dry as toast, and she downed half the glass in one long swig. "I'm sorry Judy couldn't join us for lunch today," she said apologetically. "We have a client who is a little uptight, and she needed to tie up some loose ends, but she asked me to tell you dinner is still on for Wednesday night."

"No problem. I'm glad to have the chance to meet you. Sounds like we'll be working on the Christmas potluck together." He flashed her an eager smile.

"Apparently," she said, trying to hide the apathy in her voice. "I can email you the spreadsheets Judy uses to keep track of everything. I don't think there's much to it. Just making sure the tables and chairs get set up, a little decorating, stuff like that."

"Sounds easy enough. Have you already found a tree?" he asked.

"Tree?" she repeated with confusion.

"The Christmas tree for the potluck. The tree is the star of the show," he replied emphatically. "Did you get it yet?"

"Oh," she said, feeling a little foolish. "No, but I'm sure it's on the spreadsheet."

"Good." He leaned back in his chair and rubbed his

hands together. "I love picking out Christmas trees."

"Perfect." Rachel wasn't interested in doing it, so this was going to work out better than she thought. She could keep an eye on the spreadsheet, and he can do the dreaded Christmassy tasks.

After skimming the menu, they both decided on the bourbon pecan crusted chicken, a local favorite. The server brought a silver basket of warm, seedy bread to the table then took their orders.

"How are things at the ranch? Are you getting settled in?" Rachel asked, digging a knife into a pat of butter.

Tyler nodded. "Still unpacking, but it's getting there. The farmhouse is actually in great shape for being vacant so many years. The old stove is on the fritz, but other than that, it's mostly cosmetics." He paused in thought. "Well, actually, there is one major problem..." Tyler hesitated as tiny lines formed between his eyebrows, and his smile morphed into a grimace. Rachel's mind raced with worry, imagining termite-infested walls and shotty electrical wiring. "There's a giant owl living in the attic, and I need to have it removed." His hands clenched as he spoke, and his shoulders gave a shudder.

She laughed at his disdain for a simple barn owl. It wasn't like he'd found a twenty-foot python up there. "Are you afraid of it?"

Tyler's back straightened in an attempt to attest to his masculinity. "Well, afraid is a strong word. More like hyper-aware of its presence." Rachel continued to smile teasingly, and he finally conceded. "Okay, I'm a little freaked out at night when I'm trying to sleep, and I hear scratching noises above me." He spread out his arms in a how-can-you-blame-me gesture, then leaned back in towards her. "It thinks I'm invading ITS territory." His eyes grew wide, and his voice had a serious tone. Rachel's smile didn't budge. "He flew right at me when I went up there last weekend," Tyler explained, trying to convince her of the imminent danger. " I almost fell backward down the stairs!" he added for further justification.

She envisioned the chaotic scene and couldn't hold back her laughter. Living in the country her entire life, Rachel was used to wildlife taking up residency in unusual places. Realizing the creature was genuinely troubling him, she replaced her playful tone with the softness of sympathy. "Well, don't worry. My friend Nick is an excellent trapper. He can get it out of there and find it a new home in the woods around your house."

"That would be a big help." Tyler's brow relaxed a bit at this, and the sparkle returned to his eyes. "Judy said the attic is full of antiques. I'd love to see them, but I haven't gone up there since."

"Oh, that reminds me." Rachel reached for her bag and retrieved a large envelope marked with Tyler's name in black print lettering. "Judy asked me to give you this." She passed it across the table to him. "I think these are the documents you need to sign. She talked to the zoning department at City Hall this morning and put the wheels in motion to get the property rezoned for multi-use. It should only take a couple of weeks for everything to be finalized." She watched as he carefully slid the papers from the envelope and examined them. A tiny smile formed on his lips. She knew what this would mean for him. Judy had filled her in on his plans, and Rachel couldn't be happier that he was taking on this new venture. "What's your vision for the ranch?" she asked, hoping to get more details.

"Well," he began. "Restoration is the most important thing to me. I want it to be the way it was when my mother lived there. Judy said there were small, one-room cabins along the west side of the lake...a fish camp. I haven't seen them yet, but she said they are pretty dilapidated, so I'm going to rebuild them. They will produce a good portion of my income." He paused to chew another bite of the delicious bread. "The orchards need some work, but once they're cleaned up, I'm planning to let visitors pick apples, maybe even add a storefront out by the road to sell products I make on site."

"Sounds like a great life in the country! Those trees are beautiful when they're in bloom," Rachel said, remembering rows and rows of branches covered in pink and white blossoms.

"Yeah, I remember walking through the orchard in the spring when I was little. It's gorgeous, like being in heaven," Tyler agreed.

Rachel nodded in dreaminess, remembering herself laying on her back, staring up at the tree branches against a bright blue sky while delicate blossoms fluttered around her from an afternoon breeze.

The clanking of a fork being dropped jarred her back to the restaurant. Realizing she'd slipped into a daydream, she glanced at Tyler, whose half-smile revealed he noticed she'd become distant. A little embarrassed, she let out a small laugh then tried to focus back on their conversation. "You know, when I was a teenager, I helped take care of your grandma's horses during the summer. Probably the best job I ever had."

"Really?" he asked, an amused smile appearing on his lips.

"Sure. Those summers at the ranch were amazing. She had two mares, Holly and Jolly. I'd go out every morning and muck the stalls, fill their buckets with feed and water, brush their coats. I loved every minute of it."

"Holly and Jolly... I remember them! They were Christmas gifts to my mom and Aunt Judy when they were kids."

"Yes, Judy told me that." Her mind reminisced about the time she spent at the ranch. She loved those horses and dreaded every fall when school started. "Are you planning to get any horses out there?" she asked hopefully.

"I thought about it," he hesitated. "Only I don't know much about taking care of a horse. You think you could give me some lessons?" He shot her a smile that filled her with anticipation.

"I'd love to!" She clasped her hands together, thrilled at the chance to be hanging around the ranch again, but a hint of disappointment festered inside her. She'd be moving away soon and wouldn't have much time getting to know his horses. Shaking the feeling away, she said, "You might already know this, but I think your farmhouse is the oldest house in Laurel Valley."

"I believe you're right. I've been doing some research on

the architecture." He leaned in, his hands becoming more animated as he spoke. "My great-great-grandfather built it in 1912 out of a kit he ordered from a Sears Roebuck catalog. He paid under $1800 for the entire house. Can you believe that? I found the original plans in a closet."

"That's incredible!" Rachel said, studying his features and noting the tiny wrinkles in his brow when his eyes filled with excitement. She had to admit Judy was right. He was adorable! "Did you ever live in Laurel Valley before now?"

"Yep, I was born here, but my dad got a job offer out of state when I was in second grade, so we had to move right after Christmas."

"What year was that?" she asked curiously.

Tyler glanced up in thought. "Two-thousand-five, I think."

Rachel tapped her upper lip with a finger, doing some quick mental math. "We were in the same grade," she said. After a pause, she squinted, trying to think, repeating his name out loud a few times. Her eyes widened. "I remember you..." She pointed a finger at him. "You were really shy and sat in the back next to the windows. And you had a red and blue Spiderman lunchbox." She snapped her fingers, impressed with herself for this vivid recollection.

Tyler chuckled. "You have a sharp memory. I tried so hard to be invisible in that class, and you noticed me anyway," he remarked, looking intently into her eyes. He held her gaze for a moment, and a current of attraction rippled between them, making her a bit uncomfortable.

"I guess I did," she said, shrugging her shoulders.

Rachel grabbed her napkin, clumsily unfolding it to place in her lap while trying to conjure up the memory of the beautiful fountain that appeared on her screen this morning. She needed to get Judy's "adorable" description out of her head. Grasping her water glass, she suppressed the urge to press it against her cheek and took a long, cooling drink instead.

"So, what do you do for fun here in Laurel Valley?" Tyler asked. "Hog tying? Play in a jug band?" His artificial southern drawl took her by surprise, making her laugh with an explosive spray of water escaping her lips, misting his shirt.

"Oh my gosh! I'm so sorry!" she said, attempting to stifle her laughter, which only worsened the dribbles down her chin. As she stood to hand him her napkin, she bumped the table, causing both their water glasses to tumble over and spill onto the tablecloth. Tyler jumped out of his seat to avoid a wet lap, and their eyes met for a split second before they both burst into laughter, scrambling for napkins. Once the mess was under control, they glanced around the room and noticed the eyes of the other patrons on them, apparently perturbed at their disruptive outburst.

"Sorry," Tyler said apologetically to their audience.

"So, so sorry," Rachel echoed as she regained her composure and slowly sat back down. "To answer your question," she began, squelching the giggle inside her. "I'm a big fan of the theater, but unfortunately, we happen to be dining in the only one Laurel Valley had; closed down about ten years ago. So now I attend the theater in St. Louis...with my boyfriend, Grant." She added this to avoid any misunderstandings about her relationship status. His head slightly nodded, but he held her gaze and said nothing. "When I'm not working at the law firm, I make pottery that I sell on my website. And I run a free art class for kids on Saturdays. I'm planning to open an art school for children in St. Louis soon."

"Really? St. Louis." She noticed his smile falter slightly. "That's great. How much longer will we have the honor of your presence here in Laurel Valley?" he teased.

"That's still a little up in the air. Grant found a beautiful spot and put in an offer. There are some inspections and financing contingencies to get through. I'll know for sure by Christmas." It all seemed surreal to her, moving away from her hometown. A year ago, she'd planned to open a school here in Laurel Valley, but her relationship with Grant had progressed quickly, and the plans were redirected to St. Louis.

"I see," Tyler said. "Wow, that's in just two weeks." There was an air of disappointment in his tone, and she felt a hint of it as well. Tyler was an interesting person, and if she wasn't moving, she would have liked to get to know him better. There was an easy-going vibe surrounding him, mirroring the country lifestyle she'd seen in the residents of Laurel Valley. Even though he'd been away for over twenty years, he seemed to fit right back in as if no time had passed. "Tell me about your school. What kind of art will you teach?"

"Right now, I have a small class of eight kids on Saturday mornings. We are doing ceramics this month, then I'll focus on drawing and painting. I have to keep the class size small because of the room I'm using at the community center. It's really tiny. But once I find a permanent spot, I'll be able to expand the number of classes and teach full-time."

"What's the space in St. Louis like?" he asked.

"I haven't seen it in person yet, but Grant sent me some pictures." She pulled out her phone and swiped through several images for him. The room on the screen was brightly lit by two large arched glass windows. The walls were a medium gray, and track lighting zig-zagged across the ceiling, reflecting down onto the tobacco-colored wood floors. "I can fit at least six large tables in there, enough to hold 24 students per class."

"It's a beautiful space. I'm really excited for you." His warm smile conveyed genuine happiness.

"Thank you," she replied, tucking her phone back into her purse. "So, what made you want to return to Laurel Valley?" she asked. "Our world-renowned corn hole competition next month or the chili cookoff in February?" she said with a teasing wink.

Tyler returned her cheeky tone with a grin but hesitated a moment before speaking, and she waited for a witty comeback.

"Not exactly," he said, darting his eyes away from her and fiddling with the silverware nestled beside his plate. "My mother passed away two years ago," he said solemnly. "This was her hometown. She grew up on the ranch, and I moved back to feel closer to her."

His statement was jarring to their previous

light-hearted conversation. Rachel was unable to speak for a moment, then belatedly remembered Judy taking a leave from the practice for two weeks after her sister, Gwen, had passed away. Unfortunately, Rachel hadn't put two and two together until this moment, and regret was sitting on her chest, heavy as a cement block.

"I'm... so sorry," she stammered, averting her eyes. Tyler's words pulled at her heartstrings, bringing up feelings about the close relationship she missed with her own mother. She met his eyes and could see the remnants of pain behind them.

"I appreciate that." He took a sip from his water, and the broad smile returned to his face. "I've got a steep learning curve ahead of me, but I'll be the fifth generation to live at the ranch," he said, attempting to brighten the conversation.

"That's amazing," she replied, still trying to regain her composure and move on from the shock of his revelation. The server returned with their food, and they discussed the rehabilitation of the farmhouse. As Rachel listened, she considered his reason for returning to Laurel Valley. His mother had grown up here, and living out on the ranch brought him closer to her, closer to his roots. He was embracing his past, and in contrast, Rachel hoped to move away from hers, feeling as if her roots were holding her back. She wanted a fresh start, growing in a new city with new people.

"How did the house look to you? Was there much of the original design left?" she asked.

"Yes, most of it is original. I think an extra bathroom

was added in the fifties. Everything is bright pink!" They both laughed at this, and Rachel imagined him brushing his teeth at a sink the color of an antacid. "Even my mother's old room was left just as when she left for college. I saw ribbons she won horseback riding and pictures of her and her friends when they were young. Her favorite stuffed animals were still on the bed."

Rachel felt her grumpy mood melt away as she listened to him talk about his explorations of the farmhouse. She'd been to the ranch multiple times as a girl but had never been inside the house. She was fascinated to hear him describe the historical artifacts he'd found tucked away in closets and cupboards, even a narrow staircase hidden behind a wall. The enthusiasm she saw in his eyes was heartwarming. He was obviously excited about his new venture, yet the insecurity and stress didn't appear to faze him. He had a mild confidence about him that came off as laid-back yet strong and determined.

She wasn't used to seeing this level of openness in a man. It was a stark contrast to Grant's stoic, reserved personality. When she'd met him, Grant was utterly different from anyone she'd known. He had a take-charge personality that drew her in. She knew whatever goals he'd set for himself, whatever plans he made for his future, would always spell success. He was all big city, from his ultra-modern decor style to his high energy and drive for winning. Not a speck of country in him. Since they'd been dating, the country had been seeping out of her as well, but she hadn't noticed until now as she sat with Tyler.

Although Grant seemed to have it all, there was one

thing missing...the feeling of home when she was with him. Her sister, Brianna, had assured her there was nothing to worry about. Home is where you hang your hat, and once she was settled in St. Louis, Rachel assumed that feeling would come.

As if reading her thoughts, Tyler said, "I'm just amazed at how quickly Laurel Valley feels like home again." Warmth emanated from his eyes. "I bet it'll be hard for you to leave."

She studied his face as he stared back at her. It was a kind face, full of compassion and optimism. "Yes...it will be very hard," she replied honestly.

Chapter Three

L unch with Tyler turned out to be quite enjoyable despite the way Rachel's morning had started. Laurel Valley had lost some of its vitality over the years, and she was happy they were getting a new resident to breathe some life back into the community.

"Judy asked me to deliver some paperwork in town," Rachel said as she and Tyler headed toward the restaurant exit. "But I'll email you all the information I've got for the potluck."

"Would you mind if I tag along?" Tyler asked. "I need to run into the hardware store, and I haven't had a chance to explore downtown since I arrived."

A hint of hesitation crept through her brain as she wondered if spending casual time with Tyler would give him the wrong impression, but she knew Judy would appreciate the extra extension of kindness. "Of course," she replied, hoping he didn't notice her indecisiveness. "I can introduce you to two of my favorite shop owners. We'll start with Mrs. Perry."

A flash of winter wind startled her as they stepped

outside and headed down the sidewalk, but she resisted the urge to pull her hat back on, fearing another wild hair scene. As they approached the lively strobing of twinkle lights surrounding the outside window dressing of The Curio Shop, Rachel glanced over at Tyler and noted the amusement reflecting in his eyes. She smiled to herself, knowing it served only as a small hint of the Christmas extravaganza happening inside. They were greeted by a life-size Santa Claus, standing sentry directly in front of them. Activated by a motion sensor, he shouted, "HO! HO! HO! MERRY CHRISTMAS!"

Delight sprang to Tyler's face. "That's awesome!" he exclaimed. His eyes scanned the shop, taking in the spectacular show. Twinkle lights lined every display cabinet, and swags of lighted garland crisscrossed the ceiling. Large, colorful ornaments hung from each bend in the greenery, and there was a hint of evergreen pine in the air.

A faint train whistle grabbed their attention, and Tyler headed toward the front window to investigate. "I remember seeing this when I was a kid," he said over his shoulder. "The train was my favorite part." Rachel joined him, and their eyes followed the little train as it passed the miniature Victorian houses, then disappeared into the dark tunnel running through hills wrapped in white, cotton batting.

"Mine too," she said softly. Its headlight shone brightly, lighting up the cave walls as it exited through the other side, and a tiny puff of steam rose into the air. "I remember when Mrs. Perry added the train to the display for the first time. It was a big to-do," she said.

"I was here that night, too," he remarked, smiling at her. "We were all standing outside, kids in front, right up against the dark window holding mugs of hot chocolate."

Rachel gave a small laugh. "And we all counted down THREE! TWO! ONE! Then she flipped a switch, and the entire village lit up!" The excitement she felt that night sparked again at the memory. To think they might have been standing right next to each other.

Mrs. Perry came from around the counter to greet them. Tiny ornaments bobbed from her earlobes, and a strand of glowing Christmas tree lights encircled her neck. Her brightly colored sweater had an image of Santa flying over a rooftop with Rudolf at the helm, and a fluffy red pom-pom represented his nose. Sequin shingles glimmered on the roof of the house as the cheerful store owner approached them.

"Hey, what a great ugly sweater!" Tyler said, pointing at her.

"Ugly sweater?" Mrs. Perry asked with a hint of hurt in her voice.

"Um, I mean..." he stammered, his face red as Rudolph's nose. Rachel placed a hand over her mouth to stifle a giggle.

"I'm just pullin' your leg, honey!" Mrs. Perry said, chuckling. Tyler blew out a sigh of relief.

"Mrs. Perry, this is Tyler Patterson, Judy's nephew," Rachel interjected.

"Oh yes, Tyler!" she exclaimed. "I remember when you were just a little boy." She held a hand waist high to show

27

them how tall he was the last time she'd seen him. "How's that old farmhouse? Are you staying warm?" she asked.

"Yes ma'am. It's wonderful to be back," he replied.

"Judy asked me to give this to you," Rachel said, retrieving the yellow envelope from her purse and passing it to her.

"Oh, that cranky old Mr. Merriweather is at it again!" Mrs. Perry quipped as if the lawsuit was nothing more than a library fine. "Give it a week, and he'll have forgotten all about it!" Two customers approached the counter, waiting for her to ring up their treasures. "You all have a look around if you want. Let me know if I can help you with anything." She headed towards the counter, leaving the scent of toasted marshmallow in her wake.

Tyler followed Rachel as she headed down an aisle. Stopping at a display of antique dolls, she picked one up to examine it. The top of the head was painted light brown, with swirly waves molded into the surface to mimic hair. Faded pink lips were formed into an open smile, revealing tiny teeth inside the mouth. When Rachel leaned it back, the rusty eyes closed as if it were going to sleep.

"That's so creepy!" Tyler whispered. She giggled and floated the doll towards him like a ghost. Tyler recoiled, feigning terror. Rachel let out a cackle and quickly placed it back on the shelf, then continued down the aisle, picking up items to examine as she walked.

"So, what's it like to be the owner of the biggest ranch in Laurel Valley?" she asked, hoping she didn't sound crass.

"It's not entirely mine just yet. After my grandfather passed away, my Grandma Polly lived there for several years but her health started failing. She was moved into a nursing home and the ranch was put into an estate." He picked through a box of old pocket watches, then moved further down the aisle. "Since my mom has passed, Judy and I are the beneficiaries, and she doesn't have any children, so she's going to deed her portion of it to me once it's in her name."

"Wow, quite a gift," Rachel said.

"I agree. That's why restoring it is so important to me. I want to keep everything as original as possible. Maybe get it on the National Register eventually."

"That'd be great. Our librarian could probably help you research that." Rachel smiled at him. He seemed to be in his essence here, and she wondered if moving away as a child had been difficult for him. Her mind drifted to her plans to move away with Grant. She would miss this town dearly but was excited to experience new places and people. She felt like her whole life was on display here and couldn't wait to finally have some privacy.

A group of three rosy-cheeked patrons crowded into the toasty store, and Rachel motioned towards the door, signaling to Tyler she was ready to leave. After waving goodbye to Mrs. Perry, they made their exit and headed down the sidewalk.

"Mrs. Perry seems like a real-life Mrs. Claus!" Tyler chuckled.

"I know. She's over the top when it comes to the holidays, but don't let the angelic face and ugly sweater fool you. She's a pretty sharp businesswoman and owns several commercial properties around town."

"Really? Good to know. My dad wants to open a diner here. I'll have him reach out to her."

"People around here love home cooking. I'm sure he'd get a lot of business."

Passing the shops, Tyler grew thoughtful. "How come the stores aren't decorated for Christmas? Other than The Curio Shop, you wouldn't even know it was December around here."

Rachel cast her eyes around at the street scene. He was right. The town didn't seem very festive. The streets were clean, and the buildings and sidewalks were in good repair, so it most likely wasn't a city budget issue. "Maybe Mrs. Perry's window is enough for the whole town," she said in jest.

Tyler's voice was full of sincerity. "Before we moved away, I remember lots of lights on all the tree branches down the center of Main Street, and every store had decorations in the windows and wreaths on the doors. There was a gigantic Christmas tree in the park next to the gazebo, too. My mother used to love coming downtown to see the display. Some of my best memories are with her down here at Christmas. I wonder why they don't do that anymore."

Rachel shrugged as if it was not something she had ever thought about. She was grateful the town didn't go overboard. "Maybe Judy would know," she suggested.

"What about you? How long have you lived in Laurel Valley?" His breath swirled upward in the cold as he spoke.

"We moved here the same year Mrs. Perry put the train out for the first time. Come to think of it, I do remember the town being more festive that year. But I haven't seen it like that since..." Her voice trailed off as she thought back to that night. She squeezed her eyes closed to shut out the memory. Tyler didn't seem to notice her discomfort.

"I'm so glad to be back. There's nothing I like more than wide open spaces. The farmhouse has a huge back porch that overlooks the lake. It's gorgeous at sunset." He paused, as if realizing he'd been yammering on. "Do you think you'll miss the quietness of the country when you move away?"

"Doubtful. I've lived here almost my entire life. I want to experience the excitement of a fast-paced city for a change. Something completely different from Laurel Valley."

Tyler nodded. "St. Louis is definitely different from Laurel Valley."

They walked a few more paces as Rachel considered his statement. There was so much she was looking forward to experiencing in a new environment, yet a part of her wondered if she was doing the right thing. She hoped the change would be a blossoming of her spirit and not some rude awakening.

"What does Grant do in St. Louis?" Tyler asked.

"He started a financial planning firm a few years ago. Doing quite well."

"Wow, high finance! That's great." He paused momentarily, then added, "You think you'll marry him?"

Rachel grinned at his forwardness. "It hasn't been discussed," she replied. "He's very busy with work, trying to build his business, so we don't get to see each other as often as we'd like." Thinking this might put Grant in an unattractive light, she added, "He's a great person, though. He would do anything for me. And we are similar in a lot of ways, share similar values, so overall, I think he's a good fit for me."

"A good fit," Tyler echoed. "You sound like you're choosing a reliable car."

She laughed at his comparison but admitted that her statements might seem too calculated. "I know how it sounds, but he's a good, trustworthy guy. I can count on him no matter what. Plus, he makes me strive for bigger things and stretch my boundaries. I'd like to meet people who weren't around when I lost my first tooth, you know what I mean?"

"Fair enough," Tyler conceded. They walked in silence for a moment as he processed the information. A chilly wind swirled around their legs and under their coats, urging them to step up their pace.

"Mr. Merriweather owns the hardware store," she said, pointing across the street. "We can go there next."

They scurried through the intersection and headed towards a bright blue awning that read "Merriweather's Hardware Heaven." Tyler chuckled as he said the name.

"What's so funny?" Rachel asked, not seeing the humor.

"All the shops have really cute names. I'm just not used to it. We had mostly chain stores where I lived. They drove all the mom-and-pops out of business. I don't see any big conglomerate storefronts here. It's a nice change."

She hadn't thought about it before, but Tyler's

observation made a good point. Across the country, independent business owners were being taken over or driven out of small towns. They were the unfortunate casualty of progress. Laurel Valley had managed to dodge these changes. The downtown shops were all privately owned, each with a distinctive personality. This Mayberry-like feel was what Tyler loved about it. Unfortunately, this characteristic was the very thing that was driving Rachel away.

A loud buzzer announced their arrival as they pushed through the swinging glass door of the hardware store. Tyler scanned the interior, his eyes growing wide with awe. The shelves were stocked with military-style clothing, survival kits with dehydrated food, and assorted helmets with matching bullet-proof vests, among the usual paint cans and screwdrivers normally found in a hardware store. A mannequin was posing in the corner, modeling the latest gas mask couture.

Mr. Merriweather reached their side in three long strides and gave them an official salute. Rachel was, of course, used to his quirky behavior and dutifully saluted him back in lieu of a hug or even a handshake. She could tell by the bewildered look on Tyler's face he didn't know what to make of him. The townspeople were used to his eccentricities, and nothing surprised them, but Rachel could see why this behavior might be a shock to Tyler and regretted not preparing him better.

Tyler's mouth hung slightly open as he took in the strange man standing before him. Mr. Merriweather's attire was a mish-mosh of Gomer Pyle meets Florida tourist. His olive green, military tunic covered the upper half of his plaid, pink and baby blue Bermuda shorts. Calf-high socks and brown Birkenstocks with shining buckles completed the ensemble. His silver flattop sat upon his head like a stiff upholstery brush and came to a little V-shaped peak on his forehead, A long white beard hung from his chin, coming to a point at the end, matching the one on his head.

Tyler finally gave him an awkward salute as Rachel fought back a laugh.

"At ease, soldier," Mr. Merriweather said. Tyler lowered his arm and slumped his shoulders exaggeratedly. Mr. Merriweather looked him up and down, considered his demeanor, then decided he was good folk. "What can I do for you two?"

"Hello, Mr. Merriweather," Rachel said. "Judy asked me to give you this paperwork."

"Ah! The next mission." He grasped the envelope and clung to it like he'd been given a map to the Holy Grail. His eyes glazed over as he pried open the flap and examined the paperwork, seemingly oblivious to the two of them standing there.

Rachel eyed him, taking in his wardrobe choice, and noticed his bare knees. "Mr. Merriweather, did you go out in the snow dressed like that?" His sister, Maple, usually gave him a once-over and caught him before he left the house if he wasn't appropriately dressed, but he must have slipped by her today.

"Of course not! I've got my galoshes in the back," he said, thumbing towards the stockroom.

Rachel took him by the arm and ushered him over to a rack of camouflage hunting outfits. "You know, I bet you'd increase your sales if you wore a pair of these camo pants to and from the store; it's free advertising."

"You think so?" he said, intrigued.

"Sure," Tyler chimed in, seeing where she was going with this. "Everyone would see you and want to get some, too. Could bring in some extra revenue."

Mr. Merriweather nodded slowly, appearing impressed by their business knowledge.

Tyler began flipping through the pants hanging on the rack until he found a pair that might fit. "You should probably wear them around the store, too."

"Good idea," Mr. Merriweather agreed, kicking off his sandals and slipping the pants on over his shorts. "I didn't catch your name, son."

"It's Tyler Patterson. I'm Polly Harrison's grandson."

"Pleasure to meet you, soldier." He stepped back away from them and held out his arms. "Well, what do ya think?"

"Fabulous!" Rachel said, and he beamed with the compliment. With another look, she noticed he'd tucked in the front of his jacket, leaving the back hanging out. She giggled at his inadvertent use of the latest fashion trend, the French tuck.

Tyler gave a quick snap of his fingers. "I almost forgot what I came in here for. I need a Phillips screwdriver, a roll of plumber's tape, and some window caulk." He ticked off each item on his fingers.

"You got it." They followed Mr. Merriweather around

the store as he gathered the items, then rang them up on an ancient cash register. A nostalgic chime echoed in the shop when the cash drawer opened.

"Thanks very much, and nice meeting you, sir," Tyler said as he reached for his bag.

"Dismissed!" Mr. Merriweather shouted. They turned back and waved goodbye as they headed out the door.

The sun had ducked behind the dark clouds once again, and the temperature took a nosedive. Fearing the drizzly rain would return, they decided to call it a day. Rachel pulled her hat over her ears as they began walking toward the restaurant.

"What did you think of Mr. Merriweather?" Rachel asked, amused.

Tyler laughed and shook his head. "He's quite a character. Which branch of the military was he in?"

"Oh, he's never actually been in the military, but to hear him speak, you would think he'd fought on the front line of every battle since the signing of the Constitution. He's extremely patriotic and has an enormous heart. Drives a big van around picking up the veterans who don't have transportation and brings them to doctors' appointments at the VA Hospital in St. Louis."

"That's really awesome," Tyler said.

"We have a lot of kind residents here. Patty Stevens owns the bakery," she said, pointing up ahead. "She bakes about a hundred cookies every week and sends them up to the hospital with him."

She felt Tyler's eyes on her. "You seem to know the residents here like they are family," he observed.

She allowed his statement to brew in her head for a moment. She never realized how close she was to them and had never thought of them as family until he pointed it out. "I guess they are, in a way. After my parents divorced, my mother worked full-time with Mrs. Perry. My sister and I grew up running around town, and the shop owners kept an eye on us. My mom was offered a partnership in a bed and breakfast in California about five years ago. Kind of a dream job for her." Rachel was so proud of her mom for following that dream, even if it took her far away. "She moved, and we stayed here to finish college."

It had been a comfort to have the familiarity of the townspeople around her, drying her tears after a breakup with a boyfriend and cheering her on when she completed her degree. An unfamiliar twinge of anxiety crept into her chest. All the love and support she received from them would be gone once she moved away. She hadn't ever considered how they would feel about her leaving. Maybe they would miss her more than she realized.

They arrived back at the restaurant and stood next to Rachel's car. "Well, it was nice meeting you today," she said, offering her hand.

He grasped it for a split second before giving it a gentle shake, sending goosebumps up her arm. "It was nice to meet you, too. Thanks for letting me tag along!" he grinned.

She unlocked her car and ducked inside. "I'll send that spreadsheet to you when I get into the office tomorrow morning. The potluck is in less than two weeks, so we should meet at the VFW soon to get it decorated."

"Sure, just let me know what works for you. Oh, wait," he said as she was closing the car door.

She stopped and looked up at him. His eyes grew concerned, and the crease between his brows returned.

"When do you think Nick would be able to come out and take care of my owl problem?" His weight shifted from side to side, and he held his hands clasped in front of his chest.

She grinned. "I can probably get him over there early tomorrow morning. Wouldn't want you to lose any more sleep worrying about getting attacked."

Tyler let out a sigh of relief. "Okay, perfect. I appreciate it."

"We'll get that stove fixed for you, too." Rachel gave him a wink, then pulled the door closed. As she left the parking lot, she saw him getting into an ancient pickup truck. *Yep! He fits right in here*, she thought.

Chapter Four

R achel pulled the curtain back from the front window to peer outside for the fourth time, hoping to see Grant's BMW pulling into the driveway. She watched as the moon emerged from a veil of clouds, illuminating her view, but the only movements were from the trees casting shadows across the snow-covered front yard.

Her cat, Willow, sat on the back of the couch, licking a front paw and swishing her tail. After patting Willow's head, she readjusted the throw pillows and then plopped down against them. Willow made her way down and nestled onto Rachel's lap for more petting just as her phone buzzed with an incoming text from her mother, Charlotte.

Hope you are staying warm. I miss you! xoxo

Warmth spread in Rachel's heart. Lunch with Tyler made her realize how lucky she was to know her mother was only a phone call away, and his loss resonated even more with her at this moment. She typed a quick reply. *I am. And I miss you too! xoxo*

Thirty-five minutes passed, and there was no sign of Grant. She heaved a sigh as a recent comment from her mother, accusing Grant of being a workaholic, echoed through her brain. He'd buried himself even deeper in his work lately, and Rachel had hardly seen him at all in recent weeks. But she hoped things would eventually level out, and they'd have more time together.

She reached a hand to her neck and touched the diamond solitaire necklace he'd gotten her on their six-month anniversary. She was overwhelmed and had never received a gift this beautiful. For her birthday, Grant had ruby earrings delivered to her office since he was in Boston at a conference. Roses were constantly being delivered to her desk, usually after he had canceled a dinner date. She knew he was trying, but she really wanted the one thing he couldn't seem to give her... his time.

Willow gave a loud meow, proclaiming it was dinnertime. Rachel stroked her velvet ears and scratched under her chin. "I know you are hungry. I am, too!" As she stood, her phone chirped with a message from Grant.

Hey Rach, so sorry I'm running late. I'll be there in 45 minutes.

A flash of excitement shot through her. In just 45 minutes, her life would take a new direction. Images of the dream wedding she had been conjuring up floated through her mind like iridescent bubbles, causing a tiny giggle to escape her lips.

She tapped out a response as she headed towards the kitchen, her feet light as air with anticipation. *No worries. I'm starving, so I'll just make something, then warm it up for you when you get here.* She added a yellow smiley-face emoji and hit send. After pouring kitty kibble into a dish for Willow, she thumbed through an old, love-worn recipe book her mother had left behind and decided on grilled cheese and her grandma's tomato bisque recipe.

Standing over the stove, Rachel added ingredients to a large pot prepared with olive oil. Aromas of tangy garlic and caramelized onion began filling the kitchen. As she loaded the food processor onto the counter, Willow scampered under the small worktable, knowing a racket was about to ensue. Bright red tomatoes whirled around the blades, creating a beautiful puree. She added this to the pot, along with some heavy cream, then covered it with a lid to simmer.

"Let's go lounge on the couch," she said to Willow, who obediently followed her to the living room. She regarded the snow resting on the thin strips of wood dividing the window panes, and a chill ran up the back of her neck. She grabbed an afghan her grandmother had made off the chair and snuggled into the overstuffed couch, then let her eyes drift lazily around the room. It was cozy and warm, with walls the color of soft peach and white curtains framing the windows. Most of the decor was in neutral base colors, with hints of crimson, amber, and Kelly green sprinkled throughout the accent pillows for a bit of excitement. The oak floors were a golden amber, showing decades of wear and tear, which only made them more beautiful. An antique, threadbare oriental rug anchored the other colors. It was a housewarming gift from Mrs. Perry when her sister, Brianna, had gotten married and moved out, leaving Rachel to make the cottage her own. Floor-to-ceiling bookcases were filled with colorful spines of her favorite reads, in addition to various pots and vases she'd made in her make-shift pottery studio she set up on her back porch. She remembered how bare the wall had seemed until Mr. Merriweather surprised her with these shelves he had built himself.

Her gaze rested on a framed watercolor painting of a small white cottage surrounded by a colorful garden. Painted by her grandmother, the soft colors had inspired the palette for the room, and it was one of her favorite possessions.

Rachel rolled onto her back and began clicking through Pinterest, trying to get a few ideas for the potluck, and maybe a few for a summer wedding. Willow climbed onto her chest and settled in, waiting to have her ears scratched. Rachel typed in a search for "potluck decor," then scrolled through pictures of festive table decorations, lights strung throughout rooms, and events for children she could incorporate into the dinner. Although Mr. Merriweather had graciously donated the event space for the Christmas potluck, the VFW wasn't very festive. It would take a lot of work to get it presentable. Maybe Tyler would have some good ideas.

His face flashed before her. That tall, dark, and handsome guy was not at all what she had expected, and neither was the connection they seemed to have. Aside from spending a brief time together as children, they hardly knew each other. Yet, Tyler felt as comfortable as the other residents of Laurel Valley.

She stroked Willow's head, pondering her relationship with Grant. They had been dating for almost two years, but early on, she understood his resistance to life in a small town. His criticisms of Laurel Valley were framed as harmless jokes, but she knew there was truth behind the jabs, and they had slowly opened her eyes to the opportunities she could be missing out on. Moving to St. Louis was exactly what she needed, according to Grant. He continually reminded her of the subtle intrusions she experienced. She could hardly sneeze before the ladies in town were on her doorstep, handing her a pot of chicken soup, shoving a thermometer in her mouth, and whisking her into bed with a hot water bottle at her feet. She had never thought of the gestures of kindness that way until he pointed it out.

Although she was grateful for the community support after her mother left, she admitted there were times she felt a little smothered by their continued involvement in her personal life. Despite this, she knew it would be hard to leave them when the time came. They were always there to catch her every fall. But it was time for her to experience life, make mistakes, and fix them on her own. According to Grant, she needed to move away from Laurel Valley in order to grow and mature. Once she shared her plans for an art school, Grant was completely supportive and convinced her that it would do best in a city like St. Louis. She trusted his business sense, seeing the career progress he had made in a short time, and hoped to emulate this pace in her life as well.

The kitchen timer startled her. Willow scampered off

43

her chest and darted under the coffee table as she rose and headed to the kitchen, the savory aromas teasing her taste buds. She grabbed a frying pan and added some butter, then layered in the bread and cheese. When the cheese was all melty, and the bread was a crisp, golden brown, she flipped it onto a plate, then ladled out some soup into a ceramic bowl she had made in her studio. Soft jazz music played from her phone as she dipped the crusty sandwich into her soup, then took a bite way too big for her mouth. There weren't many things better than a warm grilled cheese sandwich.

The doorbell rang at 8:05, almost 2 hours after Grant originally planned to arrive. At the beginning of their relationship, his tardiness and lack of communication would have her worried that he'd been in an accident. However, as this became the norm rather than the exception, Rachel learned to curb her apprehension and wait it out. This was the latest he'd been. But she tempered her frustration, knowing the next few moments would be worth the wait.

Rachel opened the door, and a gust of chilly December air rushed into the room, stinging her cheeks. An armful of red roses was the first thing she saw. Grant's apologetic grin peered around the bouquet. She cocked her head to one side and crossed her arms. "I was starting to worry about you," trying to keep the annoyance out of her tone.

"I know, Rach, I got caught on a conference call and couldn't break out of it. Then the traffic was terrible because I left the office late. I'm really sorry." He gave her a quick kiss on the cheek, and she stood aside to let him in, then followed him to the kitchen. He grabbed a vase from over the refrigerator, filled it with water, and then placed the roses inside.

Unable to hold back her curiosity, she said, "So, what's your big news?"

Grant turned to face her, then grabbed both her hands. She could sense the magnitude of his next words and felt ready to burst with impatience.

"The conference call tonight was with a firm in Germany. They want to acquire my company."

The words rattled her brain like a clap of thunder, causing her to lean back from him, but instantly, she realized what this meant and threw her arms around him. "Grant, that's fantastic!" It wasn't the proposal she was expecting, but she knew all the years of hard work he put in, all the sacrifices they had made, were finally paying off. He had basically just become a millionaire at the age of twenty-eight. This was it. Now he'd be ready to start their life together, and she hoped the proposal would be the next words from his mouth.

But as she pulled away, she saw the tense look in his eyes and realized there was something he hadn't told her yet. She took a step back and waited for him to continue. "I'm leaving the day after tomorrow for Germany to finalize the terms of the contract," he said, pausing and looking right into her eyes. "They want me to stay on as COO... and move to Germany."

She slowly let out the breath she'd been holding. "Germany," she repeated, slumping into a chair. She had been excited about moving to St. Louis, but the thought of moving to another country sent a shiver through her. There was a major difference between moving to another city in her state and moving to a foreign country without knowing their language, customs, or traditions. But Grant had been a cheerleader for her art school, and she didn't want to let him down. Besides, she could learn German and open an art school there just as well.

As her mind shifted into overdrive, racing to catch up with her life's new direction, she saw an apologetic look come over his face. She knew what he was thinking, and a sinking awareness fell into the pit of her stomach. He definitely wasn't proposing.

"I know a long-distance relationship would be extremely difficult, but we could try it for a while and see how it goes." He waited for her response, but her heart was in her throat, rendering her speechless. "The problem is," he continued. "I don't know when or if I'd ever be moving back to the US." She watched his expression and saw the mix of regret and excitement lurking behind his eyes. "What do you think?" he asked gingerly.

Rachel sat motionless, struggling to find her voice. What just happened here? This morning, she was contemplating the color of the linens at her wedding reception. And now, the man she loved and planned to marry was moving away... far away. She truly valued everything Grant had given to their relationship. He supported her goals and always encouraged her to reach outside her comfort zone to make things happen in her life. She knew he'd done his best to balance his personal life with his growing business and probably assumed she was okay with his lack of presence for the good of the company. But it wasn't enough for her. They'd experienced too many difficulties living in separate cities, and an international romance would magnify this problem tenfold. In order to stay true to herself, Rachel knew what her answer had to be. Before she could reply, she saw his eyes shift to the front window.

"Look, it's starting to snow," he said, leading her into the living room. Willow watched them pass by, then scooted into the bedroom. They sat at each end of the couch, watching the snowflakes fall with an airy silence. Rachel tried to wrap her head around this new reality. She thought they would be together forever. She thought their lives were finally syncing, and in a matter of months, she was going to be in St. Louis, just as they'd planned. But Grant's life was taking him in a new direction, away from her. She was being left behind to forge a new path on her own. The art school in St. Louis was her dream, a dream she wouldn't give up on, and she knew her only choice was to reimagine her life without him by her side. She just needed to figure out how to do it.

"So, what's the verdict?" he said, not much louder than a whisper.

Rachel turned her face towards him, clasping her hands in her lap for strength. "I think it would be best if we break up so you have a clear head while you are in Germany, not wondering how your decisions will affect our relationship." As the words left her lips, she felt a sense of pride to have formed such an emotionally intelligent response without any tears, although she knew they would come later. She studied his face and thought he seemed surprised by her answer, maybe even impressed. She now knew where her place in his life was, where it had always been... second to his career. Her mother was right. The angst and arguments with her were all for nothing, and that realization flooded her with regret.

He took her hand in his and nodded his head. "I understand." He blew out a deep breath and continued. "Well, I've already put down a deposit on that space in St. Louis. I want you to keep it and try to follow through with the move."

Her breath caught in her chest. Moving to St. Louis alone was intimidating enough, but purchasing a space for the school all on her own seemed too overwhelming. "I... I don't know." Her heart raced and her palms grew clammy.

Grant scoffed. "Listen, Rach. You've got a chance to own a property instead of renting someone else's. This is an opportunity you can't pass up. You need to go for it. Make your dream number one. That's how you get ahead. That's how you win." His voice grew in intensity as he spoke.

"I just hadn't imagined moving from Laurel Valley to St. Louis without you."

"Don't worry, I'll help you with the contract when the time comes," he said reassuringly. "I received a counteroffer today. The owner is a friend of mine, so I asked him for a little time to figure out the financing. If you hustle and raise the money for the down payment, the space is yours."

"How much time do I have?" she said, her voice

trembling.

"Till December 23rd."

She gasped. "That's less than two weeks away. How am I ever going to get the money?"

"You could see if your friends and family could help. Opening an art school for kids is pretty awesome and needed. I'm sure they will help."

She nodded and hoped he was right.

Grant stood and looked out the front window. "It's really coming down. I should head to the inn before it gets any worse. I'll call you next week and see how it's going."

Rachel walked him to the front door, still dazed by the turn of events. His arms wrapped tightly around her back, and she breathed him in one last time as the finality of their relationship was sinking in. "I'm really happy for you, Grant." She truly meant it in her heart. He was a good person and a hard worker. He deserved this windfall.

"Thanks, Rach. I know this isn't the way we thought this would go. But I'm really hoping everything works out for you." He pulled back and kissed her lightly on the forehead. "There is a whole world of excitement out there waiting for you. And it'd be a shame for you to waste your talent here."

"Well, my grandma always said, 'What's meant to be, will be.'" She gave a small laugh to hide the tears she fought to hold back, wanting him to remember the strength she had shown.

He smiled back at her, then headed out into the falling snow.

As she watched him drive away, she felt her world grow

dark, like the death of a close friend had occurred. There was no anger towards Grant, which might have made things easier. Only loss and loneliness. She had conjured up an entire life with him, moving to St. Louis, a beautiful wedding...dreams that would never come true.

Willow rubbed her face on Rachel's leg, and she bent down to pick her up, then carried her to bed, where they snuggled under the soft, down-filled comforter. She thought about what had happened that night and still struggled to believe that Grant was moving to Germany.

She wondered if St. Louis was still her destiny now that he wasn't going to be there to share it with her. Even before she met him, the art school had been her dream, although moving it to St. Louis had been his idea. But she loved so many things about moving away. New faces, new places to explore, and a new routine. Maybe it could work. Maybe she could raise the money for the space. She needed to dream bigger, just like he said. If it didn't work out, then... she wasn't sure what she'd do, but decided to cross that bridge when she came to it. There was still hope for a new life in St. Louis, and she had about two weeks to make it happen.

Chapter Five

Rachel stared blankly at the passing trees, as Nick's truck rambled down a muddy country road towards the ranch. A small patch of fog on the passenger window created by her breath caught her attention, and she lazily drew the shape of a heart with her index finger. The sun hid behind wind-swept clouds, and the gray cast to the sky matched her mood. The loss had seeped into her skin overnight like a heavy, wet blanket, and she'd awoken groggy and grumpy.

"What's up with you this morning?" Nick said, nudging her shoulder. Nick McCaslin knew Rachel better than she knew herself. Best friends since third grade, there wasn't much they hadn't been through together. Building forts and fighting bullies were just the beginning. When they were ten, he helped her trap a rabbit she wanted to keep as a pet, even building a cage for it in the garden shed. Her mother found it two days later and ordered them to set it free. The following year, they got matching casts on their arms after a ramshackle treehouse collapsed, sending them sprawling to the ground like Jack and Jill. And at the age of fifteen, they'd shared a first kiss together in the back of his dad's auto repair shop. The waiting room had the only soda machine in town, and on that fateful day, Rachel had come by for a Dr. Pepper. Sipping from their cans behind the shop, they concluded they were the only kids in the tenth grade who hadn't had their first kiss, so they might as well get it over with. Not much of a first kiss, but she was glad she had shared it with her best friend.

Rachel turned towards him and heaved a heavy sigh. "Grant and I broke up last night."

Nick remained silent and stared at the road ahead. She knew what he was feeling. Relief. Probably the same thing her mother would feel when she told her. Most likely, Brianna would be the only person upset by the news. She was a die-hard Grant fan. To her, Grant meant a secure life for Rachel and a husband she could count on. He was trustworthy and hardworking, the only two essential qualities in her opinion.

A small humph escaped Rachel's lips. "I know you didn't like him."

"I didn't have anything against him as a person," Nick argued. "But he worked ALL THE TIME. You hardly ever saw him. You even had to go to the Valentine's Day dance with your scruffy best friend instead of the guy who claimed to love you."

"Yeah, well, I didn't hear you complaining." She laughed at the grin stretching across his face.

"Shoot, yeah! I got to dance with the prettiest girl there." He smiled at her, then grew serious. "You deserve someone who's gonna be there for every dance," he said.

Nick was not usually good at pep talks, but these few words did a pretty good job of reminding her that she deserved more. "You're right, I do," she replied.

"So does that mean you're staying local?" he said, with a hopeful lilt in his voice.

"I don't know yet. I might try to buy the space in St. Louis on my own, but I have no idea how I'm going to pull it off." Rachel fell silent, wondering how Nick would react to this. After all, Grant was the one who'd encouraged her to move to St. Louis, and now he was out of the picture. She hoped Nick would be supportive, but she held her breath, waiting for his response.

He looked over at her, his eyes boring into hers for several seconds. There was love between them, not romantic in any way, just love. "Well, what do you need to make it happen?"

Rachel leaned her head back and closed her eyes. "Oh, not much," she said with a sarcastic tone. "Just a pile of money and a good dose of self-esteem."

Nick gave out a loud whistle. "I don't have much to give you monetarily... but I've seen you wrestle a boy twice your size and get him pinned to the ground. And I've seen you shimmy down a tree with a cat under one arm." His eyes were full of playful admiration, and she smiled back, enjoying the praise. "Not to mention fighting with the city council to get a dog park out at the lake. There are some pretty happy terriers out there because of you, so I'm betting you can figure this out. How's that for a dose of self-esteem?"

She nodded, accepting the little boost to her ego and

feeling empowered after this trip down memory lane. "I am pretty awesome."

"All right then," he continued. "Tell me about this dude, Tyler. Seem like a nice guy? Best friend material? 'Cuz I'll have to replace you when you move."

"Definitely. Fits right in here. He's planning to restore the whole ranch, even the orchard."

"Really?" Nick's ears perked up. "I'll need to find out more about that."

The ranch was an icon to everyone in Laurel Valley, and any talk of a revival was sure to raise some excitement. Nick had spent most of his youth at Lake Haven Ranch, working for Tyler's grandfather after school, repairing fences, hauling hay for the horses, and eating his weight in his grandma's apple cake. Some of their best memories were the summers they worked together caring for the horses. Seeing the ranch thriving again would be a spirit lift for both of them and everyone in the community.

The sound of tires crunching through snow filled the house. Tyler headed towards the front door and saw an oversized pickup truck pull to a stop in front of the porch. A lanky man wearing camouflage pants and a heavy brown coat exited the driver's side, then grabbed a metal cage from the truck bed. Relief washed over him. Tyler knew adjusting to life in the country would be challenging but hadn't counted on a critter invasion.

As Rachel got out of the other side, Tyler's heart raced

at the sight of her. Her dark brown hair was twisted into a side braid, and a wooley beret sat delicately on her head. He watched as she retrieved a metal toolbox from the back cab of the truck. Her face lit up with a bright smile when she spotted him coming out to greet them.

"Morning!" she said, climbing the steps and stamping the snow off her boots.

"Good morning to you both!" Tyler replied. "Thanks for coming out. You must be Nick," he said, extending his hand.

"I am," Nick replied as they exchanged a hearty shake, then headed inside. "I hear you've got an unwanted roommate."

"Sure do." Tyler couldn't hide the anxiousness in his voice. He had been listening to scratching noises overhead for too long and couldn't be happier to have Nick here to take care of it. "It's up in the attic." Tyler led the way up the stairs and noticed Rachel heading to the kitchen. "There's a fresh pot of coffee. Help yourself," he called to her.

At the top of the stairs, Tyler turned the knob of the attic door and felt resistance as he attempted to push through. Leaning in with a shoulder, he gave it a shove, and it sprang open, sending a chilly breeze pouring over them. Just inside the door, Tyler felt around on the wall for a light switch and flipped it, drenching the narrow stairwell in soft light from a bulb attached to a high rafter.

They carefully ascended each step, then stopped halfway up, peering over the edge at floor level to see if the owl was in sight. The attic walls tilted inward, forming the ridge of the roof, and light from the overcast sky poured in through large oval, leaded glass windows at each end. Assuming the coast was clear, they continued up the stairs. The time-worn floors creaked as they moved about the room.

"Okay," Tyler said in a hushed tone. "Last time I was up here, he was sitting on the back of that old chair." He pointed across the room to a worn-out rocker shrouded partially in a dusty sheet. His eyes scanned the room, darting into every shadow, searching for the beast.

"Whoa!" Nick blurted out, pointing to a feathery form perched on a beam above the center of the room.

"Shhh!" Tyler's face snapped towards him. The owl's head slowly turned downward, and its eyes glared unblinkingly into his, sending a trickle of fear down his spine.

"I didn't think he'd be so big," Nick whispered.

"But you can handle him, right?" Tyler asked, struggling to keep his voice steady, fearing the beast would dive-bomb them at any moment.

"I don't really know." Nick gave a non-committal shrug.

"What do you mean? I thought you were a professional trapper," Tyler whispered, anxiety filling his belly, causing a subtle quiver in his voice.

"Well, no," Nick admitted. "I run the Quickie Lube across town. But I've trapped hundreds of racoons, and this can't be much different," Nick whispered back, trying to sound confident.

"Oh brother. This is not going to end well." Tyler shook his head. A raccoon didn't wield razor-sharp talons and thunderous wings that could knock a man right off his feet. But there was no turning back now.

"How's it going up there?" Rachel shouted from the bottom of the stairs.

"Fine!" they quietly replied in unison.

"Need any help?" she called back.

Tyler looked at Nick, his eyes pleading for permission to allow her up to help. The three of them could surely handle this oversized pigeon.

"No way," Nick whispered to him. "We can do this, bro." His eyebrows furrowed, and his jaw muscles bulged from the clenching of his teeth.

Tyler reluctantly called down to her. "No thanks. Almost done." He turned his face back towards the owl and gave it the evil eye. This was his house, not the owl's.

"Look out!" Nick shouted. They dropped to the ground, flattening their bodies against the floor, as a fantom-like shadow circled above them.

Three minutes later, they descended the attic stairs. From down the hall, Tyler heard the click click click of a gas stove burner attempting to flare up. A soft whoosh followed.

"Stove's fixed," Rachel said as they entered the kitchen. She turned around to face them and let out a chuckle. "What happened up there?" The two men looked at each other, then down at their clothes. Feathers sprung from their shirts, hair, and shoes. A thin layer of dirt covered them from head to toe.

"We got the owl out of the attic," Tyler announced triumphantly. Crossing his arms over his chest, he felt invigorated by the accomplishment.

"The situation is under control," Nick said, jutting his chin up.

Rachel glanced down at the empty cage in Nick's hand. "Where's the owl?"

Their postures relaxed a bit and they gave a quick, sideways glance at each other.

Tyler cleared his throat. "Well, there's a window he'd been coming in and out of," he explained. "He flew out, and we shut the window." It didn't sound like much of a feat when he said it out loud. If he hadn't been so afraid to go back up, he probably could have shooed it out himself without involving Rachel or Nick. Nonetheless, he considered it a victory over his fears and gave himself a little pat on the back. He was feeling more like a cowboy every day!

Rachel giggled, and her eyes darted between the two of them. "I am very proud of you both. You know, owls can be fierce predators. I knew an old country boy who got carried away by a barn owl just last fall," she teased.

Tyler noted the playful sarcasm in her eyes and a beautiful little twinkle that warmed his cheeks. His attention turned to the amber glow rising from the open oven door. "How'd you know how to fix it?" he asked, in awe of her skill set.

"Just needed to replace the igniter. I figured that was your problem and brought one with me. Piece of cake."

"Wow, I'm impressed," Tyler said, shaking his head. "My dad and I will be able to cook for Aunt Judy tomorrow night after all. Thanks." He gave her an appreciative fist to the shoulder, then pulled his wallet from his back pocket. "How much do I owe you?"

Rachel raised a hand. "Don't worry about it. I'm happy to help. I've got to head to work, but Judy's closing the practice for the holidays starting Friday, so I can come out and make you a list of supplies if you're serious about getting a horse." She grabbed the toolbox and headed for the door.

"Sure, that would be great. Thanks again for helping me with the owl." Tyler grabbed Nick's hand and gave it a grateful shake.

"Hey man, anything you need, you just call."

"Well, in that case, I'm going to need somebody out here full-time helping me get the ranch up and running. Are you interested in a job?" Tyler asked. He noted a charge of excitement racing through Nick's eyes.

"Well, I can't say managing the Quickie Lube has been my dream job, so...yeah, I would definitely be interested," Nick replied as they headed onto the front porch.

"You got it. You can start as soon as you'd like."

"I appreciate it, Tyler. Looking forward to it. Heavy snow is in the forecast tonight, so be sure to stock up on firewood."

Tyler waved goodbye as Nick and Rachel got into the truck and headed down the driveway. Returning to the warmth of the kitchen, he gave a chuckle, marveling at Rachel's mechanical skills. She fixed his stove without expecting anything in return, not to mention bringing Nick out here to deal with the pesky owl. The kindness in the people here continued to amaze him.

Without fear of being attacked, Tyler ventured back into the attic, hoping to find some family treasures. The walls were lined with antique furniture, steamer trunks, and boxes stacked four high. He grabbed the sheet off a large piece of furniture, sending a cloud of dust fluttering into the air. A tall chest of drawers was hidden underneath. Tyler ran his hand over the wood, feeling the decades of wear. After yanking the sheets off the other pieces, he took inventory of what he had uncovered. Three upholstered chairs in varying condition, a cane-seat rocker the owl had been using as a perch, two steamer trunks, and an ornately carved headboard and dressing table that matched the chest of drawers. His attention was caught by a high-back, floral print chair. Memories of his Grandma Polly swam through his mind. He could still remember crawling onto her lap and listening to her sing, her lavender-scented perfume lulling him to sleep.

Glancing over at the dressing table, he noticed a small stool tucked underneath and gingerly took a seat in front of the faded glass mirror. His hands ran across the top, feeling each curve and imperfection in the wood, then slid open the slender drawer by its glass pulls. Several photographs were scattered inside, and after gathering them, he set them on the table to look.

There were several of Grandma Polly doing all sorts of things: cooking a batch of her famous fried chicken, standing in a boat holding up a bass the size of her forearm, and others sitting in a ladder-back rocking chair on the back porch gazing out at the lake. She was so full of life and always had special activities planned when they visited.

Family trips to the ranch were rare, and he remembered counting down the days until it was time to make the long flight to Laurel Valley. After a few years, his father's job became more time-consuming, and unfortunately, the summer trips became less frequent and shorter in length.

He took another stack of photos and quickly flipped through them, landing on one with two teenage girls sitting on the hood of a bright blue pickup truck in bikini tops and jean shorts, posing with big smiles. He knew the truck immediately as the same one parked outside the farmhouse. He ran his finger gently down his mother's young face and recognized the other girl as his Aunt Judy.

Setting the picture aside, he shuffled through more of the stack and found several of an older woman he didn't recognize. She was with Grandma Polly in some of them and alone in others. In one photo, she was sitting at a table painting the face of a small doll. With another look, he noticed it had wings on its back and realized it was an angel. There were more photos of the two women in various scenes, having fun together.

His watch vibrated with an alarm. After gathering the photos, he scanned the room and studied the window suspiciously. Just to be sure there would be no more uninvited guests, he gave it a quick shake, then headed back downstairs.

Chapter Six

P eppermint mocha lattes had made their annual debut at Valley Brews, and Rachel couldn't wait to put her hands around a warm mug of her favorite velvety concoction. The heels of her boots made a determined clop-clop-clop as she made her way across Main Street, speeding up with anticipation the closer she got.

The previous night's storm had dropped four inches over the town, and mounds of snow were piled up along the sidewalks from the freshly plowed streets. A chilly breeze swept the last few crimson leaves from the tree branches, hinting at more snow in the coming days.

Valley Brews was a favorite haunt for everyone in town. You could sample a variety of espresso flavors, stretch out on an old leather sofa to read, and catch up on the gossip all in one spot. The owner, Ben Carmichael, had an enormous selection of coffees and teas from around the world. Ben had opened the store just three years ago with his wife Ellen and had already attracted regular customers from neighboring towns. Brightly colored tattoos covered his forearms, and his impressive wiry mustache curled up on the ends like an old western saloon barkeep. He was a fun-loving, incredibly smart guy, and Rachel adored him and his family.

"Good morning, Ben. How's baby Lily doing? Is she cutting any teeth yet?"

Ben grumbled. "I think so! She's been a little grizzly bear lately and keeps us up all night. Makes it hard to get here at 5 am." He gave her a wink. "How about a peppermint mocha with a little cinnamon sugar sprinkle?"

"That sounds heavenly." After swiping her card, she headed for a table to wait.

In a booth by the windows, she spotted Tyler sipping from a steamy mug while reading a newspaper. The sun was streaming down onto the table, reflecting onto his face, giving his skin a warm glow. He glanced up and smiled as she approached him. When their eyes met, her face flushed, and tiny bolts of electricity shot through her, making the tips of her fingers tingle. *Stop it!* she thought to herself. She hadn't even been single for forty-eight hours. *Stick with the plan. I'll be moving away soon. Friends only!*

"Nice coincidence seeing you here!" Tyler rose to greet her and offered her the seat across from him. She happily accepted and placed her purse next to her. After removing the beret from her head, she quickly remembered to smooth down her hair and noticed a suppressed grin from Tyler.

"Well, I'm addicted to Ben's famous brews, which means I'm here every morning... and sometimes in the afternoon, too! So, it's probably not much of a coincidence," she said with a quick laugh.

"Are you on your way to the office?" he asked.

"Yep. The office Christmas party is in a few days, and my sister is catering it. I'm meeting her there to see what she's planned.

"Judy invited my dad and I, so I'll get to sample her food."

"It should be really fun," Rachel said. "I know the food will be outstanding. You'll be able to meet lots of people, too."

"Great," he said. "That was quite a storm last night. A lot of branches down around the ranch this morning."

"I didn't hear a thing. Last I remember was my cat kneading the pillow next to my face, and then it was morning."

"Wow, you are quite the deep sleeper!" His eyes widened, and she saw those beautiful caramel rings again. She stared for a moment, almost hypnotized by them.

Ben jolted her back to the present. "Here ya go. Enjoy!"

Rachel grasped the mug with both hands and blew over the surface. The first sip was pure heaven. She felt Tyler's eyes on her and attempted to make small talk. "So, other than the lack of Christmas decor, does the town feel much different to you?"

"Definitely! The stores seem a little more upscale. I also noticed a fountain in the park. Seems a lot cleaner, too."

"Judy is on the beautification committee. They keep everything pristine around town so you can give your compliments to her."

"I'll do that. I wish I could have been here to see the

transformation," he said. Rachel saw a hint of sadness in his eyes, but it quickly vanished, and his smile returned. "I've missed this town. And I'm thrilled we'll be here for Christmas." His eyes lit up when he said this, and reminded her of the excitement seen in a child.

"Yes, it's beautiful here in December, but I don't really get into all the hype."

"You don't like Christmas?" he asked, his voice full of exaggerated consternation.

She shook her head and giggled at his antics. "Nah. Seems like a lot of time wasted."

"Wow," he said, leaning back in his seat. "A real-life Scrooge." He gave her a playful wink.

Rachel laughed. She considered sharing the events that led to her aversion to the holidays, but decided against it. He was in a good mood, and she didn't want to put a damper on his spirits. "Very funny! I just feel that my time is better spent on pursuing my goals than wasting it on silly traditions."

Tyler nodded. "And how is your goal coming along?" he asked. "Still on track for the move to St. Louis?"

"Yes, I think so. Might have to make a few adjustments to the plan, but I'm full steam ahead."

"I'm so happy for you. Kids definitely need a creative outlet."

She nodded. "It has been my dream for a few years, and I feel like I'm really close to it becoming a reality if I can overcome a few obstacles." Her tone had a hint of doubt, knowing there was a chance it may not work out right now.

Tyler didn't seem to pick up on it. "That's fantastic!

I'm really excited for you. I can tell by your passion that the school will be a huge success. Totally worth any sacrifices you've made."

All of this was a big step for her, and his encouraging words filled her with hope. His gaze fell heavy on her, and they were both silent for a moment. "I agree," she said, breaking the tension. "It's just that some things have changed, and I'll have to purchase the space in St. Louis on my own. I've got to come up with the down payment by the twenty-third." She forced a smile and tried to sound positive, but she couldn't help averting her eyes from his. She felt him staring at her and hoped he could figure out the breakup without her having to say the words. It was all a little embarrassing since she had just been singing his praises at lunch two days ago.

"Oh." His tone fell slightly and had a hint of empathy. He knew what she meant. "Is there anything I can do to help?"

Rachel gave a small laugh. "Not unless you have a background in fundraising."

Tyler shook his head. "Sorry. I know as much about that as I do about critter control... or appliance repair, for that matter."

Rachel dissolved into laughter at the memory of the owl encounter. "It's alright, I'll figure something out. But if you come up with any stellar ideas, let me know!" Her phone chirped, and she retrieved it from her purse to read the text. "Oh, no!" she said, gripping the phone. "Judy said the roof on the VFW collapsed last night with all the snow."

"That's terrible! Was anyone hurt?"

"Doesn't sound like it. But we were going to have the potluck dinner there. Mr. Merriweather owns the building and donated the space to us. I don't think there's money in the town's budget for a venue." Her hand dropped into her lap as her mind raced. "Plus, how will I find a new location this late?" Her fingertips tapped the table in a rhythmic drumming.

"We could have it out at my ranch if you think it would work," he offered.

Her eyes shot up to his in disbelief. "Are you serious? You would do that?"

"Sure! The barn just needs a good cleaning. It's got electricity, plenty of room..."

"You are a lifesaver! I can't thank you enough. I'll text Judy and let her know." Her fingers flashed across the keyboard. "She says, 'Awesome! Tell him it will be perfect.'" She placed her phone on the table. "I just need to call the rental company and change the delivery address for the tables and chairs. I can help you clean it up when I'm out there on Friday."

"Nah, my dad and I can handle it. But I'll let you know if I need any machinery fixed. You're quite the Handy Andi."

Rachel laughed at his exaggeration. "Only with a few things. I learned a lot from my mom. You'd be surprised how quickly you figure out how to change a fuse or replace a leaky faucet when there isn't any money to pay someone."

"Doing is the best kind of learning," he said.

She saw Tyler's eyes move past her shoulder, and he held up a hand to wave someone over. Getting to his feet, he said, "Hey, Dad. This is Rachel Noelle. She's Aunt Judy's assistant."

Rachel turned and saw a handsome older man approach the table. She noticed the resemblance right away: the warm brown eyes, the perfect smile. If it weren't for the gray hair and charming laugh lines at the top of his cheeks, he could pass for Tyler's brother.

"Well, hello, young lady! Jack Patterson, at your service." He did a slight bow at the waist, and Rachel giggled.

"Good morning! It's a pleasure to meet you, Mr. Patterson." She stood and began putting on her coat.

"Please call me Jack. You aren't running off on my account, are you?" he said with an apologetic look.

"Not at all. I need to get to the office," she replied.

"Well, it was a pleasure meeting you. And thanks for giving Tyler a head's up on Mrs. Perry for me. I think she's got a property that might work for the diner."

"Glad I could help. See you Friday around nine, Tyler. And thanks again for hosting the potluck." She gave them a wave, then turned and headed out the door.

Tyler watched as Rachel stepped out into the blustery weather, then turned back to face his father, who was sliding into the booth. He returned to his seat and waited for Jack's reaction.

"Well, Rachel seems very sweet." Jack observed. "Is she single?"

"Dad," Tyler said with a hint of annoyance. "I hardly know her." He already knew the answer but didn't want to give Jack any false hopes.

Jack shrugged and held up his hands in surrender. "Okay, okay, none of my business. So, what was that about hosting the potluck?" Jack asked.

"The roof caved in over at the VFW. They needed a new venue, and I offered the ranch." Tyler explained.

A conspiratorial look came over Jack's face. "Ah, the knight-in-shining-armor routine," he teased. "Smart move."

Tyler laughed. "So how did it go with Mrs. Perry? Anything good?"

"She's got a building that would be perfect. The first floor is split in half, with the empty space for the diner on one side and Patty Cakes on the other side. The bakery is a strong tenant and additional income. The second floor is living space for me. I told Mrs. Perry we can see it tomorrow morning."

"Sounds good." Tyler slipped a spoon into his coffee and gave it a swirl. He eyed Jack for a moment, hesitant to ask his next question. "Have you asked Judy if you can use Grandma Polly's recipes for the menu?"

Jack shook his head. "No, I don't feel right asking for them. These were her mother's family recipes. They should stay in the family."

"Dad, you're her family, too," Tyler reminded him. "I think you should ask her. She might be honored that you even want them."

Jack smiled back at him, waiving off the advice. "So, what's the story with Miss Rachel?"

Tyler laughed at Jack's insistence on butting in. "She's really nice but she's moving to St. Louis soon."

"Really? I can't imagine anyone wanting to leave this little town. Maybe she'll come to her senses!"

Tyler grinned at his dad's optimism. Thinking back to their walk around town yesterday, he remembered seeing a hint of adoration in her eyes when she talked about the shop owners, and from what he could see, they loved her as well. Something told him there was more sentimentality in her heart than she admitted to.

Chapter Seven

R achel tossed the end of her scarf over her shoulder as she headed towards the firm. Passing the colorful shops, she saw the town with fresh eyes. The majority of the town's renovations were completed when she was in elementary school, so she didn't have many memories of the way it was before. The architectural details of the buildings were beautifully restored and painted in historically appropriate colors. The windows of the storefronts were sparkling clean and displayed a variety of treasures to entice the shoppers. A row of scarlet oaks flocked with snow lined the center of Main Street. Their branches created a shady canopy of green leaves every spring, then turned fiery red in the fall. Rachel marveled at how beautiful everything was as if seeing it for the first time. It must feel pretty magical to Tyler, coming from...where was he from? Another small town? She hadn't even asked him yet, but she figured it must be smaller than Laurel Valley if he thought this was so grand.

Tyler's encouragement had lifted her spirits, and she arrived back at the office in a surprisingly good mood.

Sitting at her desk, she placed her purse in a drawer then picked up the phone and dialed her sister. Brianna answered on the fourth ring and sounded out of breath.

"Hey, Rach, sorry. I couldn't find my phone! I could hear it ringing somewhere in the bedroom, but I couldn't find it."

Rachel laughed, imagining Brianna tearing apart her bedspread and sheets to find the phone. Her sister was notorious for misplacing it and had left it in almost every shop around town. "Are you on your way?"

"Yep! Just about to head out the door. I'll be there in about fifteen minutes."

"Okay, drive carefully. I'm not sure if they've cleared all the roads yet. Call me if you get stuck."

"Sure thing. I'll see you soon. Love you!"

"Love you too." Rachel stared at the phone and wondered how she would break the news about Grant. Brianna only focused on the good in him, citing his stability and honest nature as rare qualities in a man. She came off as dismissive whenever Rachel brought up a problem, glossing over any fault on his part as a non-issue. In contrast, their mother had only focused on the bad, comparing him to their father, who was absent most of their lives. But Rachel knew they both only wanted the best for her. Their advice, even when unsolicited, always came from a place of love.

Her phone gave a chirp, jolting her from her thoughts. It was a text message from Grant. Her heart began to race. Closing her eyes, she tried to guess what the text would say. Had he changed his mind? Was he willing to give it all up for her or maybe even try to convince her to come with him?

Good morning. I hope you slept well. I'm heading to the airport soon and just wanted to tell you how much I appreciate your understanding of everything.

She slumped in her chair, feeling a little deflated. Although she knew they were doing the right thing, knowing he would leave her behind so quickly stung a bit. Would she do the same if the situation were reversed? She considered her feelings for Grant and knew that if he had proposed last night, she would have accepted without hesitation.

But strangely enough, the breakup hadn't rocked her to the core. Tears were shed initially, but she was able to regain her footing quickly and move on. She didn't even fight for the relationship. Was she mourning the loss of Grant, or was it the loss of a settled life and the plans they had? She began tapping her response.

Of course, this is your dream, and you have to pursue it. I would never want to stand in your way. If it were me, I would do the exact same thing. She wondered if this last statement was true.

Thanks Rach. I'll be back in a week and call you to see how the fundraising is going. Maybe we could grab dinner, and I can show you the spot in St. Louis.

Okay, maybe, she replied. Rachel wasn't sure if she wanted to see the space yet. If she couldn't raise the money, it would be harder to walk away if she saw it in person. First things first.

B rianna arrived at the firm precisely on time, carrying a large satchel of items to show Rachel. After exchanging hugs and kisses, they headed for the elevator.

The building was constructed in 1926 with four stories of stunning architectural detail. The law firm occupied the first three floors with a reception area and several conference rooms on the first level, and offices on the second and third levels. Most of the fourth floor was a grand ballroom with wood-paneled walls and brilliant chandeliers. A wall of French doors led to the outdoor patio space.

"I plan to have the buffet indoors with tables surrounding the dance floor," Brianna explained as they entered the room. "The patio area is a little bland, so I'm having some couches and a couple of fire pits delivered tomorrow." Rachel walked beside her as they crossed the room and peered through the glass doors. "I think a few high-tops would be good out there, too, more intimate."

"Sounds perfect," Rachel agreed. Brianna began pulling items from the bag she had brought.

"I'm doing an Evening Under the Stars theme," Brianna said as she held up a ring of fabric swatches and weeded through them until she found one in a silvery gray color with a very subtle sparkle. "This is the color of the tablecloths, and each table will have a small vase of holly and a red candle to give them some color."

"Ooo!" Rachel squealed. "It's going to be so beautiful!"

Brianna waved a hand toward the ceiling. "I'm stringing twinkle lights across the ceiling tiles to give it the look of the night sky." She placed her hands on her hips and waited for Rachel's reaction. "What do you think?"

"Everything is perfect! I love the theme! Judy will love it, too." Rachel was always amazed at Brianna's creativity. Even as a child, Brianna had a flare for decorating. She was always begging Rachel to help her rearrange their bedroom furniture. She'd even made little throw pillows for their beds by attaching iron-on decals to pillowcases, then stuffing them each with a rolled-up towel to give them some shape. Rachel cherished her pillow to this day, proudly displaying it on her bed.

Brianna began walking around the room, pointing out the locations of the various activity stations. "Food over here, band over there. I'll have speakers on the patio so the guests can hear the music out there. And Sam knows a caricature artist who's agreed to come for free to get some exposure. We can set him up over here."

Rachel tried concentrating on Brianna's plans, but her mind wouldn't stop focusing on the enormous financial challenge she faced. When Brianna grew silent, Rachel realized she'd asked her a question. "I'm sorry. What did you say?"

Brianna's eyes narrowed. "I asked if there were any extension cords in the storage room. What's up? You seem like you're on another planet."

Rachel turned her face away from her sister's gaze, contemplating the best way to break the news. After a moment of indecision, she decided it was best to get it over with, like yanking off a bandage. "Grant and I broke up last night. He sold his company for millions of dollars, and he's moving to Germany." The words spilled out of her in one long breath, and she braced herself for her sister's impending meltdown.

Brianna's eyes glazed over, and her mouth hung open slightly, apparently speechless at the unexpected outpouring of information. She shook her head back into the moment and flung her arms around Rachel. "Rach, I'm so sorry!" She pulled back to look deep into her sister's eyes. "When did this happen? How are you feeling about all this? You must be devastated!"

Rachel shrugged. "Monday. I'm shocked, of course. I mean, I knew he was going to be successful. But, wow! Huge change for him."

Brianna stared at her with disbelief in her eyes. "So," she spoke slowly, trying to reconcile the devastating news with Rachel's dispassionate response. "You are okay with the handsome millionaire leaving you... it doesn't even faze you; life as usual..." Her eyes had yet to blink.

"It's not life as usual," Rachel argued. "It broke my heart. But there isn't any point in wallowing in self-pity when there is nothing I can do about it. He's moving to Germany. It might as well be the moon."

"So that's just it? End of story?"

"We had a long talk and decided it was best to break it off. A long-distance relationship has been hard even from St. Louis. I hardly ever saw him. It would be impossible from another country. It's really for the best."

Brianna's shoulders relaxed, but the concerned scowl

on her face hadn't disappeared. "Well, you seem to be handling it better than I would expect. What about the art school?"

"Grant said I could keep the deposit and try to buy the space myself. But I have to raise the money for the down payment by the twenty-third, or the offer will be canceled."

Brianna's hands went to her cheeks, and she let out a small gasp. "How much do you need?"

"I don't have the exact number yet." She paused, knowing the task would be almost insurmountable. "But he said it will be twenty percent of the sales price." Rachel had been saving for a couple of years but knew it wasn't even half of what she needed.

Brianna put an arm around Rachel's shoulders and pulled her in close. "Okay then, we will just have to put our heads together and figure it out."

There weren't many things better than a hug from her sister, and Rachel felt the heavy vice of anxiety around her heart begin to loosen its grip. Grant's suggestion of asking friends and family for help was fair, but she hadn't gotten the nerve yet. She knew her mother didn't have that kind of money, and Brianna struggled financially after her recent divorce.

The elevator doors parted, and Brianna's assistant, Sam Fitzgerald, entered the room, struggling with a box under one arm and a tall ladder balanced on his shoulder.

"Hey Sam! Thanks so much for bringing up the ladder." Brianna grabbed the box and set it gently on the ground.

"No problem. I've got another box in the van, be right back. Hey Rachel!" Sam waved a hand at her, then headed back to the elevator. Sam was a student at the culinary college and paid his tuition by working for Brianna for the past two years. They planned to form a partnership once he graduated in the summer. The catering business was growing rapidly, and Brianna needed a partner to help carry the load and share the pressure of running the business.

Rachel waved back at him and wondered if there could finally be a romance budding between them. They would be so cute together, but she doubted anything would ever happen. Brianna was too wrapped up in building her business to have any romance in her life, and Sam was too shy to make the first move. But there was a definite connection between them when they cooked together. They just seemed to click. It was like watching a ballet. Every movement seemed effortless and timed in perfect accordance with each other.

"What's new with Sam?" Rachel said in a hushed tone. "Have you two gone on an official date yet?"

"Are you kidding?" Brianna rolled her eyes. "I don't have time to date." She opened the box and started pulling out jumbled balls of twinkle lights. "Besides, Sam is just a friend and soon-to-be business partner. I don't really think of him like that."

Rachel shrugged. "Some of the best relationships start out as friendships." As soon as she said this, she realized she and Grant had not become friends before dating. A mutual friend introduced them, and he asked her out on a date that same night. They had been together ever since.

Brianna waved off the comment. "I don't know. I'm just too busy. Okay, let's start in that corner and work our way across." She dragged the ladder over, then ascended the steps to reach the ceiling. "So, how is the potluck planning going?"

"It's fine, but did you hear about the VFW?" Rachel asked.

"No, what happened?"

"The roof collapsed, and now we can't have the potluck there."

"Oh no! Do you have another venue you can move it to?" Brianna quickly scanned the room. "I think this room is too small for it."

"Actually, I do have another venue. Judy's nephew, Tyler, offered to host it out at his ranch. He's helping me with the planning, too."

"Well, that was nice of him," Brianna said as she fought with the hooks in the ceiling.

Rachel continued. "I met him at lunch Monday and found out we were in the second grade together! Isn't that funny? He's planning to restore the farmhouse and build a business at the ranch. We talked for over an hour about his plans. He made me laugh so hard I spit water right in his face! Oh, and he's coming to the office party Friday night, so you'll get to meet him."

Rachel smiled as she pictured Tyler yesterday at the ranch, his face smudged with dirt from the battle with the owl. "And I ran into him again at the coffeehouse this morning. You should see how excited he is about being here for Christmas. It was really sweet..." Her face turned up towards Brianna, who had stopped fussing with the hooks and eyed her warily.

Brianna descended the ladder and stood in front of her. "Rach, are you falling for this guy?"

"No way!" Rachel stared at her, shocked by the question. Of course she wasn't falling for him! They just met two days ago, the same day she and Grant broke up. Besides, she wasn't staying in Laurel Valley, so it didn't matter anyway. Rachel shook her head for emphasis but had trouble denying it a second time. "He's a nice guy, but... um, no..." She looked up at Brianna. "Not really."

"Rach," Brianna pleaded. "Please don't give up your dream in St. Louis for a guy you hardly know. He just moved here. I'm sure he doesn't even have a steady income yet."

Rachel knew there was some truth to Brianna's warning. Security in a relationship was important. But what about having a deep connection and being madly in love? Over the past couple of days, she realized she had never been able to form a deep connection with Grant because they didn't spend enough time together, and she wasn't going to make that mistake again.

"Bri, I'm not giving up anything. I'll find a way to raise the money for the school. He's just a nice guy, that's all." She thought of his dark hair that curled up at the ends and his perfect smile. "A really handsome, nice guy," she added with a sideways smile.

Brianna couldn't help letting out a chuckle. "As much as I would love to keep you in town, I want you to stay because you want to stay. Not because you fell for the new guy in town. Just focus on your dream and see where it takes you." She gave Rachel a quick hug. "Now, let's get this place finished."

They worked through the rest of the afternoon, transforming the plain, empty space into the magical, starlit vision Brianna hoped to capture. As they hung the last of the string lights, Rachel thought about seeing Tyler here, all dressed up for the party, with the soft light reflecting in those dreamy eyes.

Chapter Eight

T he dark waters of Lake Haven came to life in bits of color as the sunset reflected off its icy ripples. Tyler gazed out the large kitchen window of the farmhouse. Stretching out beyond the back porch, the land seemed to shiver in the chilly December wind. His new home was something of a silver lining on the dark cloud his life had been since his mother passed away, and the beauty of the land before him stirred a suppressed longing in his heart for someone to share his life with. Returning to the ranch meant a new business venture, time to reconnect with his hometown, and the chance at a new love with someone who could appreciate the quiet life in a small town.

Things were going well so far. The farmhouse was in great shape, and the orchard should be ready for picking by next summer. The people in town were so welcoming and made him feel right at home. He already had a freezer full of homemade casseroles and pies, and jars of preserves filled an entire cabinet in the kitchen. But in the love department? Not so great.

After a painful breakup with his ex, battle scars were

etched into his heart. It turned out that she was more interested in marrying someone with deep pockets than finding true love. Laurel Valley seemed like the perfect place to find romance with a kind, unpretentious person who could love him for who he was and the values he held. Rachel seemed to fit that description, but she had just ended a relationship and wasn't keen on staying in a small town. It would take nothing less than a miracle to overcome this obstacle. But as Tyler spent his day cleaning the house before his dinner guests arrived, she kept popping into his mind, no matter how hard he tried to avoid it.

Headlights appeared through the parlor window, signaling the arrival of his Aunt Judy and Uncle Frank, and he stepped out onto the wide front porch to greet them. Just as the sun disappeared from the horizon, the wistful call of an owl echoed over the snowdrifts from somewhere deep in the woods. Tyler smiled, wondering if it was the same owl they evicted from his attic.

"Hey, there's the guy!" Frank called out as they climbed the steps. He gave Tyler a hearty thump on the back, then pressed his wire spectacles towards the apex of his prominent nose.

"You already have your Christmas tree up!" Judy said, her eyes sparkling with enchantment at seeing the brilliantly lit evergreen displayed in the front window. She leaned towards Tyler with a warm, affectionate hug.

"It's practically the first thing I did after we arrived," Tyler said as he led them down the hall toward the kitchen. Jack was tending to an iron skillet sizzling on the resuscitated stove. His face brightened as they came in.

After exchanging greetings and more hugs, Judy peered into the skillet, eyeing the source of the savory aromas that filled the house. "That smells like Mama's fried chicken!" she said, clasping her hands in delight. Judy's sister Gwen dated Jack through high school, and her mother, Polly, had considered him a son. When her girls showed little interest in learning to cook, Polly enlisted Jack for the apprenticeship, and he eagerly learned all of Polly's tricks, sparking the foodie in him.

"I found a few of her recipes tucked in a drawer," he replied, turning back to the chicken and lowering the burner flame. "We can't fill up on fried chicken, though." He motioned to the worktable. "Tyler brought some apples to the bakery in town, and the owner made us a cake for dessert."

"That's beautiful!" Judy said as she bent down to inhale the aromas of cinnamon and baked apple. "Everything Patty makes is wonderful." Warm, gooey filling peeked out from star-shaped cutouts, and sugar crystals sparkled like tiny gems over the entire crust. "I'm surprised there are any apples left on the trees out there," she said, motioning toward the orchard.

"Not many, but I gathered a small basket full," said Tyler. "The trees are covered in vines, so I'll need to do some work out there to get them cleaned out."

Jack began placing crispy fried chicken into a serving dish. "Have a seat in the dining room. Tyler and I will bring everything to the table."

"This house is still gorgeous!" Frank said, admiring the

woodwork on the way. "I haven't been out here in years. Can't wait to see what you will do with it, Tyler."

Natural-colored beadboard ceilings ran the length of the long central hallway, and remnants of tattered floral wallpaper lined the walls, hinting at its past beauty. Leaded glass windows were in almost every room. The heart pine floors gave a satisfying creek with every step. Tyler followed close behind with a large bowl of sauteed green beans and a cheesy, crusted squash casserole. A basket of honey-buttered biscuits was snuggled beneath a cloth napkin to keep them warm, and a pitcher full of chilled lemonade completed the feast.

"Have you had a chance to explore the attic?" Judy asked, sliding out a chair and taking a seat at the table.

"Just briefly," Tyler replied. "Lots of beautiful furniture up there. And I found these pictures." He grabbed the stack off the buffet and handed them to her to sift through. Frank came around the back of her and peered over her shoulder.

"Oh, look at Mama reeling in that fish. Lord, she could out-fish anyone in the county. And here's me and Gwen on dad's old truck," she cooed. A wide smile crept across her face, but her eyes glimmered with the sting of loss.

"You still got that bikini?" Frank teased. Judy gave him a playful swat. The next photo was of the elderly woman painting the angel.

"Who is that?" Tyler asked.

"That's Liz Parsons. She was the mayor of Laurel Valley back then. She was so talented! Loved to paint." She studied the picture more closely. "That's the angel we used to have at the top of the town Christmas tree every year. I think she made some ornaments for us, too. You should see if they're up in that attic. They'd be beautiful on your tree." Looking up at Tyler, she said, "Liz was Rachel's grandma. She and your Grandma Polly were best friends."

"Really?" Tyler wondered if Rachel knew this. She hadn't said anything about it at lunch. "That reminds me," Tyler said, thinking back to his exploration of the town with Rachel. "Do you know why the town doesn't decorate for Christmas? I didn't see any twinkle lights strung around the trees or anything. Seems like the town went all out when I was a kid."

"Yes, I remember that too," Judy said thoughtfully. "Your Grandma Polly used to be on a committee or something that would handle the lights and decorations around town. Come to think of it, they used to put on all kinds of Christmas activities, including a toy drive for the kids in the community. I'm not sure what happened. They just stopped having it at some point, and everyone became wrapped up in their own lives."

Tyler felt a pang of disenchantment. His Christmas memories of Laurel Valley were of parades, the big tree lighting, visits with Santa at the VFW, and lots of fellowship with the other people in town. He was so looking forward to the hustle and bustle the season brings. Unfortunately, it sounded like the town had changed a lot since he'd lived here, and there weren't many activities planned.

"I hear you and Rachel are spearheading the potluck this year, Tyler," Frank said. "That will take a huge load off

Judy."

"Ah, yes, Miss Rachel," Jack said, entering the dining room with a platter of steaming fried chicken. "I met her this morning. Your assistant, right?" He motioned towards Judy.

"Yes, she's my beautiful, smart, talented assistant," Judy bragged. "She and Tyler had lunch together Monday, and they are both angels for doing this for me." She was smiling from ear to ear. Tyler noticed the devious twinkle in her eye and realized why she hadn't come to lunch with them: a clever attempt at playing cupid! "She's really great, isn't she Tyler?"

"She is..." Tyler hesitated. "Sounds like she has her mind set on living in St. Louis, though. It doesn't seem like she's happy out here in the country. She told me she's ready for a change and wants to live in a place where she doesn't know everyone."

Judy nodded, acknowledging the roadblock. "That's what she says, but I'm not sure it's what she truly wants. Keep in mind that Rachel has lived here almost her whole life. She's never had the money to travel or experience anything really exciting. She might think she wants to leave everything behind, but I'm not so sure." Judy's smile gave Tyler a bit of hope. "Just keep an open mind and an open heart. Maybe she's the one, and maybe not. Just wait and see. Your Grandma Polly always said, '*What's meant to be, will be.*'"

He laughed and shook his head, his fork playing with the food on his plate.

"What are your plans here, Jack?" Frank asked.

"Well...as you can tell, I love to cook. So, I'm going to open a diner downtown. I talked to Ellen Perry today, and she might have the perfect spot."

"How wonderful!" Judy said. "This food is delicious!"

"And how about you, Tyler? What will you tackle around here first?" Frank continued, as he spiked a few green beans with his fork.

"There aren't any major structural problems that I can see, but I've got an inspector coming out to give the house a once over. I want to get the stables cleaned out as soon as possible." He glanced over at Judy and smiled. "Rachel thinks I need some horses."

"Well, I think that's a great idea!" Judy exclaimed. "I loved owning horses when we were kids! Holly and Jolly. Gwen and I would open our windows at night and listen to them talking to each other out in the stable. This time of year, Dad would have twinkle lights all over the ranch, and we'd hang edible wreaths inside each stall for them on Christmas morning."

"Sounds beautiful," Jack said.

Tyler nodded. "Rachel loved taking care of those horses. It's a shame she's moving. I could have used her help."

The party moved into the parlor, and the conversation turned to more important matters... college football. As they enjoyed the apple cake, Frank and Jack bantered back and forth about the town's beloved Missouri Tigers. Tyler sat stewing about Judy's comment. *What's meant to be will be.* He wrangled with this concept. How is he supposed to know what's meant to be? Maybe Rachel is meant to be in the city. It is her dream, after all. But was she really a city girl at heart? She seemed to feel the close-knit community was more of a burden than a comfort. But she knew every detail of these people, and maybe she would miss them all too much to move away. He could only hope.

Chapter Nine

T hursday morning brought frigid temperatures mollified by hints of warmth from the bright sunshine. Tyler was in the attic sifting through boxes before he and Jack were to head downtown to see the proposed site for the diner. He shivered, noting that even with the window closed, it was not much warmer up here than outside.

Moving towards the window, he spied a box labeled "ORNAMENTS" and removed the lid. It was full of fragile objects wrapped in tissue paper. Excitement ran through him, hoping these were the ornaments Rachel's grandma had made. He began unwrapping them and admired their intricate details. They were made of ceramic and shaped like stars and blocks. Abstract designs in vibrant colors adorned the stars, while the blocks were more detailed, with circus animals painted on each side. At the bottom of the box, he found a set painted with images from the twelve days of Christmas. These must have been the ornaments Liz Parsons painted for Grandma Polly. They were so beautiful, and he thought about them sitting up here all these years instead of being displayed on Rachel's Christmas tree. She would be thrilled to have them.

The next box had the words "SILVER BELLES" written in thick, black lettering. Tyler removed the lid and found several manilla folders. The first was labeled CHRISTMAS FUNDRAISER and was full of receipts for rented tables and chairs, bulk food items, newspaper clippings, and invoices. He remembered Judy mentioning a club Grandma Polly belonged to that organized charity events for Laurel Valley. Noting the header at the top of the invoices, he surmised the club was called The Silver Belles. A Christmas fundraiser? Rachel had teasingly asked him if he had a background in fundraising. Definitely not, but maybe there was enough here to figure it out. Pulling out his phone, he dialed Judy's number.

"Good morning, Tyler!" Judy said in her cheeriest voice.

"Hey, Aunt Judy. I was just up here in the attic and found the ornaments Liz Parsons painted."

"Oh I'm so glad! Aren't they beautiful?"

"Gorgeous! I also found some boxes labeled Silver Belles. Was that the club Grandma Polly belonged to?"

"Yes, that was it. They did such great work in the community."

The wheels in Tyler's mind began turning. "Can you tell me anything else about it?"

"I don't really know much, but you should ask Mrs. Perry. She knows everything about Laurel Valley."

"Thanks, I'll do that." He clicked off the line, then

began gathering a few things to bring into town.

Tyler shivered as he and Jack drove towards downtown. Unfortunately, the heat in his grandfather's truck had given out, making for a chilly ride. Tyler admired the charm of Main Street as they cruised by the shops and started a mental list of what he would do if he were on the decorating committee. Twinkle lights in all the trees would be the top priority. There would be a nativity scene outside the courthouse, clusters of holly tied with red ribbon hanging from each lamppost, and every store would have a giant wreath on its door. The little town seemed sad to him. Maybe he'd talk to the mayor and spearhead this next year.

Mrs. Perry was at the door of the building, struggling with the key when Jack and Tyler approached her. A sign hung in the window, fastened with scotch tape, FOR SALE OR RENT.

"Good morning, Mrs. Perry! Let me help you with that." Tyler took the key from her hand, unlocked the door, and allowed her and Jack to pass by.

"Good morning, boys! I hope you're staying warm out there in that drafty old house."

"Yes, ma'am. Cozy as can be," Jack replied.

Tyler's eyes scanned the interior of the building. The wall to the left divided the space from Patty Cakes. He admired the black and white tile floors and the original antique chandelier in the center of the room. The large front area had plenty of room for seating, and an original wood counter spanned halfway across the back, making the perfect spot for bar seating. "I did a little research on this place. It used to be a post office, right?" he said.

"That's right, until 1967, when they built the big one at the end of Main Street. It's been vacant for about a month, but I had an inspector come through it after the last occupant moved out, and everything is in great shape," she said, walking towards the back of the room. "The kitchen is a little small, but there is plenty of room to expand it." She headed through a swinging door and pointed towards the stainless-steel refrigerator and gas stove. "The appliances are fairly new, so you might be able to salvage some of them." A large metal work table stood in the center. She motioned for them to keep following her past the kitchen and opened a door to allow them in. "You've got a small office here. You're welcome to the furniture." An old desk and chair sat facing a wall, and two large metal shelving units were on the opposite wall. "There's a door back here that passes through to Patty Cakes. She is a wonderful tenant, always pays on time." She glanced back at Jack. "And she's single," she said with a wink.

Jack laughed at the comment, then turned towards Tyler. "What do you think of the place?"

The air smelled of old dust and grease, but Tyler knew they could get it cleaned up. He turned around and gave it one last look, hands on hips, and a big smile crossed his face. "I think it's perfect!"

"Terrific!" said Mrs. Perry, delighted. "I'm so glad to get this place sold." She handed Jack a copy of the contract.

"Take a day or two to review it. If everything looks good, you can sign it and drop it off to me." They all headed towards the door. "Are you planning to serve Miss Polly's fried chicken?" she asked over her shoulder.

"You've had Grandma Polly's fried chicken?" Tyler asked.

"Sure! The town used to get together at your ranch on the first Sunday of every month for a potluck dinner. Now, we just do it annually at the VFW for Christmas. It's not the same, of course. But I'll never forget that chicken!" Her eyes closed as she relived the memory of each savory bite of crispy goodness.

Tyler considered this. What a great tradition...a monthly potluck dinner out at the ranch.

"I think I could persuade Judy to let me use Polly's fried chicken recipe. It would be a shame to deprive the town of the chicken they loved so much!" Jack chuckled.

"Miss Polly was the best cook in all of St. Louis County. Folks looked forward to that Sunday every month. It was all we could do to sit still through Pastor Henry's sermon that morning." They reached the door, and Mrs. Perry turned back to them. "Tyler, I want to tell you how much I appreciate you hosting the Christmas potluck this year! I think it will be a lot more festive out at the ranch. That VFW building doesn't have much Christmas spirit."

"I am excited to do it," he replied. "Hey, Mrs. Perry, can I ask you some questions?"

"Shoot!" she said, nodding.

"Well, I was rummaging around the attic at the farmhouse this morning, and I found a box of things from a club called the Silver Belles. Do you remember anything about them?" he asked.

"Of course! I was a member!" she replied. "We organized events to raise money for our residents in need. It was just a small group of older ladies, hence the Silver Belles!" She laughed as she pointed at her own silvery hair.

"And Polly and Liz, they were members too?"

"Oh yes! They were the founding Belles—both such smart ladies. Miss Polly ran the Laurel Valley Foundation and got the town cleaned up with some beautification projects. Judy heads the foundation now. Thanks to her, we have that gorgeous fountain in the center of town."

"What else can you tell me about the Silver Belles Club?" Tyler said, trying to keep her focused. He needed as much information about the fundraiser as he could get.

"Well, Miss Liz got the idea to start a club dedicated to raising money for the Christmas fund. They put their heads together and decided on a big festival."

"A festival?" Tyler asked.

"The Laurel Valley Christmas Festival or some called it the Silver Belles Christmas Festival. We used to have it every year. There was a big feast and music, a bake sale, and all the shops donated items for the silent auction. The money we raised went into a Christmas fund to buy toys for the children in the more rural areas outside of town. Sometimes, we even paid an electric bill for the families—anything they needed to have a happy Christmas. The entire town got involved. It was our favorite tradition."

"That's incredible! It must have benefited so many

families." Tyler couldn't believe the impact the Silver Belles had on their community. "What happened to the club? Why don't we have a big Christmas celebration anymore?" he asked.

"Well, I believe it's because the members sort of lost their way when Liz passed. She was the glue of the group, so to speak. Without her, the club had no leader, and no one wanted to take on the amount of work needed to get things done. Polly tried to keep a brave face, but when Liz died, a part of Polly died too. She just didn't handle the grief well and couldn't keep it going."

"Hmm, that's a shame. What do you remember about Liz?" he asked.

Mrs. Perry's face brightened. "Miss Liz was a talented artist. She painted every one of the houses in my little village." She pointed to the display in the window. "And there were some exquisite ornaments she also made. We used to decorate the tree with them for the feast."

"Yes, I found those in the attic this morning, too," Tyler said. "They are really beautiful."

"I'm so happy you still have them! I hope the angel is up there, too." She put a hand over her heart in prayer. "Every year, we had a tree in the park for the festival, and that angel was always on top, watching over all of us."

Tyler's interest piqued. "The festival sounds so great! What else did you do?"

"Oh, lots of things." She looked up in thought, trying to remember. "We had a bake sale, cookie decorating, and a big potluck dinner. We didn't charge an entrance fee but requested donations instead."

Anxiety began pricking at Tyler's chest. A festival would be a great way to raise money for Rachel's school. But how could he ever pull this together on such short notice? He didn't know the first thing about fundraising or coordinating an event. Maybe this former Silver Belle could help. "Mrs. Perry, do you think we'd be able to turn the potluck into a fundraiser?" Tyler asked hesitantly.

"A fundraiser?" she asked.

"Rachel's planning to purchase a space in St. Louis for the children's art school. But she has to come up with a down payment by the 23rd."

"Oh dear!" Mrs. Perry exclaimed, putting a hand over her mouth. "Now, that's a pickle."

"It was sprung on her all the sudden, so she's in a tight spot to raise the money quickly," he explained. "Do you think everyone would be willing to help even though she's planning to move to St. Louis?"

"I should think so! Back in the day, the Silver Belles raised money for a local boy whose dream was to study music at Julliard. And now he's a successful concert pianist in New York."

"That's awesome!" Tyler marveled.

"Honey, it didn't matter to us where your dreams led you, as long as you followed them!" Her sweet face showed the years of love and devotion to this town, a common thread among the people here in Laurel Valley. With their help, Tyler knew Rachel could follow her dream.

"So you think the festival would work?" Jack asked.

She put her hands on her hips and shook her head. "Well, that sweet girl does so much for all of us. It'd be a shame if we couldn't make it happen for her." She tented her fingertips and stared up at the ceiling in thought. "We might be able to pull it off with the help of the shop owners. I know they will be thrilled at the chance to help her, but the best way to find out what kind of response you'll get is to let everyone know at the town hall meeting. It's tomorrow night, 7 p.m. at the library. If you can make it, I'll let Mayor Oldwick know so he can add you to the agenda."

"We'll be there!" Tyler replied. "I appreciate your help, Mrs. Perry. See you tomorrow night." He prayed Rachel had come up with a solution herself, some easy fix, like a long-lost wealthy relative. Mrs. Perry seemed optimistic, but Tyler wasn't so sure. There was a lot to do in a week. But bringing back the Silver Belles Festival sounded like a lot of fun and a great way to help Rachel, so it was worth a try.

She gave them both a quick hug and headed towards the door. "I'll start spreading the word about the fundraiser. And Jack, let me know if you have any questions about the contract." They waved goodbye, and she headed down the sidewalk.

Tyler turned to Jack. "Do you think we could pull off this fundraiser?"

"If you can get the town on board, I think so."

Tyler nodded. "Let's stop at the bakery to return this cake pan to Patty."

Patty Cakes was identical in size to the diner space. It had the same black and white tile floor, but a soft buttercream paint covered the wood paneling on the walls and reminded Tyler of his mother's lemon-frosted cookies. Aromas of crumbly shortbread and blueberry almond scones filled his nose. Two display cases were in the middle, facing the door, one filled with colorful pastries, cookies, and small cakes and the other with grainy loaves of bread, assorted bagels, and flakey croissants. Three sets of tables and chairs were positioned in the front window.

Tyler's eyes darted from case to case, his sweet tooth aching at the sight of the confectioneries. Behind the counter on a marble-topped worktable, he spotted three pies with tendrils of steam curling upwards from their flakey crusts. Patty popped her head around the back doorway.

"Hey, Tyler! Welcome back." She approached the counter, wiping her hands on her bright pink apron. "This must be your dad. You boys look like brothers!" Patty's face lit up when she smiled. Her auburn hair was styled in a short, layered bob with blond highlights, and her jade-colored eyes shone like polished stones behind her rimless glasses. Tyler watched carefully for any sign of a spark. Jack reached his hand over the counter to shake hers. He was smiling from ear to ear, and Tyler noticed a slight blush in his cheeks.

"It's nice to meet you, Patty. Looks like we are going to be neighbors." Jack said.

"Well, that's a bit of good news. Are you renting, or has Mrs. Perry decided to sell? Last I heard, she was renting it out again." Patti said.

"I'm buying. But I promise to be a nice landlord," Jack teased, putting his hand in the air like a boy scout. "I'm going to open a diner over there. Just need to get through permitting."

"Oh, permits don't take any time at all in Laurel Valley. You'll be open for business quick as lightning."

Tyler handed her the white ceramic cake pan, embossed with the words Patty Cakes in scrolly letters.

"That cake was delicious," Tyler said.

"That was Miss Polly's Apple Cinnamon Cake recipe," Patty said.

Tyler's eyes lit up. "Really? It was awesome. I think I ate most of the cake myself."

"She gave me that recipe when I opened the bakery as a little housewarming gift. I get orders from all over St. Louis County for them, especially this time of year. Gotta keep my freezer stocked full of them." She thumbed towards the cake pans cooling on the back table.

"How long have you been in business?" Jack asked.

"Oh, about 25 years now. I've baked wedding cakes for two generations of families. Watched kids grow up and have their own kids."

Tyler's heart warmed as Patty spoke. This hometown feeling was exactly what he'd been missing all these years. He knew Rachel wasn't keen on everyone knowing your business, but Tyler felt it had pros and cons. It was better to know everything about your community than nothing at all.

"Are you going to Judy's Christmas party Saturday night?" Jack asked Patty.

"Sure. It's just about the only time I get to throw on a pretty dress and act like a girl!" Patty laughed. "Judy's been throwing that party for years. It's her way of doing something special for the business owners in town. She and Frank are exceptional people."

"I agree," Jack replied.

"How are things out at the ranch? I haven't seen that old place since Miss Polly left it," Patty remarked.

"Pretty good," Tyler said. "Considering its age and neglect for so many years. I don't know how Grandma Polly kept it up by herself for as long as she did. Surprisingly, everything seems to be in good repair."

"I'm sure it is," Patty confirmed. "Nick was a big help. He did what he could to keep the place running after your grandfather passed away. Some of the ladies in the garden club went out there every week to help with the housework and laundry, light yard work, stuff like that. And we all pitched in with food when she wasn't feeling well. Miss Polly and that ranch were well taken care of."

"I appreciate that so much, Patty. This town has been wonderful to me and my family," Tyler said. Jack nodded in appreciation.

Patty tilted her head to one side. "It's the least we could do for all she did for us. Miss Polly holds a special place in all our hearts." Her voice was filled with sentimentality. "Now, if you boys will excuse me, I've got a wedding cake in the back needing to be frosted."

"Looking forward to Saturday night," Jack said as they turned to the door, his eyes hardly moving off Patty's face. It thrilled Tyler to see his dad look at someone that way again. It had been a long and lonely two years for him, and Tyler was happy that moving here seemed to be giving Jack the courage to move on.

"Hang on, let me give you a little something to bring home." She grabbed a paper bag and began filling it with an assortment of goodies from the pastry case. Tyler's mouth watered as he watched orange-glazed cinnamon rolls, two slices of banana walnut bread, and several blueberry scones drop into the bag. She folded down the top, then added a pink Patty Cakes sticker to keep it closed. "Gotta keep your strength up to be ready for all that dancing at the party." She said with a wink.

"Thanks so much," said Jack, taking the bag from her.

As they walked down the sidewalk towards the truck, Tyler quickly glanced at Jack, who still had a smile on his face.

"Patty is really nice, isn't she?" Tyler asked as they climbed into the truck.

"She sure is." Jack replied quietly, and Tyler knew what he was thinking.

"It's okay, Dad. Mom wouldn't want you to be lonely." Tyler placed a reassuring hand on his father's shoulder. He could see the angst Jack was feeling. How could you ever love someone else when the love of your life still held your heart? But Tyler knew it was time for them both to shed their past lives and start new ones here.

Chapter Ten

F riday morning arrived with bright blue skies. After filling a thermos with coffee, Tyler headed outside to figure out his plans for the ranch and inspect the barn for the Christmas potluck. Rachel would be arriving soon, and he thought it would be good to have a to-do list started. Crumbling fences needed repair, the vegetable garden was unrecognizable, and the stalls for the horses had been filled with old tires and rusty tools no longer useful. The tables and chairs were being delivered next week, so cleaning out the barn was his first priority.

Tyler grabbed a small spiral notebook out of his back pocket. In the morning sun, he could see the signs of wear on the exterior boards of the old barn. The town's residents had done what they could to keep up with it, but years of winter snow and summer heat had warped them pretty badly. They would need to be replaced eventually, but for now, the most important thing was to inspect the interior and be sure it was suitable for hosting an event.

As he passed through the large sliding door, the smell of dust and old hay filled his nose. He spotted a light switch on the wall and gave it a flip. Six incandescent bulbs glowed overhead, flooding the space with light. The rafters appeared to be in good shape, just a layer of cobwebs a broom could take care of. Bales of old hay were scattered about and would need to be moved to the stable. He ran his boot over the floor to sweep away the years of dust. The broom could take care of that as well.

Jack appeared at the door. "How's it look in here? You think it's suitable?"

"I think so." Tyler said. "We just need to get the junk out and give it a good cleaning."

"Okay, let's get to it." Jack grabbed a large industrial broom and whisked the years of dust and hay out through the open door. Tyler teetered on a ladder, batting the cobwebs from the rafters with a metal rake.

"Tyler," Jack called to him. "I'm proud of you for having the integrity to stick to your beliefs.

"What do you mean?"

"You had an excellent job back home. Good pay, benefits, a promotion on the horizon." Jack paused, wiping the sweat from his brow. "You always said Laurel Valley was where you were meant to be. You gave up everything to move back here. Shows a lot of character."

Tyler smiled down at his father. Jack was right. He'd been offered a promotion but already spent more time at work than he liked, leaving little time for anything else. He enjoyed weekend trips hiking and camping, but as his work responsibilities grew, his free time dwindled away. It became increasingly clear that he was on a fast track to burnout and wanted to step out of this lifestyle before it was too late. When his mom passed away, it reminded him that our time on earth is precious and limited. He graciously turned down the promotion, and after a two-month notice, he packed his bags and moved back to his hometown.

"I'm glad you came with me, Dad."

"It was time for a fresh start for both of us."

While Jack finished sweeping the floors, Tyler carried the hay bales outside and sat them on the back of the tractor bed. Although a little run down, the ranch was a treasure to him, and he joyfully tended to each repair, loving every inch of its thirty-two acres. The entire homestead sat on the sparkling waters of Lake Haven and had provided multiple sources of income for his ancestors, and Tyler intended to bring it all back to life. He regarded every speck of peeling paint, loose fence post, and torn screen door as opportunities. To him, every flaw was a reminder of where he was and the possibilities ahead.

The tractor sputtered across the snow. After pulling into the stable, Tyler hopped off and yanked each bale of hay off the bed and stacked it against a wall.

"A lot of great memories out here."

Tyler turned and saw Rachel standing in the doorway, her small stature appearing even more fairy-like in the wide opening. A cowboy hat sat perched a little sideways over her dark hair. The sun illuminated her from behind, giving her an angelic appearance. She wore a puffy gray vest over a purple and blue plaid shirt. Her light blue jeans were tucked into brown leather knee-high boots that had seen a good deal of work. Tyler noted her appearance seemed different today, more relaxed, but even in worn-out boots, she was stunning.

"I'd say it's seen better days, but I think I can get it shaped up and ready for a couple of horses." He looked into her eyes, trying to gauge her mood. After thinking over the enormous undertaking of the festival, he wasn't sure if it was right to get her hopes up just yet and decided to see how she was feeling. It was possible she'd already come up with a solution on her own.

"I made a list of what you'll need for the horses." She handed him a folded-up piece of paper, then continued walking past him towards one of the stalls. "Nick will be able to help you get set up." She sighed, then added, "If I'm not here."

Tyler noted a subdued vibe from her and wondered if the sudden disruption in her life was getting to her more than she let on at the coffeehouse. It must have been quite a shock, and he was sure she was still hurting from the blow.

She was quiet as they walked the rest of the way to the stalls. Rachel slid her hand along the cold metal gate. "This was Jolly's stall. Holly's was there." She motioned to the next stall over. Her eyes grew distant, and he knew she was deep in thought, savoring the memory of a place she loved. She climbed up a rung of the gate and rested her chin, staring into the space Holly once occupied.

Tyler came and stood beside her and draped his arms over the gate. He deliberated the next few moments, wondering if he should let her think in silence or unload the worry onto him. He hoped she thought of him as someone she could trust, someone she could count on, but they hadn't known each other very long, and he wasn't sure what she was thinking. "You wanna talk about it?"

She hesitated, and he heard a long, slow breath seep out of her lungs. "Yeah, I do." She turned her sapphire eyes toward him, and he was thankful there weren't any tears in them. "Grant and I had a future planned together in St. Louis." Her tone carried an edge of frustration. "We'd talked about spending our lives together, starting up my school. The plans were in motion. Everything was coming together." She shook her head, and he saw a wave of disappointment crash over her. "And now he's moving to Germany and leaving me here to figure everything out by myself. Everything is up in the air, and I feel so unsettled."

Tyler was quiet for a moment, not sure of what to say. It was risky to tell her about his idea for the festival fundraiser when so many things could go wrong, leaving her with nothing. Putting together a festival in a week would be incredibly hard, and he hoped there was another path, maybe one where she could stay in Laurel Valley. "What are your options?" he asked.

"My first option is to buy the space in St. Louis myself. Grant's letting me keep the deposit money. But I haven't found a way to raise the rest of the down payment."

"And option two?" he asked.

She let out a small laugh. "Option two is giving up and staying here until I figure out a new plan." She shrugged her shoulders.

Tyler's hopes of an easy solution fell. It didn't sound like she had come up with anything to dig herself out of this mess. "I bet that would make the whole town happy, especially your sister. They all really love you." He saw the far-off look in her eyes again, the longing for something more, or at least something different.

A smile finally crept across her face. "I know they do."

As much as Tyler wanted her to stay in Laurel Valley, he knew experiencing the city was her dream, and he couldn't let her go down without a fight. A feeling of resolve overcame him, and he began pacing down the middle of the stable.

"Well, you can't give up." He turned back to her, crossing his arms over his chest.

"Why? Have you found a pile of money hidden in the attic?"

"Not exactly, but how about a fundraiser? Like...a festival or something?"

She turned her gaze slowly towards him, one eyebrow raised with skepticism. "A festival?"

"Sure. I'm thinking we could add some activities to the potluck and have a Christmas festival instead. Maybe a silent auction, bake sale...stuff like that."

Rachel laughed and shook her head at him. "Tyler, I don't know anything about putting on a festival. I barely know how to coordinate the potluck. How are we going to do this in a week?" Her voice rose at the sheer absurdity of him even suggesting they try.

"I bet we could figure it out," he said with determination. The pace of his words quickened as his thoughts raced. "There used to be a club here in Laurel Valley that raised money for people in need. They put on a Christmas festival every year. Mrs. Perry was a member and can give us some guidance. And I found some boxes in my attic that might help us out. You want to go through everything and see what you think?" He knew it was crazy to take on something like this. But this might be her only hope of raising the money in such a short period of time.

"But why would everyone want to help me raise money for a space in St. Louis?" she questioned.

Tyler was surprised she even had to ask. "Because it's for you. It's your dream."

A slight raise to her brow told him there was a hint of optimism growing behind those beautiful blue eyes.

Chapter Eleven

Rachel's mind buzzed with energy as they entered the house. She couldn't imagine putting together a festival in only a week, but Tyler seemed willing to try, and it might be her only hope.

After helping her out of her coat, he led her into the kitchen and picked up the stack of photos. "Check these out," he said, handing them to her.

She stared at a photo of her Grandma Liz and Miss Polly looking right into the camera with their cheeks pressed together and radiant smiles on their faces. "Judy said they were best friends, like sisters," Tyler explained.

"That's so sweet! I never knew they were close." She flipped through a few more photos then stopped on a picture of her grandmother painting the angel, and her heart filled with love.

Tyler continued talking. "I found some boxes in the attic full of stuff about a club called The Silver Belles. I asked Mrs. Perry about it yesterday. She said our grandmothers started The Silver Belles together."

Rachel stared at him wide-eyed. "Really? How does

this help us with a fundraiser?"

"I'll show you everything I found," he said, leading her towards the stairs.

"Wow!" she exclaimed as they entered the attic. "Look at all this cool stuff!" She went over to the chest of drawers and ran her hand along the cold wood.

"There are some folders from the club over here," Tyler said, heading towards the box by the window. They began flipping through the folders, filled mostly with invoices, inventory lists, and important names and phone numbers. Rachel spied a piece of newspaper and carefully unfolded it. "Here's an article about them."

The heading read, "The Silver Belles Bring Christmas to Families in Need." Tyler began reading the article out loud.

Volunteers are the heart and soul of every community—a food drive here, cleaning up a park there. But volunteerism is a way of life for the founders of the Laurel Valley Silver Belles, Elizabeth Parsons and Pauline Harrison. What started as an annual coat drive one chilly October in 1990 grew into an annual Christmas Festival that has raised almost thirty thousand dollars for families in need since its beginning.

"It's all about gratitude and service," says Harrison. Her role in the club includes recruiting volunteers, called Belles, for their charitable projects. "The Belles create special bonds with the population we serve. Our goal is to bless these families while instilling a sense of selflessness and gratitude in the volunteers."

And it is not just toys the Belles provide these families.

They have partnered with their local tree farm to give out Christmas trees, even paying rent or utility bills for some residents in the surrounding communities.

"We aren't just handing out presents," said Parsons. "We are giving these families the spirit of Christmas."

Rachel tucked the article back into the folder. "I can't believe they did all this for the town." Rachel became thoughtful. She had been unknowingly shunning a holiday that meant so much to her grandmother. It was more than decorations and spending money on presents. This club pulled the entire town together for a greater cause.

Tyler grabbed a rolled-up poster and unfurled it. "Join us for the eleventh annual Silver Belles Christmas Festival," he read across the top. Pictures of brightly colored Christmas trees, gingerbread men, and presents decorated the border. A list of events was in the center, including a toy drive, fruitcake contest, silent auction, cookie decorating station, s'mores, and bake sale. At the bottom, in big block lettering, it read "All proceeds benefit the Laurel Valley Christmas Fund."

"I have vague memories of a Christmas party or something we would go to," Tyler said. "Must have been this festival." He opened the box containing the ornaments. "Mrs. Perry said your grandma painted all these, and they would hang them on a tree in the park downtown."

She handled them carefully, in awe of the exquisite details painted on each one. When she reached the bottom of the box, she found a smaller container and pulled it out. Wrapped in green tissue paper was a beautiful angel Christmas tree topper, the same one in the photo of her grandmother. Rachel stroked the angel's delicate porcelain face. She wore a long burgundy velvet dress with gold wings carefully attached to her back. In her hands were two tiny lights with wiring that ran into the sleeves of her dress and connected to a cord under her skirt.

Rachel sat down on the floor, surveying the files, the ornaments, and the boxes of photos.

"I'm just amazed at all the things our grandmothers did to help people. It must have been so much work," Rachel said wistfully.

"What do you think about my idea? We've already got the groundwork done for the potluck. We just need to ramp it up with activities and get the word out to surrounding areas."

Rachel winced. "I just don't know. With only a week to plan? How can we possibly get all that organized?"

"We have to try. You said Judy's office is closed next week, so that will give us time to work out the details."

A hint of panic rose in her voice. "There's more to this than just details. Are you sure we should even attempt this?"

"There's a town hall meeting tonight at seven. Mrs. Perry said you could speak to everyone there and ask for volunteers."

She balked at the thought of this. "I hate speaking in front of people! I once lost my voice reciting the preamble to the constitution in front of my US Government class." The memory flooded her with angst, and a tightness coiled in her chest.

"It'll be okay," he said sympathetically. "You can do this! And I'll be there to cheer you on."

Rachel stared into Tyler's face. She couldn't understand why he would be willing to do all this work for her. They hadn't even known each other very long. Not only was he putting his own work on the ranch aside to help her raise this money, but his efforts would be spent on helping her move away from Laurel Valley. It was an incredibly noble thing for him to do.

After gathering the boxes of ornaments and carefully re-packing the angel, they headed downstairs. In the kitchen, Tyler served up the cinnamon rolls he'd received from Patty, and they discussed the plans for the festival. Rachel pulled a small notebook from her purse and reviewed the checklist items. "I've got the spreadsheet for the food updated. I think we'll have a nice variety this year. I need to contact the rental company about the tables and chairs. We might need more than we originally planned for."

"What were some of the activities listed on that poster?" Tyler asked.

Rachel closed her eyes, trying to remember. "Fruitcake contest, silent auction, bake sale..." She kept thinking. "Oh, and cookie decorating. I bet we could bake all the cookies at Patty's bakery." She continued scribbling down their thoughts.

"Maybe we can charge three for a dollar," Tyler offered.

"Hmmm, we really want all the children to have cookies to decorate, and some families might be unable to afford it. I think we should just ask for a donation."

"That's a great idea. Mrs. Perry also said they didn't charge an entrance fee; everyone just made a donation for that, too."

"Perfect. I bet we raise even more money doing it that way."

"You know that Victorian village in Mrs. Perry's window with the train?" Tyler asked. Rachel nodded. "Your grandma painted all those little buildings."

She smiled at him with awe. "You know what? You've learned more about my grandmother in a couple of days than I've ever known."

"Yes, I'm a regular Sherlock Holmes," he teased. "But there's another mystery I'd like to solve." He paused, giving her a smirk. "Why does Rachel Noelle hate Christmas? Even your name is Christmassy!" he said, playfully goading her. A spark of humor glinted in his eyes.

Rachel gave a quiet laugh while debating whether or not to confide her reasons to him. She didn't want to darken the mood, but she wanted him to know she wasn't really a Scrooge. "I don't hate Christmas," she countered. "It's just a reminder of a sad time in my life."

Tyler leaned towards her. "Oh, I'm sorry, I didn't know. You don't have to talk about it if you don't want to. I was just teasing." His voice was soft and apologetic.

"I know, it's okay." She paused for a moment, wondering where to start. "The night of the train unveiling at The Curio Shop, my sister and I were spending the night with my grandmother, and we wanted her to take us to see the train. She wasn't feeling good but took us anyway."

Tyler stared at her intently, listening to her every word. "What happened?"

"She got sick and passed away late that night."

"I'm so sorry," he said, reacting to the pain in her eyes.

" I always wondered if she'd still be here if she hadn't gotten sick that night. I don't mean to be a Scrooge, but this time of year brings up those memories, so I've always focused on other things in my life instead."

"I can see why Christmas isn't something you look forward to. I'm sure you were very close to her."

She gave him a small smile, appreciating his sympathy. "Yes, we were very close. I got my interest in art from her." Rachel smiled proudly. Her grandmother had always encouraged her to use art as a way to connect with others and brighten someone's day. "She had a quaint little cottage somewhere she used as an art studio. It had windows overlooking beautiful flowering trees and wildflowers." She allowed her mind to reminisce about the wonderful memories. "We'd spend hours there together, going for walks, painting the scenery we saw out the window, talking together. She would always add a little fairy to her pictures and swore she had actually seen it out the window, fluttering over a dandelion or hiding under a mushroom!" Rachel laughed, remembering the magical world they'd escaped to together.

"And now you've been inspired to create that same feeling in other children with your art classes." Tyer said with an air of admiration in his voice that filled her with pride. "Were there any happy Christmases after that?" he asked.

She gave a small humph. "Not really. My dad left shortly after that, and my mom didn't have much, so we eventually got out of the habit of celebrating. As I got older, I became more practical and wanted to spend my time being productive and saving money." Rachel became thoughtful. "To be honest, I think Grant put that philosophy into overdrive." She was piecing together a connection between her avoidance of Christmas and her ex. She'd always felt it was due to her grandmother's death, but Grant didn't celebrate Christmas with his family either, so it was much easier to forget about the holidays.

"Wow. I'm really sorry you had such a rough time growing up. At least you lived in a town surrounded by people that cared about you," Tyler said.

Rachel pondered this. She thought about the people in town, how they had stocked her mom's freezer with casseroles so she wouldn't have to cook, how they came to her holiday plays at school, and how they all pitched in a bit of money to help her buy her first car. Tyler was right. In both good times and bad, this town had been there for her and her family.

They turned their attention back to the fundraiser and came up with a quick speech for the town hall meeting. Tyler walked Rachel to her car and opened the door for her. She paused before getting in and turned to him, putting her arms around him in a quick hug. "Thank you for discovering all this, Tyler. You don't know how much it means to me." He raised his arms to return the embrace, but she quickly let go and got into her car. Friends only, she reminded herself. Her heart was beating wildly in her chest, but she had to ignore it.

"I'll meet you at the library tonight at seven," he said.

She nodded, then closed the car door. She saw him wave in her rearview mirror as she headed down the driveway, and thoughts of regret swirled through her mind.

Chapter Twelve

A bitter wind swept through the streets as people hurried into the warmth of the library. A table in the foyer offered an assortment of cookies, coffee, and hot cocoa. Tyler and Rachel helped themselves to the carafe of hot cocoa and spooned in some mini marshmallows. The first sip of sweet chocolate brought her mind back to visits with Grandma Lizzy, and she felt the presence of her grandmother giving her a hug of encouragement. She knew this was where she needed to be tonight.

Thanks to Mrs. Perry, news of a proposed festival had already spread, and a charge of excitement filled the room. Rachel wasn't sure how many attendees the town hall meetings usually drew, but she hoped the large crowd was here to support her request. She scanned the crowd, noting all the seats were filled, with more people standing around the sides. She quickly waved to Brianna as Mayor Oldwick approached the podium and tapped the microphone. His silvery hair was combed back away from his face and hung slightly below his earlobes. Wild brows hung over his baby blue eyes, and the apples of his cheeks were rosy and plump, reminding her of the Wizard of Oz.

"Welcome, everyone! Let's all quiet down so we can get on with our business," he shouted, trying to be heard over the chatter. "Since you are all obviously excited to hear about the festival, let's get through our other business as quickly as possible. Then I'll bring Rachel Noelle up to fill you in. Maple Merriweather would like to discuss our first issue."

Tyler and Rachel stood in the back, waiting patiently for her turn to address the crowd. The first order of business was a complaint of sticky sidewalks outside the ice cream store. Rachel heard Tyler chuckle when the topic was announced.

Mr. Merriweather's sister, Maple, stood at the front, no taller than five feet, and waited for Mayor Oldwick to adjust the microphone for her. "I would like to propose a ban on consuming ice cream within the city limits, particularly on the sidewalks. It should be sold in containers and eaten elsewhere. Sticky sidewalks are a nuisance."

"You're crazy!" Mr. Merriweather shouted at her from the back row. "Git down from there, Maple. This ain't California!"

"And you ain't Clint Eastwood, mister smarty pants!" she yelled back at him. The crowd roared with laughter at the exchange, and the poor mayor had to hustle her back to her seat before they started throwing punches at each other. Tyler shook with laughter.

"What on earth are they talking about?" Rachel asked.

"Carmel-by-the-Sea is a little city in California, and

they had actually banned eating ice cream because it was messy," Tyler whispered back. "Clint Eastwood was their mayor back in the late eighties and repealed the law."

Rachel stared at him in amazement, shaking her head, wondering how any of them knew such an arbitrary bit of trivia. The crowd finally settled down, and Mayor Oldwick asked if anyone was in favor. Of course, no one but Maple Merriweather responded with a defiant aye. After the rest of the crowd feverishly shouted nay, the motion was denied.

"Next up, Patty Stevens is requesting a temporary stay on the ban of selling alcoholic beverages within city limits to sell her homemade Spirited Eggnog at the bakery." Mayor Oldwick paused momentarily, and Patty twisted in her seat to give everybody a wave. "Are there any questions?" he asked the crowd.

"How much alcohol is in a serving?" asked Mr. Merriweather.

"Oh, about two shots, one each of white rum and amaretto liquor," she beamed. A collaborative gasp escaped the crowd.

"All in fav-"

"AYE!" shouted the entire room, practically shattering the windows. Jack gave Patty a celebratory fist bump.

"Any nays?" Mayor Oldwick asked half-heartedly. The room was silent. "Motion approved. And finally," he continued. "Rachel Noelle will speak on the proposed festival."

Rachel stood and made her way to the front, feeling her knees shake as she tried to focus on her breathing. She took a glance back at Tyler, then instinctively raised a hand and smoothed down her hair.

"Uh, good evening, everyone," she said, hoping no one noticed the crackle in her voice. "Thank you for giving me this chance to speak tonight." She looked out into the crowd and saw Nick making his way over to Tyler. Her eyes darted around, scanning the crowd, and spotted Judy and Frank in front. Beside them were Mr. and Mrs. Perry, and off to the right, she saw Jack, Patty, Brianna, and Sam. All the other shop owners were present as well. It seemed that everyone in the room was a relative or a friend. She knew them all. There were no strangers in Laurel Valley. Each set of eyes quietly encouraged her, willing the nervousness out of her. A calm came over her heart, and she found a steady voice.

"I've dreamed of opening a children's art school for many years, but until recently, I hadn't found a space large enough. Last Monday, I was offered the opportunity to purchase a location in St. Louis. While it's not here in Laurel Valley, it's the perfect size for the school and the chance for me to put my dreams into action." She swallowed hard as the nervousness began creeping back into her throat. "Unfortunately, there have been some changes to the finances, and I only have until December twenty-third to raise the money for the down payment, or I'll lose the contract." She heard the audience let out a small, sympathetic gasp.

Her eyes went back to meet Tyler's, and she could see the warmth in them even across the room. "After some brainstorming, our newest resident, Tyler Patterson, and

I came up with an idea for a festival fundraiser." Murmurs of delight spread throughout the crowd, and Rachel was pleased with the response she was getting so far. "Although I don't have any experience putting together a festival, we recently found some information about a Christmas club called the Silver Belles, founded by my grandmother, Elizabeth Parsons, and Tyler's grandmother, Pauline Harrison.

"You all remember Elizabeth, my Grandma Lizzy, as your town's beloved mayor. She was an incredible woman. It left an enormous hole in my heart when she passed away, and I know it affected this whole town. I was just a little girl, but you all had the privilege of knowing her much longer." Her words began spilling forth without hesitation. "You saw her as your hope, your leader. And when she was gone, it was as if a light dimmed in all of us." She blinked hard, fighting back the tears that threatened to form in her eyes. Every eye in the crowd was on her, and a heavy silence spread around the room. "Through the Silver Belles Club, Grandma Lizzy and Polly Harrison hosted numerous events throughout the year to raise money for our neighbors, who struggled financially. The biggest event was the annual Christmas Festival. Not only did this event bring a happy Christmas to our local families and others throughout the county, it brought our community together in fellowship and service." Her voice faltered slightly as she wondered if she was rambling too much. All eyes remained on her, so she pushed ahead.

"My hope is to transform the potluck into the twelfth annual Silver Belles Christmas Festival to raise money for the school while reviving Laurel Valley's giving spirit." The crowd stood and clapped.

Mayor Oldwick returned to the podium, raising his hands to quiet the crowd. "Okay, everyone, simmer down, simmer down." He turned to Rachel. "Now, Miss Rachel, I know I speak for everyone here tonight. We would love to help you raise the money you need. We trust you'll put it to good use, whether you're here, St. Louis or Timbuktu. You just follow your dream where it takes you." Cheers of encouragement rang out.

"Thank you so much!" She leaned in for a hug from him, then turned back to the crowd, wiping a tear from her cheek. "We are planning lots of activities, including a bake sale, cookie decorating booth, and a silent auction. I've created a flier advertising the event we can post in your store windows. I will email it to each of you so you can share it on your social media pages. We have posted the volunteer sign-up sheets along the bulletin boards on the back wall. Please be sure to sign up for whatever activity your heart draws you to. I appreciate your help with this. Thank you all for helping to make my dream a reality."

The clapping continued as she joined Tyler and Nick in the back. These were the people she'd come to know as her family. The outpouring of love she saw in their eyes was heartwarming, and she knew that no matter what the GPS said, this place would always be home.

As she reached them, Nick raised his fists to declare victory. Tyler gave her a congratulatory hug, then pulled back and looked straight into her eyes. "I think it's pretty clear there isn't anything this town wouldn't do for you."

As the crowd filed out of the library, Tyler and Rachel stood in the back, answering questions and assisting with the volunteer sign-up sheets.

Mrs. Perry pulled Rachel aside. "Thank you for inspiring this tired old town." Tears filled her eyes, and she swiped them away with a tissue. "We needed a good cause to pull us together again. Laurel Valley has had too many years without any Christmas spirit."

Rachel glanced over at Tyler, who was talking to Mr. Merriweather. "So have I," she replied.

"Well," Mrs. Perry continued. "If we can't keep you here, we'll be sure you are a success wherever you go, sweetie. You'll bless many hearts whether you're here or St. Louis."

"Thank you so much." She gave her sweet old friend a warm hug, then headed towards Tyler. He had made this all possible for her. He believed in her dream and devised a solution, even though its success meant leaving her hometown. His eyes watched her as she came towards him, and she felt a warmth in her heart growing.

"You were incredible up there! Not a single eye left your face," he said.

Rachel was proud of herself as well. Hope was bubbling within her, and she began to feel the disparity drain away.

As they headed towards the parking lot, Tyler said, "I've got an idea. Let's visit a true Christmas town before the office party tomorrow and get some inspiration."

"I can't tomorrow. I'm teaching an art class at 9 a.m." She saw a hint of disappointment on his face as his smile faded. "How would you like to come?" she asked hopefully. "We are working with clay tomorrow."

Tyler's eyebrows raised. "Clay? Okay, I'd love to. Then maybe we can get our Christmas inspiration on Sunday if you're free."

"Sounds good."

They said goodbye, and she headed towards home. Warm air flooded towards her as she entered her little cottage. She collapsed down into the plush cushions of the couch, exhausted from the day's emotional twists and turns. Willow climbed onto her lap and demanded a chin-scratching. Rachel stroked her fluffy white fur and dreamed about her art school. The faces of the crowd tonight appeared in her mind, and she smiled at the outpouring of their generosity. She'd always known the people of Laurel Valley were as kind-hearted as they come. But she had to admit, she was a little surprised at the level of support she received.

And what a turn of events! The simple potluck she'd been dreading was now the most important thing to her, the one thing that might save her dream and save this town from more gloomy Decembers. Grandma Lizzy started The Silver Belles Club to bring the town together and to rally around those who struggle during the holidays. And now it would impact Rachel's life as well.

Chapter Thirteen

Tyler arrived at the community center a few minutes late and entered the art classroom. The air was heavy with the damp scent of earthy clay. Two square tables dotted the center of the room, and shelves with pottery lined the side wall.

He spotted Rachel standing at a table, demonstrating a loop tool to a young boy. She hadn't noticed him enter the class, and he was able to stare at her unnoticed for several minutes. Her dark hair was tied back into a high ponytail, and a small lock fell down the side of her face. He watched as her hand reached up and tucked the rogue strand behind her ear, showing off her sharp cheekbones. Long dark lashes fanned out across the tops of her cheeks. She bit her bottom lip in deep thought as a tiny furrow formed between her brows. She was so beautiful he could hardly blink.

Tyler heard Rachel's soft voice speaking to the boy as her hands worked to mold the clay. They laughed at something he said, and then her eyes shot over to where Tyler stood in the doorway. Her whole face brightened as she put down her tool and approached him.

"Hi! I'm so glad you came," she said, taking his arm and guiding him to a table. "I've got a spot right over here for you." Three children were surrounding him, each with a lump of clay they were transforming into something beautiful. Tyler gazed down at his small gray pile, trying to figure out where to start.

"Any ideas on what I should make?" he asked the little girl beside him.

"Well, I'm making a Christmas owl," she said proudly, holding up her masterpiece for him to admire.

"A Christmas owl?" he asked, the word sending a little shiver down his spine.

"He lives in a Christmas tree, and he brings presents to the other animals in the woods, like Santa," she said matter-of-factly.

"I love that idea," he said with a serious tone in his voice. "I'll make one too." Maybe this would get him past his owl phobia.

Before long, the lump had taken on the shape of a small bird with tiny, pointed ears and big round eyes. He worked at trying to make a triangular-shaped piece of clay stick to its face to form a beak. After it fell off for the third time, he motioned to Rachel for assistance.

Her vanilla perfume filled the air between them. As she reached for the little owl, their fingers brushed against each other, and they exchanged a playful glance. Seeing her here, doing what she was most passionate about, caused Tyler's heart to flip-flop.

"You have to rough up the surfaces that you want to

connect so they will bind together," she explained. "It's called scoring." She used a small tool to etch tiny lines in the owl's face and the back of the beak, then dotted on a bit of water with a small brush. He watched as she carefully placed the beak on the face, then used a tool to tie in the edges.

"Here you go," she said, handing it back to him. "Now take this little brush and smooth out the rough area around the beak."

Tyler dipped the brush in water, then carefully swept it over the clay. "How's that?" he asked.

"Adorable!" she said. "Let me show you a couple of ways to make the feathers." Using a wire tool shaped like a U, she created rows of imprints in the clay. "Or you can do it like this." She turned the owl upside down and used the same tool to dig into the clay and pull slightly, creating a curl of clay. She continued three more times to demonstrate.

"That looks really good!" he said as she handed the owl to him. She left his side to help another child, and Tyler put the finishing touches on his little mascot.

After twenty minutes, a timer on Rachel's phone chimed.

"Okay guys, it's clean-up time. Find a spot on the drying rack for your pieces, then wipe down your tables."

Giggle-filled chatter echoed through the room as they lined up to return their tools to her at the large stainless-steel sink. Tyler found a place on the rack for his owl, then went to the sink to help Rachel clean the tools.

"That was really fun," he said. She looked adorable in

a bright red smock. The gray smudges on her face did nothing to hide the joy in her face that these children brought. It was reflected in her adoring eyes and the smile that wouldn't quit. His time with her was like a charge to his internal battery.

"The kids love it. Once I'm in St. Louis, I'll have three times the space and can accommodate more."

"What types of programs will you offer?" he asked, reaching for a paper towel to dry his hands.

"Summer camps, after-school programs. And classes during the week for home-schooled kids. It'll be a full-time job once it's up and running."

After turning off the sink, she set the clean tools on a counter lined with a large towel. They each grabbed a broom and swept up the tiny specks of clay sprinkled all over the floor, and soon, the room was as good as new.

"Thanks for inviting me to join the class today. Hopefully, my owl's beak will survive the kiln!" He clasped his hands together in prayer. Rachel laughed as they headed through the door.

"Thanks for accepting the invitation," she stared into his eyes for a moment, then broke away and headed to her car. "I've got to drop this key off at the receptionist's desk. I'll see you tonight at the party," she called to him.

"Sounds good," he answered, watching her head around the building and wondering how different Rachel's life would have been if his family hadn't moved away. They would have grown up together and attended school and festivals together. Maybe she would have even been his high school sweetheart, and maybe she wouldn't feel she needed to leave Laurel Valley to live her dream. Her personality seemed to fit here so well. He just couldn't imagine her living a life in St. Louis, surrounded by strangers. But it wasn't for him to decide.

Chapter Fourteen

Rachel took one last look at herself in the mirror, scanning head to toe for imperfections. A crystal barrette secured her hair up on one side, and the rest cascaded down her back in soft waves. She chose a sleek silver dress for the office Christmas party, and she was stunning.

Hurrying towards the door, she wriggled into her full-length coat and grabbed her evening bag, giving Willow a quick pat on the head as she passed by. It was only a 10-minute drive, but it gave her some time to get her thoughts straight about Tyler.

She was a little angry with herself for allowing a small spark to develop for him. She hardly knew him, but strangely enough, he felt so familiar to her. Knowing the struggles of a long-distance relationship, she wasn't about to repeat the same mistake and resigned herself to putting the brakes on her feelings.

After circling the lot behind the building, Rachel finally found a parking space and hurried inside towards the elevator doors. Her heart was beating a mile a minute, imagining Tyler dressed in a handsome suit under the twinkle lights.

The doors opened to the open ballroom filled with jazzy music and savory smells. The room appeared even more magical than she'd imagined it would be. A low glow fell over the entire space from the overhead twinkle lights, giving it a romantic feel. Each table had holly leaves and berries encircling a lit candle, and the amber flicker reflected in the guests' eyes.

She recognized most of the attendees from her office. Some were employees, and others were clients. The rest of the guests were business owners around town. She even spotted Mr. Merriweather and Mrs. Perry chatting away as if a lawsuit wasn't looming between them. Rachel smiled at them. No one stays enemies long in Laurel Valley.

After mingling around the room, she accepted an hors d'oeuvre from a passing waiter, then devoured the delicious crab and gruyere cheese crostini in two bites. As nonchalantly as possible, she gave the room a quick scan for Tyler. Judy caught her eye and strolled over, wearing a red sequined dress with matching ruby lipstick. Her blond hair was tied back from her face, revealing her sharp jaw and beautiful skin.

"You look gorgeous!" she said, grabbing Rachel's hands and holding them out to get a good view of the dress. Rachel beamed and returned the compliment.

"How is the party going?" Rachel asked, trying not to sound overly anxious. She continued to scan the room as Judy gushed over the food. Each of them grabbed a dinner plate and began picking through the selections of meats and vegetables. Brianna and Sam had prepared a scrumptious dinner buffet comprising pancetta-wrapped beef tenderloin bites with horseradish cream and a smoked salmon souffle for the entrees, and cider-glazed carrots with walnuts, balsamic green beans with pearl onions, tossed greens with apples, grapes and goat cheese for the side dishes. As they reached the end of the table, Nick emerged from a curtain carrying a tray full of shrimp cocktails in sparkling crystal bowls.

"Nick!" Rachel exclaimed.

"Well, hello, ladies!" he said, glancing up at them.

"Are you planning to eat that entire tray yourself?" Rachel teased.

"Nah, just helping Brianna out." He carefully set each bowl on the buffet table, ensuring none of the garlic-roasted shrimp escaped. Rachel watched him, amused by the care he was taking.

"Sam couldn't make it," Judy explained. "He received a call from his mother a couple of hours ago. His father is ill, and he had to fly home."

"Oh, I'm so sorry to hear that." Rachel glanced back at Nick, who was scooting the larger dishes around to make room for the shrimp. He was truly one of the kindest people in Laurel Valley.

"Let me know if I can get you anything." He flashed a quick smile, then disappeared behind the curtain. Judy and Rachel each helped themselves to the shrimp, then returned to the table. Judy's phone chirped just as they were sitting down.

"Hello?" She paused, listening to the caller. "Hi, Tyler!"

Judy winked at Rachel. "Oh, I'm sorry to hear that." Her smile faded, and Rachel's heart sank, assuming he wasn't coming. "Okay, drive safe, and we'll see you soon!" Ending the call, she turned to Rachel. "The old truck wouldn't start. Poor Tyler got some grease on his shirt and had to change his clothes, so they are running late," she said. Rachel felt a wave of relief come over her, then quickly scolded herself for caring so much.

"Were you looking forward to seeing Tyler here tonight?" Judy gave Rachel a shrewd glance. Rachel felt a blush fill her cheeks, and she weighed her answer before responding.

"Well, um," she stammered. "I just know how much he was looking forward to meeting some new people." Judy continued to eye her curiously, forcing Rachel to avert her eyes.

"Listen," Judy leaned in and lowered her voice. "It's okay to have a good time tonight and get to know Tyler better."

Rachel sighed. "It's just a little confusing. I'm not planning to stay in Laurel Valley. I just felt it would be wrong to lead him on."

"Well, don't worry. Tyler's a big boy. He knows the situation. Just have fun tonight!" Judy gave her a wink as another guest grabbed her attention, and she turned away. Rachel sat quietly, pretending to listen to their laughter-filled banter.

Another twenty minutes ticked by, and she was losing hope that Tyler would make it to the party. Judy had left her side to schmooze the partygoers, and Rachel was stuck keeping polite conversation with the rest of the people seated at the table. While feigning interest in old Mr. Wadsworth's battle with a ten-pound bass last fall, a light tap on Rachel's shoulder got her attention.

"Is this seat taken?" Tyler flashed his captivating smile down at her. He was even more handsome in his black suit and tie than Rachel had imagined. She stood to greet him and held her breath, watching his eyes taking her in.

"You look incredible," he said breathlessly. Their eyes locked, and neither spoke for a moment. The sounds of the party grew faint, suspending just the two of them together. She could feel the motion of her heart in her chest, not faster, but stronger. As if by magnetic force, the distance between them closed and she forgot the promise to herself to pull back the reins on her feelings.

"Well, good evening, Miss Rachel!" Jack exclaimed, appearing in the gap between them. "You and your sister did a wonderful job with the room."

"Thanks, Jack." She smiled back at him. "You two clean up pretty good!"

Tyler laughed. "Not quite as comfortable as jeans and a flannel, but it's nice once in a while."

"You kids have fun." Jack left them and headed towards Patty, who greeted him with a side kiss. Rachel was happy to see these two lovely people hitting it off. She hoped Tyler was happy for them as well.

"I'm glad you guys made it. Are you hungry?" she asked him.

"Yes, but I'd hate to take you from that riveting conversation with Mr. Wadsworth. Are you sure you can pull yourself away?" Tyler teased.

Rachel giggled as she led him towards the buffet table. Brianna appeared, carrying a large tray of hors d'oeuvres.

"Hi, Rach," she said, setting the tray on the table then giving Rachel a quick kiss on the cheek. "You must be Tyler. I'm Rachel's sister, Brianna."

"Nice to meet you, Brianna. The food looks delicious."

Rachel noticed Brianna's eyes narrow, trying to size him up, but a smile appeared on her lips, and her voice was warm and kind.

"Thank you. I've got a pretty good variety out here, so grab a plate and dig in." Brianna quickly headed back towards a prep area concealed behind curtains, and Rachel guided Tyler down the food line.

"Everything is fabulous." She handed him a plate and pointed to the items she'd already tried while filling her plate with things she hadn't. They made their way through the crowd and headed out to the patio to find a table away from the loud chatter of the guests. Warming lanterns lined the patio's perimeter while soft music played through the speakers, making the space cozy and romantic.

"Are you warm enough out here? We could sit inside instead," he offered.

"I'm fine. It was a little stuffy in there."

After settling in at an intimate table, they enjoyed light conversation about Tyler's plans for the ranch and the history of the farmhouse he'd uncovered. Rachel told him about Willow and was happy to hear he was not allergic to cats. She talked about her work at the law firm and how she'd thought about becoming a paralegal, but Judy convinced her to follow her dream.

"I really love teaching the classes at the community center," she said. "Most of the children are from the more rural areas around Laurel Valley. I think it brings me as much joy as it does them!" Her mind flashed on each of their smiling faces, and she was thrilled to be able to help develop their creativity. She glanced at Tyler and noticed a touch of sadness in his eyes. She knew what he was thinking. What will they do once she moves away? Would someone be willing to take over the class for her? It suddenly dawned on her how much would change and the lives that would be affected when she left. She'd been so wrapped up in breaking out of this town that she hadn't stopped to think about the people she was leaving behind. The move to St. Louis wouldn't just affect her life. There were people here who depended on her. Could she really just move away and not look back?

Tyler described his experience of acclimating to his new home. Rachel nodded her head, enamored with his description of the town. "I enjoy walking down the street and saying hi to everyone by name," he said. "There is a sense of community here. Everyone is eager to lend a hand when you need it."

This type of thing had bothered her in the past. Sometimes, she felt smothered and yearned for the new and unknown faces in the city. Tyler felt completely different about the people here. She wondered if he'd get tired of it at some point as well. Or could she have just seen these acts of kindness as intrusions because this was how Grant saw them?

Tyler's voice broke into her thoughts. "I can't tell you how many times people I haven't even met have greeted me by name on the street and offered to help with unpacking or repairs."

"I'm glad everyone is making you feel so comfortable. Things are going just the way you'd hoped."

"I agree. I couldn't ask for a better life than the one I'm living now. Laurel Valley is a special place, a dream come true for me." She was touched to see how this quaint little town had captivated him.

Rachel felt him drawing her in with his eyes as the strand of twinkle lights overhead swayed in the chilly breeze. An acoustic version of "Have Yourself a Merry Little Christmas" began playing. "Would you like to dance?" he asked.

"Yes," she said, a little breathless, placing her hand in his.

He held her close, one hand resting at the small of her back and the other gently holding her fingertips. She rested her temple against his jaw, feeling the warmth of his skin and taking in the scent of his cologne, his nearness sending a tingle down her spine. As they swayed to the rhythm of the music, she closed her eyes and tried to burn this memory into her brain. She knew there would come a time when Tyler would not be close, and she wanted to carry this feeling with her.

"I'm really glad Aunt Judy introduced us," Tyler said.

Rachel's heart raced with apprehension. She wasn't sure what to say. "I'm..." she hesitated, then slowly looked up at him, staring into his eyes. "I'm happy, too." She knew he wanted to kiss her. She could feel her skin warming as he drew her in closer. Everything inside her wanted so badly to feel the softness of his lips. She looked away, not wanting this to end and not wanting it to go further. It was so difficult to keep from falling for him, and it was wrong for her to lead Tyler on when the trajectory of her life was still uncertain.

Tyler could see the hint of both longing and hesitation in Rachel's eyes. He knew what she was thinking. The breakup with Grant was still so fresh, and their bond wasn't completely broken yet. She'd hardly had time to wrap her head around being single. Throwing in a new relationship on top of everything else going on would be too chaotic for her, especially since she was still planning to leave soon.

But there was a connection between them that was undeniable. They both knew it. Now, they needed to figure out what to do. The festival was in a week, plenty of time to fall even further for her, and he wasn't sure he had the strength to deny it. He knew she needed to do what she felt was right, and right now, she felt like she belonged in St. Louis. It would be wrong for him to sway her feelings.

The soft beat of the music picked up as an electric guitar thrummed the intro to "Jingle Bell Rock," breaking the spell between them. He could tell things had gotten too heavy and regretted making her uncomfortable.

"I noticed a hot cocoa station inside, and I bet they

have little marshmallows." He held her hand and pulled it slightly towards the door. "You want to go in and warm up?"

She nodded, and he saw the relief wash over her face as they headed inside.

They made a beeline to the beverage table as they entered the room and grabbed two mugs. Tyler filled each cup with steamy hot cocoa, then topped both off with marshmallows and a sprinkle of cinnamon sugar.

Tyler spotted Jack dancing with Patty. Until now, his father hadn't been ready to let go of the loss in his heart. But Tyler felt that he was witnessing this release right before his eyes. Jack deserved happiness, and Tyler was glad he'd found it here.

After savoring every sip of their cocoa, they had their caricature portrait made. The artist captured their faces perfectly, then added disproportionately small bodies, exchanging gifts in front of a Christmas tree. He even added Willow peeking out from the branches. It was adorable!

"It's almost midnight. I'd better head home," she said to Tyler, eyeing her watch.

"Okay, Cinderella. I'll walk you to your car," he teased.

Rachel giggled. "Thanks. I just need to stop and say goodbye to Bri."

They headed towards the exit and spotted Brianna chatting with Mr. Merriweather. As Rachel and Tyler approached, they heard her saying, "I agree. The police department should definitely add a small tank to their vehicle fleet."

Tyler shook his head and chuckled quietly, and Rachel elbowed him.

"Bri, everything was perfect," Rachel said, hugging Brianna.

"Really delicious," Tyler chimed in.

"Thanks so much. Are you heading home?" Brianna asked.

"Yes, I'm exhausted from all the drama I've created these past couple of days!"

Brianna laughed. "Everything's going to work out. Drive careful. I'm catering a conference in St. Louis on Monday but I'll be back late that night. Chloe and I are still planning to come over Tuesday afternoon to make the snowflakes for the barn."

"Okay, perfect." The sisters gave a quick cheek kiss.

"It was nice to meet you," Tyler waved to Brianna.

"You too, Tyler."

Rachel and Tyler stood quietly while waiting for the elevator doors to open.

"Who is Chloe?" he asked.

"She's Brianna's daughter. I promised her she could help with the decorations."

Tyler nodded and stood silently beside her. "I had a great time talking with you tonight," he said softly.

"Me too." She smiled up at him, and a silent conversation passed between them.

If things were different, I bet we'd end up together.
I think so, too.

Suppressing their feelings was the right thing to do...the only thing they could do. The doors finally parted, and they stepped inside, feeling a brief jolt as the elevator began its descent.

"So, I was thinking about what you told me about your grandma. Whatever happened to that cottage? Do you ever visit it?" he asked.

"No, unfortunately, I don't even know where it is. I just remember things about it. I asked my mom a few years ago, but she didn't know either."

He felt a pang of sadness at hearing this. That magical place she visited with her grandmother was gone. It might have offered her comfort if she'd been able to spend time there growing up.

They stepped outside into the frigid night air and walked towards her car. "I'll pick you up tomorrow morning for our Christmas spirit field trip."

"Where are we going?" she asked inquisitively.

"Not sure yet, but don't you worry! I will have it figured out by the time I see you."

He bundled her into her car and watched her leave as feelings of discouragement festered within him. Why did she have to move away?

Chapter Fifteen

Tyler sat in his favorite spot by the window of Valley Brews, taking in the bustling downtown activity. The festival was sure to be a huge success, judging from the support they received at the meeting. He knew Rachel was feeling overwhelmed, so visiting a neighboring town, well-known for their Christmas spirit, would be a nice escape and give them plenty of ideas to bring home.

Nick slid into the booth across from him. "Morning!" he said brightly.

"Hey, Nick! Good morning to you, too. Great party last night."

"I agree. Judy and Frank never disappoint."

Tyler eyed Nick curiously. "I bet you were a big help to Brianna." He watched Nick's face for a reaction. An unmistakable sparkle appeared in Nick's eyes, and his face blushed slightly at the mention of her name.

"I guess. She got a little frantic when Sam had to back out. I couldn't just stand around enjoying the party." He tried to wave it off like it was nothing more than an act of kindness, but Tyler could see a subtle change come over him.

"Have you thought more about coming to work at the ranch?" Tyler asked, changing the subject. Nick's brow drew in a bit, and the sparkle in his eyes dimmed.

"I don't think I can leave the shop. My dad wants to retire, and my brother was supposed to take it over, but he's moving to Florida. His father-in-law offered him a great job." Nick's face grew sullen. "So, I think my dad wants to leave it to me."

Tyler's hopes fell, and tension resumed its perch on his shoulders. He knew he was taking on a mountain of work at the ranch, but he'd hoped to find someone to help him acclimate to the inner workings of life in the country. Before moving back to Laurel Valley, he'd dreamed of the tranquil setting of evenings on the porch listening to crickets and watching the moonlight dance on the ripples of the lake. But this picturesque setting hadn't been the reality thus far. Problems were popping up almost every day. Aside from creating a profitable business, there were a multitude of expensive repairs needed.

"I can still help you on weekends, probably a few evenings during the week too, at least until I know for sure about the shop." Nick gave him a reassuring smile.

"I appreciate that. I think I got into more than I bargained for with this old ranch." Tyler hoped his smile hid the anxiety that crept back into his chest. Refocusing on the day planned with Rachel, he said, "Hey, I'm planning an excursion with Rachel today. She needs some Christmas spirit, so I wanted to take her to a nearby town that does it right. Have you got any ideas? Maybe within a

45-minute drive."

"St. Charles is about 30 minutes east. Just hop on I-70, and you'll see the exit. It's a beautiful town."

Ben came by the table and set a steaming mug before Tyler. "St. Charles is awesome," he said in agreement. "We were going to take our little one there to see Santa." He paused. "Unless you are planning to have Santa at the festival." Both Ben and Nick looked at Tyler, waiting for a response.

Tyler considered this. He'd need to find someone to volunteer for the part, and his mind immediately went to Mr. Meriweather. He had a nice wooly beard and would look great in a furry red coat. "I think we might just do that!"

Ben nodded. "Me and the Mrs. are heading to McMillan's this afternoon to pick out a tree. You want me to get an extra for the festival?"

With so much left to plan, Tyler was grateful for one thing to be off his to-do list. "That'd be great, Ben. I appreciate it."

"No problem," he said, turning away, then stopped. "You know, I drive past Rachel's house every morning on my way here. Noticed she didn't put up a tree again this year. You think she might like one, seeing how things are different? I could drop it off while you guys are in St. Charles."

Tyler considered this. He loved the idea of decorating a tree with her but hoped this wouldn't be overstepping a line. He cast his eyes toward Nick, who gave him a nod of approval. "I think she'd love it, Ben. Thanks so much!"

"You two have fun today," Nick said, sliding out of the booth. I'm heading to work. Give me a holler if you need anything." He thrust his hand at Tyler, who gave it a hearty shake.

"Thanks, I really appreciate you, Nick."

Tyler grabbed his phone from his back pocket and quickly searched for St. Charles. A picture appeared on his screen. Snowy streets, antique iron gas lamp posts... it was a scene straight out of a Norman Rockwell painting. He poked around the site some more, scribbled down an agenda on a napkin, then gathered his things and headed out the door to their Christmas adventure.

As he pulled into Rachel's driveway, he first noticed its lack of Christmas decorations. The little cottage was cloaked in snow but had no Christmas vibe, not even a small wreath on the door. Ascending the front steps, he admired the craftsman bungalow architecture, then spotted a little white kitty peering out at him through the window. Rachel answered after a quick tap on the door.

"Hey, I'm almost ready." She greeted him with a broad smile. "Come on in; you can meet Willow."

Willow was curled into a small loaf on the back of the couch, tiny paws tucked underneath her. She raised her head as Tyler approached and eyed him suspiciously. He allowed her to sniff his hand, then she granted him permission to pet her soft fur.

"Wow," Rachel said with surprise. "You must have a golden touch. She usually runs under the bed when anyone comes over."

Tyler counted that as a huge point in his favor. "Well,

back home, I was known as the Cat Whisperer," he said jokingly. She giggled, then sat down on the couch to lace up her boots. Tyler looked around her place and smiled when he spotted the caricature drawing displayed on her mantle. His eyes drifted to the colorful bookshelves. After perusing some of the titles, he noticed the unusual pieces of pottery displayed.

"These are really unique. Where'd you get them?"

She laughed. "I made them."

He gingerly took one into his hand, marveling at the beautiful colors. "Really?" he asked.

"Yep. I have a makeshift pottery studio out back on the porch. It's hard to work out there in the winter. That's why I want to move to a bigger location, so I'll have space for a classroom and a pottery studio," she said, completing the bow on her second boot. "You want to see it?"

"I do!"

She led him through the kitchen, where he noticed the original cabinetry and period appliances. The bright red stove caught his attention. "Incredible! This is a vintage 1940's O'Keefe and Merritt gas stove." He ran his hand over the smooth chrome edge. "Red is tough to find. Where'd you get it?"

"It was here when we moved in. I've had to repair it several times, but I love it. Gave me the practice I needed to fix yours." She gave him a wink.

They passed through a door at the rear of the kitchen and stepped out onto the porch. Tyler could see what she meant by makeshift. Panels of plastic had been fastened to the columns around the perimeter to create walls and keep out the harsh weather while allowing sunlight to shine through, although they weren't doing a very good job of keeping out the cold. Three metal shelving units lined the wall that backed up to the house, and several pieces of brilliantly colored pottery filled the top two shelves. Tyler stared at them in awe. There was an iridescent metallic hue to them he'd never seen on pottery before.

"You made these?" he asked, gently touching the surface of a scalloped edge bowl. His eyes scanned the other items. There were plates, cups, vases, and bowls, all made with the same technique, each different from the next.

She laughed. "Yes. That technique is called copper matte raku. I've been experimenting with it. I use a copper oxide wash before firing them. It's a bit tricky; still working out the kinks."

Tyler plucked a coffee mug from the shelf. It had the same brilliant coloring as the sunset over the lake at his ranch. "It's stunning," he said, replacing it.

Rachel walked over to him, picked up the mug, and held it out. "You can have this one."

"Really? Are you sure? I am happy to pay you for it."

"No way! It's my gift to you for helping plan the festival."

After helping Rachel with her coat, they each gave Willow a pat on the head and descended the front porch steps.

"So where are we going?" she asked as they got into the truck.

"Nick told me about a little town nearby that is the

epitome of Christmas spirit, called St. Charles. I thought we could walk around for some inspiration."

"Sounds great. I haven't been there before."

A snowplow had cleared the roads, creating drifts that sparkled like tiny diamonds in the morning sun. Tyler gave the steering wheel a squeeze of appreciation as he felt the warm air blow through the vents.

"Your house is really nice. How long have you lived there?" he asked.

"I grew up there with my mom and Brianna. Then my mom moved to California." She stared out the window in reflection. "Brianna moved out when she got married, so it was just me after that."

"Has it been hard here without your mom?" Tyler felt he might be treading in choppy waters, but he thought they had known each other long enough to be on a more personal level.

"Yes, until recently. Seems like every time we talk, we end up in an argument about my love life. She didn't particularly like Grant; said he was a workaholic like my dad.

"Was he?" Tyler asked inquisitively.

"I guess so, although I hadn't admitted it until after we broke up." She was quiet for a moment. Tyler glanced over at her, but she continued staring out the window. He heard her sigh before saying, "I just kept making excuses for him."

"Did your grandma live in the house before you?" he asked, leading the conversation away from Grant.

Rachel nodded. "She and my grandfather built it when

they got married. We moved into it after she passed away. It's paid for, so my mom doesn't charge me any rent, which is nice. Gives me more money for art supplies."

"That's a sweet deal," he said.

"So, you never told me where you lived before moving here," she said. "Was it a lot like Laurel Valley?"

"Actually, no, nothing like it. I grew up in a high-rise in Manhattan."

Rachel turned to face him. "Are you kidding?" Disbelief rang in her voice.

"Nope. It was beautiful. Overlooked Central Park. Had a doorman and everything, just like you see in the movies."

"Manhattan," she repeated dreamily. It was the end-all-be-all of exciting cities in her eyes. "So, you're a real-life city slicker! How could you ever want to leave such an exciting place?" she asked with shock.

Tyler laughed and shook his head. "Living in a big city isn't for everybody. I love the outdoors and space and being in nature. Unless you count Central Park, I didn't get much access to it."

Tyler stole a quick glance at her and saw the wheels turning in her head. The bewildered look on her face made him chuckle. He knew she thought he was just another small-town guy, so this revelation must be quite a shock to her. "I can see how living in a big city might seem really exciting," he continued. "And there are a lot of things I got to experience that I wouldn't have otherwise. It's just not for me."

"But wasn't the vibrance and the anonymity better

than everyone knowing your business?" she asked.

"Sure, for a while. But being just another face in the crowd gets lonely, and ultimately, I wanted to feel like my town was a part of my family. There is a closeness and quietness of a small town that I couldn't live without. Besides, Laurel Valley is where my family started; my roots are here, and every time we visited, it was harder and harder to leave. I always knew I would return someday and make it my home again." They drove silently for a moment while he allowed her thoughts to process.

"What about college?" she finally asked.

"I have a PhD in American History from Columbia."

She laughed out loud. "I had no idea, Tyler!" She shook her head. "Or should I say, Dr. Patterson! Why didn't you tell me?"

"I guess it never came up," he said, shrugging his shoulders. He felt her staring at him with astonishment, and it occurred to him that Rachel had been attracted to Grant because he was from a big city, highly educated, and different from the boys she'd grown up with. Now that she knew his background, was there a chance she would see Tyler as the best of both worlds?

Chapter Sixteen

The truck sputtered down St. Charles' historic Main Street. Beautiful old brick buildings lined the street, all dressed in Christmas cheer. Colorful wreaths adorned every door, and swags of garland hung loosely across each second-floor balcony. They gazed out at the black antique lamp posts wrapped with evergreen garland. Red bows were fastened towards the top, just under the light, giving the appearance of a dapper gentleman with a black top hat and bright bowtie.

"This is really beautiful," said Rachel. Snow had gathered against the buildings and settled in all the windowpanes. Thinking back to the streets of Laurel Valley, she could see how Tyler would have been disappointed.

"I think Laurel Valley could look like this with a little work," Tyler replied.

They parked in front of a small red brick cottage with black shutters attached to a larger building. A quaint white picket fence surrounded an area to the left, and multiple snowmen had been constructed, each with its own personality. A green checkerboard sign hung over the door that read Main Street Marketplace.

"This store has some great stuff. Let's run inside for a minute," Tyler said.

Once inside, Tyler headed to the counter and started a conversation with an older gentleman as Rachel browsed around, admiring the displays of local honey products, delectable jellies, spices, and teas. The interior was beautifully decorated for Christmas. Holiday throw pillows, table decor, and candles were displayed throughout.

"Hey, Rachel," Tyler called out to her. She headed towards his voice at the back of the store. As she approached him, she noticed the coffee mug she'd given Tyler sitting on the counter. "This is Mr. Ewing," he said, gesturing toward the elderly man.

"Hello, young lady, it's a pleasure to meet you. This your work?" he said, pointing at the mug.

"Yes, sir," she replied in confusion.

"I think my customers would love them. How'd you like to bring in a few pieces on consignment?"

Her eyes flew to Tyler, and he grinned back at her. Her face broke into a broad smile. A stranger liked her work, and she was honored that he would want to take up shelf space with her pottery. It was a huge compliment.

"Of course! I have a few different styles you can choose from." Her heart was pounding inside her chest, and she hoped the nervousness wasn't showing in her voice.

"That'd be great. You pick whatever you think my customers would like. Just bring them in when you can.

Thanks for stopping in." He shook both their hands. "Can't wait to try that cider wine, Tyler."

"Thanks, Mr. Ewing. I know it will be a hit with your customers."

They exited the store and headed back to the truck.

"Well, that was a nice surprise," Rachel said as they sat in the truck to warm up.

"I've got a few more tricks up my sleeve," he said mischievously. "Lunch at Tompkins is next. It's this great little historic place. Supposed to have excellent food. Then, at 2:30, we are going to see Elf the Musical at the performing arts center."

Rachel inhaled sharply with excitement. "That's my favorite Christmas movie," she said, a little embarrassed.

"Well, then...after we travel through the seven levels of the candy cane forest," he began quoting. She gasped with delight. "Through the sea of twirly-swirly gumdrops..." He paused for dramatic effect. "We'll watch the St. Charles Christmas Parade at six!"

Rachel clapped her hands with excitement. "How did you plan all this so quickly?" There was a hint of wonder in her voice.

"Google's an excellent travel agent. I want to be sure we get plenty of Christmas spirit to take back home with us."

They found a parking spot and walked the streets, taking in the lovely decorations and buzz of the town. Carolers from the local choir sang on a street corner, wearing colorful, turn-of-the-century costumes, complete with top hats and crinoline skirts. Tyler stopped to sing along with a deep, exaggerated, baritone voice, making

Rachel laugh so hard she couldn't join in.

Lunch at Tompkins was a magical experience in itself. In addition to the incredible food, Tyler was a fountain of wealth when it came to Missouri's rich and colorful history. Rachel enjoyed watching the passion dance in his eyes as he described the differences in the architectural styles of the buildings and the importance of historical preservation.

With their bellies full of food, they headed to the theater for a hilarious performance of Elf. As Buddy shook the little snow globe, Rachel noticed his connection with Tyler.

"Hey, you went on an adventure to find your roots, just like Buddy," she whispered with a giggle.

"Yeah, thankfully, my roots were in a ranch, not the Empire State Building!" he agreed. "And I think I'd fit in better at the North Pole than New York City," he said with a laugh. Rachel agreed. Tyler would never be happy in a crowded city again. He'd gotten to see both of these very different worlds and knew he was making the right choice by following his heart back to Laurel Valley. She envied this about him. It must be so nice to feel settled and know where you are meant to be.

After enjoying the musical, they found a spot along the parade route with hot chocolate in hand. Their faces lit with delight as the colorful floats passed. Every business, club, and organization in St. Charles was represented. As the high school band performed "We Wish You a Merry Christmas," the cheerleaders danced to the beat, gaining heartfelt applause from the crowd. Tiny ballerinas from the ballet school fluttered around in white tutus on a trailer transformed into a scene from The Nutcracker. Even the local preschool joined in the fun. Colorful lights illuminated a caravan of ten little wagons gliding through the streets carrying gleeful toddlers, their cheeks rosy from the cold.

As the parade's final float appeared with a jolly Santa waving from a gold and red velvet throne in a scene from the North Pole, Rachel reflected on Laurel Valley's paltry take on the holiday. But everyone at the town hall meeting seemed ready to change, and she hoped their enthusiasm would carry into the new year.

Once the crowd began to dissipate, Rachel and Tyler headed down the block to grab a bite to eat before heading home. The music from the play and the lights from the parade filled her heart with joy, and she brimmed with excitement at their plans to transform their hometown into a Christmas wonderland.

"Did you enjoy everything?" Tyler asked.

"It was just beautiful!" She looked up at him as they walked along the brick sidewalk and could hardly believe this grand gesture. It was so thoughtful of him to plan all this for her just to get her into the holiday spirit. She knew what was blooming in her heart, and it was more than friendship. Like the approach of a winter storm on the horizon, there was no way to stop the swift progression of their relationship. It was happening so quickly, creating feelings of both exhilaration and confusion within her. Like a force of its own, it was stronger than either one of them.

The sky was dark as they made their way towards a little cafe, but a canopy of Christmas lights strung overhead cast a soft glow onto the snowy ground, illuminating their steps. The streetlamps had come alive with tiny flames, and all the twinkle lights were sparkling.

They arrived at the cafe and settled into a cozy table nestled in the bay window. The table was dressed with embroidered napkins and vintage teacups at each place setting.

Rachel grasped the cup in front of her and turned it around in her hand. Tiny pink and lavender rosebuds were scattered around the white exterior, and a thin line of gold encircled the rim. The handle was curved in an "S" shape and tapered at the end like a feather. She ran her finger over the intricate details, and a memory flashed through her mind. Her grandmother had a teacup collection. They had been displayed on a wood hutch in her dining room. Rachel used to climb up on a chair and take each one off the shelf, studying its delicate floral design. What had happened to them? She hadn't thought about them since her grandmother passed away, and it saddened her that she didn't have them.

Her eyes slowly raised to meet Tyler's gaze. The intense look in his eyes told her he'd been staring at her while she admired the teacup.

"What are you thinking about?" he asked.

"My grandma had teacups like these," she said, sighing. "I'm hoping my mother knows where they are. I'd like to have them."

He nodded his head with understanding. She knew

Tyler would understand how she was feeling right now. She wasn't sure why, but things she hadn't thought much about in years were suddenly becoming treasures to her, and she was desperate to surround herself with the comfort of their familiarity. "Do you have anything special from your mother?" she asked, hoping this wouldn't bring on any sad memories for him.

"I do. My dad got her a bracelet for Christmas right before I was born. It has little blue topaz stones and diamonds for my birthstone and her birthstone. Hoping I have a little girl someday to pass it down to." His eyes held a mix of emotions, filled with both sadness of the past and hope for the future.

Rachel thought about what she and Tyler had in common. They were both missing their mothers, and she regretted not working harder to get along with hers. She hoped things would be different now that Grant was gone. Pangs of remorse echoed through her. Tyler had no choice but to let his mother go, while Rachel's was only a phone call away. She suddenly missed her deeply. "It sounds beautiful. And what a special way to celebrate the birth of a child."

As he sat across from her, she wanted so badly to reach over and grasp his hand. The hum of conversation inside the cafe was soothing to her, like the wind's soft howls beyond the window. She was filled with so much joy from the day's events, and she couldn't wait to hear his ideas. "So, what kind of inspiration have you seen here in St. Charles?"

He rapped his fingernails on the table a few times in

thought. "Well, the first thing I noticed were the lamp posts. The greenery really stands out against the black metal. The lamp posts down our Main Street are black, too, so I think that would look great!"

She grabbed her handbag and pulled out her small notebook and pen, then scribbled down their ideas.

"One difference between Laurel Valley and St. Charles is the median down the main road into town," Tyler said. "There are trees in our median. The lights strung over the street here are pretty, but maybe we can wrap twinkle lights around all the branches instead like Bedford Falls in 'It's a Wonderful Life.'"

Rachel grinned at the sparkle in Tyler's eyes. "That sounds perfect! We need to decorate the gazebo, too." Her hand flashed across the page in her notebook, writing down the details bouncing around in her thoughts.

"I told Ben we'd have a Santa Claus for the kids. Mr. Merriweather will do it, don't you think?" Tyler asked.

"No doubt. He loves feeling needed. I'm sure he'll do it."

"How about the items for the silent auction?" he asked.

"It's all in a conference room in Judy's building. Where can we set all of it up at the ranch?"

"There's a room attached to the barn. Must have been storage for tools or something. It's all cleaned out and ready to go. I can come by your office with the truck and pick everything up."

"That's perfect. It's all coming together. Now, it's just a matter of getting everything decorated." Rachel sat back, amazed at how easy the festival planning had been with

Tyler. Their ideas had fallen into perfect harmony, making the work seem almost effortless.

They enjoyed a light meal, then decided it was finally time to head back home, armed with more than enough Christmas spirit in their hearts to make the festival a success. Rachel was pleasantly surprised at how much she enjoyed visiting St. Charles. It felt good to experience happiness towards the holiday for a change.

As they arrived back in Laurel Valley, Tyler turned the truck down Main Street, heading toward Rachel's house. Passing the shops, they were surprised to see wreaths hanging from doors and lights around all the front windows. Large potted poinsettias dotted the sidewalks. Some of the buildings had icicle lights hanging from the eves. Even the trees in the median had been strung with white twinkle lights. It was as if someone had read their minds while they were in St. Charles. The transformation was amazing.

"Are you sure we are in the right town?" Rachel said, completely bewildered. From the warmth of the truck, they could see fliers taped to the store windows advertising the festival.

"I can't believe they did all this while we were gone," Tyler said. "I thought we'd be spending days decorating the town."

Rachel's speech must have inspired everyone more than she'd realized. So much of the work Rachel thought they had before them was already done, and it was done by the wonderful people of this town, coming together to make the Silver Belles Christmas a reality.

As they approached the park in the center of town, he slowed the truck so they could see the gazebo. Garland, infused with twinkle lights, was strung around all the pillars and woven around the perimeter of the handrails. The interior ceiling had rows of tiny lights extending from the center like a star. A stately twelve-foot evergreen had been erected in the center of the park.

"This is amazing," she whispered.

A misty rain started to fall, and they could see the droplets turn to snowflakes in the headlights as the truck rambled down her street. As they pulled into the driveway, the truck's headlights shone brightly onto her front porch, illuminating a large dark object in the corner.

"What's that?" Rachel asked.

"I don't know, let's go see."

She looked over at him. He had a tight smile pulling at his lips. Once she ascended the porch steps, she saw the object was a six-foot evergreen, its middle branches creating a wide girth, giving it a plump appearance.

"How did this get here?" she asked in disbelief.

"I think it was a special delivery from a Christmas elf!" Tyler said, beaming with excitement. "Let's get it inside."

A stand was already fastened to the bottom, and after setting it upright next to the couch, they stood back, inhaling the fragrant scent of the evergreen.

"Seriously," Rachel said. "How'd you pull this off?"

Tyler grinned. "Ben was getting a tree for the festival today and offered to drop one off here for you."

Rachel was speechless. With everything he'd planned for the day, he even thought to have a tree delivered for her as well. She hadn't had a Christmas tree since she was a teenager, and seeing it here before her, full and fragrant, almost brought tears to her eyes.

"I'm assuming you don't have any lights," Tyler looked at her skeptically.

"Bingo," she admitted. "I'll pick some up at the hardware store tomorrow. Judy and I are going shopping for supplies."

"Okay, well, I'm gonna head out." Tyler's hand reached for the doorknob, then stopped. "If you want, I can give you a hand decorating your tree when you get back." His voice was slightly hesitant.

After all he'd done, there was no way she'd deny him. "Yes, I would love some help," she said, seeing a tiny sigh of relief escape him. Just as he was going out the door, she touched his arm. He turned back, and she slowly put her arms around him, resting her cheek on his chest. She could smell the woodsy cologne he wore that mixed just right with his body chemistry. Intoxicating.

"Thank you so much for giving me this special day," she said. Holding back her emotions was not an option at this moment. She wanted him to feel the gratitude welling up within her.

She felt his arms slowly rise to embrace her, knowing he was hesitating because she stepped away the last time he had tried to hug her. This time, she let his arms surround her with warmth and comfort. He pulled her in closer, and they stood for a long moment. She could feel his heart pounding against her cheek. It was so difficult to let go, but she knew it was the right thing to do and reluctantly loosened her arms.

He followed her lead and released his grip as well, allowing the space between them to grow. Without another word, he headed down the porch steps and got into his truck, not looking at her again as he backed out and sped away.

Chapter Seventeen

T he festival was only five days away, and Rachel felt overwhelmed with all that had to be done. Judy arrived at her house promptly at nine to pick Rachel up for their shopping excursion. Rachel couldn't wait to ask her about the beautifully decorated town. Hopping into Judy's car, she said, "Wow! Main Street looked fabulous last night! Who did all that work?"

Judy smiled. "We have a lot of kindhearted people in this town. Once you lit the fire under them, they all jumped into action and got it done. Mr. Merriweather took on the role of Official Christmas Coordinator, barking orders like it was wartime. It was like watching Santa's soldiers scurry all over town."

Rachel could just imagine the scene. Visualizing the chaos made her laugh out loud. "How about the big Christmas tree next to the gazebo? Will there be a tree lighting ceremony?"

"Yep, just a small one tonight at eight o'clock, with a few of the townspeople performing in the gazebo. I'm not sure we will have many attendees. There hasn't been much time to attract people from neighboring towns."

"That's okay. It will have a more intimate and magical feel," Rachel said happily.

Her heart warmed with the scene as they made their way down Main Street. In just a few days, the town had experienced a reawakening of its spirit, and everyone was joining in on the fun. It thrilled her to see so much activity. She had seen the town busy with shoppers before but never against a backdrop of fabulous Christmas decor. It gave the atmosphere a totally different feeling.

Their first stop was Valley Brews for an energy boost via two mocha cappuccinos, but finding a parking space was proving to be a little more difficult than usual. "It's pretty crowded down here this morning. I wonder why," Judy said. She finally found a spot in the next block, and they bundled up in their coats and headed across the street. Valley Brews was packed full of customers. Rachel and Judy exchanged a confused look, then patiently waited for their turn at the counter. At last, they were face to face with Ben.

"Ben, where did all these people come from?" Judy asked.

Ben's face lit up with a smile. "All the shop owners posted Rachel's flier to their social media accounts. I'm assuming that's what brought in all these new visitors. The store has been packed since seven a.m. You ladies have a seat, and I'll bring these out to you."

They made their way to a small table just as the previous occupants vacated it. Thankful to have found a spot, they patiently waited for their coffees. Judy didn't waste any time prodding Rachel for details of her visit to St. Charles with Tyler.

"Sooooo," Judy began. "How was St. Charles?" A gigantic grin appeared on her face.

"It was..." Rachel hesitated. She wanted so badly to be completely honest about her feelings for Tyler but felt that putting it into words somehow committed her to a path she wasn't ready to go down. Throwing caution to the wind, she said unsmilingly and with a completely level voice, "It was the best day of my life."

Judy blinked, trying to reconcile her words with the stark look on Rachel's face. A tiny grin finally formed on Rachel's lips, and Judy's eyes widened with realization.

"I'm so happy!" she whispered back. "I knew you two would hit it off. I told Tyler, 'What's meant to be, will be.'"

"My Grandma Lizzy used to say that!" Rachel said, then paused. "Wait, did Tyler talk to you about me?"

"Well, not recently. It was last week when Frank and I went to the ranch for dinner. Tyler was talking about wanting a fresh start here, and we got on the subject of relationships. And I said you two would be great together, but he feels he should back off since you want to move to St. Louis." Deep down, Rachel agreed they'd be great together, and a pang of regret echoed within her.

Ben arrived at the table with their to-go cups. "Here you go. Let me know if I can get you anything else."

"Thanks, Ben," they replied in unison. Judy leaned in again for more details. "So, how are you feeling about the breakup?"

Rachel wasn't sure what to say. With all the planning

going on, Grant had been shoved to the back of her mind. "Honestly, I haven't had much time to think about it." She shrugged her shoulders noncommittally. "I'm still upset about the abruptness of how it ended, but I guess I'm getting over it quicker than I thought I would."

"So, you do have feelings for Tyler, right?" Judy prodded.

Rachel laughed, then gave a very slight nod. The day she spent with Tyler in St. Charles had opened her eyes to the beauty of a small town and the many facets of a small-town guy. She was finding herself questioning everything she had planned. Her feelings for him continued to grow deeper. And resisting the urge to kiss him last night was almost unbearable.

Judy wiggled in her seat while tapping her fingertips together in a mini clap.

"Don't get excited just yet," Rachel warned. "I don't know how long I'll be here. It just depends on whether I'm able to buy the space in St. Louis." She ran a finger over the rim of her cup, "Living in a big city has been my dream for so long, Judy, but now I'm not so sure. I really like all the excitement of a larger city. And Tyler wants no part of that. He's had his fill and wants to live a quiet life here. I just don't know if I'm ready to give up my dream."

Judy nodded and draped her arm around Rachel's shoulder, offering her a reassuring squeeze. "Sweetie, I want nothing more in this world than your happiness, whether here or in St. Louis. But I want you to consider all that you'd be giving up. Life in a big city can be rough, especially when you don't know anyone. It might get lonely. Here, you are surrounded by people who love you. I know they can go a little overboard, but they mean well. They only want your happiness, too."

Judy had such a warm, motherly look on her face. She had seen Rachel through life's dramas, big and small, but her words conflicted with the advice she received from Grant. Moving to St. Louis would give her the autonomy she'd always wanted, but was that better than having the love and support of a community around her? It seemed like a big tradeoff, and she wondered if she needed to reconsider what she wanted. Rachel looked up at the ceiling. "I'm just really confused," she said, heaving a sigh.

Judy's face brightened, and she started gathering up her purse and gloves. "Come on," she urged. "We can fix anything with a bit of shopping!"

Chapter Eighteen

A light snow fell around Tyler as he rolled a large ball of fluffy white power around in Rachel's front yard, its girth growing with each rotation. Rachel would arrive home soon from her shopping trip with Judy, and he wanted to make the front of her house seem a little more Christmassy. As his body warmed up from the exercise, his mind buzzed with the conflicting emotions battling for control of his heart.

The move to Laurel Valley was meant to be the beginning of a new chapter in his life, one that didn't involve a girl who needed the excitement of a big city. He'd had his fill of that already and incurred plenty of emotional damage from his ex. As high school sweethearts, he and Sophia seemed like the perfect match, but once they entered college, it was clear their personalities were growing in different directions. She joined an elite sorority, which looked down on modest living. Her materialistic new friends drove expensive cars, purchased clothes with fancy name brands, and didn't bat a false eyelash at charging a hundred-dollar manicure to their parent's credit card. It was a lifestyle Tyler wanted no part of.

They managed to keep the relationship held together by threads until graduation. Tyler hoped that once they headed into their careers, Sophia would settle down. It was going fine for about a year, but the discontentment started when she accepted a position with a prominent investment firm. She constantly complained about her small apartment and economy car, always comparing herself to the jetsetters at her firm.

Thinking back, he was thankful the relationship had ended before marriage. Their priorities and values were askew and would have ended at some point anyway, and he was glad he could start a new life here without feeling he'd been a disappointment to someone. Still, the task of finding your soulmate was a daunting one.

He thought about Rachel and could feel their connection deepening, but he knew he couldn't be the reason she stayed. She would need to realize all on her own that life in a small town, surrounded by family and friends, was better than the excitement in a big city, even if Tyler wasn't in the picture. The last thing he wanted was for her to forgo her dream of running a school in St. Louis and stay here just because of him.

Tyler saw some similarities between Rachel and Sophia, mainly their independence and passion for their careers. But they differed drastically in all other ways, mostly their kindness and compassion. Rachel was nothing like Sophia in the areas that really mattered.

He'd also seen Rachel's aversion to Christmas melt away these past few days. The transformation was remarkable. He saw how her face lit up when they arrived in St. Charles. She didn't hate Christmas. She just forgot how to love it. And even if they weren't meant to be together, he knew that her Christmas spirit had been rekindled because of him.

Just as he was rolling the ball of snow for the last time, a car pulled into the driveway. Tyler saw Judy wave at him as Rachel got out and gathered some bags.

"Are you playing in the snow?" Rachel asked, laughing.

"Yep! I thought you needed a snowman to greet you when you came home," he said, taking the bags from her and placing them on the porch. "Didn't quite get him finished. You want to help?"

"Sure! I haven't made a snowman since I was in elementary school." She started forming a ball that would become the snowman's tummy, and Tyler came along beside her to push it through the snow, then hoisted it onto the bottom third. Rachel plopped a pile of snow on the top and mashed the sides to form the head.

"Okay, what's next?" she asked, standing back to surmise the project.

"A scarf and hat," he said, jogging over to the porch. He rummaged through a cardboard box, retrieving a red and green ski cap with a large fluffy ball and a tattered blue and green plaid scarf. Tyler balanced the hat on top, wrapped the scarf gently around the snowman's neck, then handed a carrot to Rachel, which she dashed into the snowman's face like a dagger. They each shoved a stick in his sides for arms. Tyler added two rocks for eyes.

"How does he look?" Rachel asked, standing back to admire their creation.

"Lonely," Tyler replied. "I think he needs a Mrs. Snowman." He bent down and started rolling another ball. Rachel giggled and started working on the middle.

"Do you have another scarf and hat for her?" he asked, heading towards the porch.

"Yes, in the seat of the hall tree by the front door."

Just as Tyler reached the porch, he heard Rachel's phone buzz with an incoming call.

"Hey, Grant, how are you?" she said. Tyler heard a touch of unease in her voice. His cheeks grew warm before he'd even entered the house. He couldn't tell much from the bits of the conversation he could hear, but something didn't feel good about this. "Super busy with the festival," she said. With the front door open, he could hear her end of the conversation. He searched through the hall tree and found an extra hat and scarf. "Friday night? Um, yes, we could do that," he heard her saying. Friday night, he thought to himself, as a heaviness settled in his chest. Were they going on a date?

Feeling guilty for eavesdropping, he decided to give her a few minutes of privacy while he made them each a cup of hot cocoa in the kitchen. As he walked back toward the porch, he overheard the end of her conversation. "Love you too." He winced and stood frozen just inside the doorway. Maybe the breakup didn't take, and they were getting back together. Apparently, the day they'd spent together in St. Charles was already a distant memory to her. Regrettably, he'd allowed his heart to take full control of his emotions, and now he was paying the price. Frustration gripped his mind. What was he thinking? This was precisely what he'd wanted to avoid. It was time for him to see their relationship for what it was: just two friends working towards a goal, then moving on. He made a commitment to help her with the festival, and now they needed to get through it without any tension between them.

He shook his head slowly to clear the dark mood out of his brain, dismissing it before it took hold. Turning around, he pushed through the screen door with his back, carrying a steaming mug in each hand, a large, fake smile pasted across his face.

Rachel turned and laughed as she saw him approach. Without extra hands, he'd placed an old pink sunbonnet on his head and had a fluffy red scarf hanging over his shoulders. She took the hat from his head and placed it on Mrs. Snowman, then pulled the scarf from around his neck and tied it in a giant bow under the snowy chin.

They stood together admiring the couple they had just created. "Now he won't be lonely," Rachel said, smiling. Despite his resolve to consider Rachel nothing more than a friend, Tyler's heart lurched, and the warmth of the cocoa did little to soothe his angst.

Chapter Nineteen

After the lights were tightly wound around every branch, Rachel and Tyler flopped onto the sofa for a little break. The pizza she'd popped into the oven ten minutes ago filled the house with mouth-watering aromas of garlic and tomato.

"Should we hang the ornaments your grandma made?" Tyler asked.

"I thought we would use them for the Christmas tree at the festival," Rachel replied. She hadn't wanted to put them on the community tree but felt selfish for keeping them to herself.

Tyler shook his head. "I don't think so. Those ornaments are too precious. People will touch them, and they might fall off the tree and break."

"Are you sure it's not wrong for me to keep them for myself?"

He turned his face toward her and smiled affectionately at her. "I think your grandma would be thrilled to know they are hanging on your own personal tree."

A wave of relief swept over her, and she dashed into

the bedroom and returned with the box Tyler had found in his attic. They gently unwrapped the tiny works of art and found the perfect spot for each one. When all the ornaments glistened on the branches, Rachel pulled the angel from the tissue paper and handed it to Tyler. He carefully placed it on top, then plugged the cord into a light strand. The angel's face glowed from the tiny lights attached to her hands, and Rachel felt the warmth of her grandmother's love surrounding her.

"Okay," he said. "We need to do a quality check."

"Quality check?" Rachel asked with amusement.

"Of course! Now, stand here next to me." He grabbed her hand and pulled her back two steps. The warmth from his touch spread up her arm and into her cheeks. "Squint your eyes a little and see if all the lights are evenly spaced." They both squinted, giving the tree a once-over. "How does it look?" Tyler asked.

"It's the most beautiful tree I've ever seen," she said, her voice catching, trying to hold back a tiny sob. She swallowed hard to regain her composure. It had been so long since she stood gazing at the beauty of a Christmas tree in this room, and she was flooded with happy memories of the good times during her childhood. Tyler's hand gave hers a light squeeze. Rachel's heart pounded in her chest as she turned her face towards his. Their eyes locked, and the room was so silent she could almost hear the snow falling.

The oven timer chimed, breaking the spell, and she blinked back a tear that had formed on her lash line. Reluctantly, she dropped his hand and then hurried to the kitchen to get the pizza.

"We've got a couple of hours before the tree lighting downtown," Tyler called to her. "I'm going to see if there are any Christmas movies on." After clicking through several channels, she heard a familiar scene from "It's a Wonderful Life." Rachel returned with a tray carrying two plates of pizza and two soda bottles. As George Bailey happily pulled ZuZu's petals from his pocket, they chomped at the butter and garlic-basted crust in unison.

"This was always my favorite part," Tyler said. "It's the moment he realizes he hasn't lost his family, and the joy washes over his face. Gets me a little teary every time."

As Rachel watched the light from the television flicker on Tyler's face, she finally understood what Laurel Valley meant to him. Much like George Bailey, Tyler was getting a second chance at life. It must be so exciting for him to be here in a completely different environment where he felt truly connected. She will also get this experience if things work out at the festival. The thrill of exploring a whole new town raced through her mind but quickly fizzled out, and she wasn't sure why. There were so many things to look forward to in St. Louis. She'd have what she always wanted. Nonetheless, an emptiness was growing in her chest, and it dawned on her that when her turn came to venture into the unknown, Tyler wouldn't be there to share it. A crucial fork in the road was before her, and she was again questioning where her true happiness resided.

Tyler turned towards her, catching her staring at him. "What are you doing?" he said, smiling bashfully.

"I'm just thinking about how similar you and old

George are." She motioned toward the television. "He got a do-over, just like you. I'm really happy you've found a new beginning here." Rachel felt something stir in her heart that she hadn't felt in a long time. "And I'm thankful you brought Christmas spirit back to Laurel Valley...and me."

"Really?" he asked, sounding hopeful. "No more Scrooge?"

She laughed. "No more Scrooge."

They munched on the pizza, watching the movie for a while. Rachel wondered about his childhood and the wonderful Christmases he must have had in Manhattan. "Did your family have a big Christmas celebration in New York?"

"No. It was just the three of us. We had a tree, and Santa brought gifts. Dinner was always good. Not much else. Not like the Christmases I remember having out at my grandma's ranch. How about you before your grandma passed away?"

"The last Christmas Day I spent with my grandmother was at our house in Stone Canyon, right before we moved here. I remember a big dinner and lots of family visiting. My parents got along so well that day, and everything seemed perfect."

Tyler nodded. "What about your dad? Did you see him much after the divorce?"

"No, he moved out of state. Apparently, he sent checks for a while, then even those just stopped, and we didn't hear from him again." It was hard for her to understand how a parent could go years without speaking with their child. But as time passed, she learned not to blame herself for her father's shortcomings.

"Have you ever thought about trying to find him?"

She shook her head. "I figured if he wanted to see us, he knew where we were, so..." her voice trailed off, and she stole a quick glance at him from the side of her eye. He was getting pretty personal, and she wondered if he'd be as forthcoming as she was. "Can I ask you a super personal question?"

He shrugged. "Go for it."

"Back in New York, did you have a girlfriend?" She kept her eyes focused on the TV, feeling slightly embarrassed for asking.

He chuckled, then nodded. "Long story, but I'll give you the edited version. I was dating a girl for a couple of years, thought we loved each other, but she realized she needed someone..." His eyes looked up at the ceiling, trying to think of the right phrase. "Who was willing to give her the life she thought she deserved," he said, carefully choosing his words.

Rachel admired his tactful answer. "Uh-huh, so she was a gold digger." Rachel smiled, nudging him in the arm playfully. The spot-on observation made Tyler laugh out loud.

"Well, I guess you can put it that way. My parents did well, but they made me work for anything extra I wanted. Gave me a good work ethic, and I appreciate them giving me that gift. She probably thought I was a trust fund kid or something. After college, I thought we were ready to get married, but when I proposed to her with a small diamond ring and saw the disappointment on her face, I knew we'd never be happy together. Before she could even answer me, I closed the box and said, 'Never mind.'" His hands formed the shape of a clamshell and snapped shut for effect. "Then I got up and left. Never saw her again."

Rachel gasped. "You did not say, 'never mind'!" They both laughed hysterically.

"I did, I swear! It just came out!"

Once their laughter subsided and they wiped the tears from their eyes, he looked at her and said, "So, now it's my turn to ask you a personal question." A smile crept across her lips, bracing for something crazy. "Are you and Grant still broken up?"

Rachel turned to him, surprised by the question. She wasn't sure why he would think otherwise. "Yes, why?"

Tyler shifted his position to face her. "I thought I heard you tell him you love him on the phone."

She frowned, trying to figure out what he was referring to. "You mean today?"

He nodded. "When we were building the snow couple."

Realization set in, and she grinned at him. "I was talking to my sister, Brianna. She beeped in while I was talking to Grant. I said, 'I love you' to her, not him." She watched his face as he took in this new information, relief relaxing the rumple on his forehead. She knew he had developed feelings for her and must have been hurting after hearing that phone call. "He'll be in St. Louis on Friday and asked if I'd like to see the space for the school."

Tyler nodded. "How do you feel about seeing him?"

"A little nervous. But I'm more nervous about seeing the space. I've been trying not to get my hopes up about it since it might fall through."

It was difficult for Rachel to leave her destiny up to the success or failure of a fundraiser. She'd always felt in control of her future and didn't like the wishy-washy state she was in now. She wasn't even sure what outcome she was hoping for. Laurel Valley had always seemed so stuck in the past. But the town didn't feel as slow now that Tyler was here. A bigger question tapped at her brain, demanding an answer. Was she ready to give up this town, these people, the Christmas magic she had come to love so much?

"Might not be so bad if it doesn't work out," she added.

Tyler turned and faced her. "Really?"

She nodded. "I mean, I've been assuming I'd end up in St. Louis, and it's still my first choice, but ultimately, my goal is to secure a space large enough for the kids, so I'm realizing that whether it's in St. Louis, or somewhere else, won't matter. We'll see what happens."

"It's good that you're keeping an open mind about it," he said. "You deserve to be happy wherever life takes you."

"Even if it's St. Louis?" she ventured.

"Even if it's St. Louis. No one should have to live where they don't feel comfortable, where they don't feel like themselves. Or worse, where they have to pretend to be something they are not."

"Like you in Manhattan," she said.

"Exactly. Hopefully, Laurel Valley will keep you, but you need to live your dream life. Don't let anybody hold you back."

His words were heavy with meaning. Rachel knew exactly what he was trying to say. If her heart was yearning for the big city, he didn't want her to stay put for him or anyone else. It would only end in resentment down the road. Tyler had refused to change himself for a girl who wanted a flashier guy. She respected that about him. He gave up a lot to move here, but it didn't seem to faze him. He seemed at peace with his decision to relocate and was thriving in his new home. She wondered how life in St. Louis would change her. Would she thrive just as well?

Arriving at the park for the tree lighting, they noticed a large crowd had gathered to watch. Rachel didn't even recognize half of them. "Who are all these people?" she wondered out loud.

"Apparently, word got out about or plan. This is great! We'll probably have a good turnout for the festival," Tyler said.

A light flurry of snow fell around them. Rachel spotted a quartette settling into place in the gazebo under the warm glow of lights strung above them. Tiny piles of snow had settled on the branches of the evergreen that stood a few feet away, waiting to be brought to life. Tyler and Rachel wiggled between the onlookers and found a spot near Brianna. As the musicians raised their instruments, poised to begin, a hush settled over the crowd. The melodic tune of "Silent Night" began to stream through the chilly night air. A soft "Ahhhh," was heard as the colorful lights on the tree slowly began to glow, gently increasing in strength until a rainbow of lights illuminated the park, reflecting off the snow. The crowd sang along, surrounding the beautiful tree they had right here in Laurel Valley.

Rachel was speechless. She couldn't take her eyes off the tree. A hand gently closed around hers, and she looked up to see Tyler staring down at her. Her heart rate sped up as she looked into his eyes. They were so familiar to her now. She knew every little caramel ring inside them. Tiny snowflakes had fluttered to rest on his wavy brown hair, and the tips of his ears were an adorable pink from the cold.

She knew she should release his hand but couldn't let go. They stood this way till the end of the song, and everyone clapped and cheered. The moment was over, and they both took a small step back from one another. The musicians began playing Christmas songs, and the crowd loosened up. They could see Jack and Patty sitting together, enjoying the lovely music, mesmerized by the beauty of the tree. It was indeed a magical night.

Judy found her way over to them. "Can you believe all these people?"

"It's incredible!" Rachel agreed. "Hopefully, they will all come back on Saturday. I noticed many of them had fliers in their hands."

"Yes," Judy explained. "Frank made those up, and we handed them out to the crowd. Fingers crossed, our festival will be a big hit!" She gave them each a quick hug, then joined Frank, who was in a deep discussion with Mr. Merriweather about the rising cost of spark plugs.

Thankfully, the heat in the old truck was working as they headed back towards Rachel's house, hearts warmed and smiles on their faces. Rachel's Christmas tree glowed in the front window, and she could see Willow's silhouette on the back of the couch. The tree was a simple gesture, but it held such meaning to her, filling her home with the Christmas spirit she'd been missing all these years.

"Are you free tomorrow morning? I'm going to visit my Grandma Polly at the nursing home. Maybe she could tell you something about your grandma."

Rachel hesitated. "Are you sure I wouldn't intrude on your time with her?"

Tyler shook his head. "I don't think she'll even know who I am. Judy said she has some memory issues. But I know she'd be happy to have another visitor."

"Okay, I'd love to meet her," she replied. A flicker of excitement rose through her. It would be wonderful to talk with someone who knew her grandma so well. Maybe she'd know where her grandma's art studio was.

"I'll pick you up around ten."

"That sounds good." They exchanged smiles, and she hopped down into the snow and headed towards the porch. Once she was safely inside, she heard his truck sputter away.

Chapter Twenty

A blast of warm, mulberry-scented air greeted Tyler and Rachel as they passed through the automatic glass sliding doors of Whispering Waters Nursing Home. Rachel took in the soaring Christmas tree twinkling in a corner of the lobby. Presents wrapped in brightly colored paper were nestled under the spindly branches. Several residents seated in cozy plaid armchairs were enjoying the peaceful view of the snow falling outside.

"Good morning, welcome to Whispering Waters. How can I help you?" A jolly-faced receptionist beamed at them over her thin, gold-rimmed glasses. She wore a bright red sweater with a delicate lace collar encircling her neck. Her cheeks were the color of a kitten's nose, and silvery hair sat upon her head like a fluffy cloud.

"Hi, I'm Tyler Patterson. My grandmother lives here, and I was hoping to visit with her. Her name is Pauline Harrison."

"Oh yes, Miss Polly. She is such a delight! I believe she's in the music room. Let me call someone to escort you there." As she reached for her phone, a woman emerged from the office behind the desk.

"I can take them to Miss Polly, Clara. I'm Maggie Hayes, the site director." She extended a hand, and Tyler shook it.

"It's nice to meet you. This is my friend Rachel," Tyler said, motioning toward Rachel.

"Hello," Rachel said. "This place is so lovely."

Maggie smiled appreciatively. "Thank you. We try very hard to make the atmosphere as close to home as possible." She led them down a brightly lit hallway towards large double doors. After swiping a card through a receiver on the wall, they slowly swung open, allowing the trio to pass through. Rounding a corner, they heard a piano playing "The First Noel" and made their way towards the music. After passing the dining hall, they entered a large room filled with elderly men and women singing along. A stage with emerald green velvet drapes stretched across the back wall and a deep shelving unit on a sidewall held several instrument cases. Two large baskets held tambourines and colorful maracas.

"What a fun room!" Rachel exclaimed.

"Miss Polly, you have visitors," Maggie called out.

The music stopped, and the pianist turned to face them. Polly watched as they approached, her gray eyes moving back and forth, trying to recognize them. Her eyes halted on Rachel, and she squinted slightly, then a beautiful smile brightened her face. "Oh," Polly said, tears forming in her eyes. She reached out her arms toward Rachel for a hug. Feeling a little hesitant, Rachel came towards her and bent down to embrace her. Polly's fragile arms wrapped around Rachel's back and held her tight. After a moment, she let go and allowed Rachel to step back. Tyler gave her a confused look.

"Elizabeth, I'm so happy you've come to see me. How are you feeling?" Polly clasped her hands together at her chest.

Realizing Polly thought she was her Grandma Lizzy, Rachel replied, "Um, I'm doing well," and returned the smile. She glanced at Tyler, who gave her a subtle shoulder shrug.

Polly's eyes went to Tyler. "And who is this handsome young man?"

"I'm Tyler, Grandma Polly. I'm Gwen's son." He came towards her and gave her a hug.

"Gwen's son!" she repeated. "Why, you're all grown up now! She must be feeding you my good old fried chicken and sour cream biscuits."

Rachel felt a stab of pain for the both of them. She saw Tyler's smile falter ever so slightly, then brighten up again. He'd lost his mother and had to live in the world without her, but thankfully, Polly had blocked out the loss of her daughter and lived blissfully in a world where Gwen was still parenting her only child.

"Yes, she's a great cook, just like you."

"Let's go to the sitting room so we can have a nice visit." Polly rose with hardly any difficulty and led the way out of the music room. Maggie offered a compassionate smile to them as they passed her.

They settled into a small sitting room with a loveseat and two armchairs. The room was painted a soft cream

197

color, and the low light through the windows gave it a soothing feel. Polly eased into an armchair covered in floral tapestry, and Rachel and Tyler chose the loveseat next to her.

Polly questioned Tyler about his age and if he'd gone to college. She recalled visiting the fire station with him for his first-grade field trip and taking him to see the miniature train at the Curio Shop with his mother and father. "You had a hot cocoa mustache and whipped cream on your nose every time I looked at you!" she laughed. Rachel marveled at how well she could remember the tiniest of details from that evening.

Polly turned her attention to Rachel. "Now, Elizabeth, are you taking care of yourself? I'm surprised to see you out and about. You know what the doctor said." She wagged a finger at Rachel.

Rachel's mind raced with confusion. Had her grandmother been sick? "Yes, I'm taking it easy. I was just looking forward to seeing you again."

Polly sat back in the chair, her eyes full of worry. "Are you going to tell Charlotte?"

Tell Charlotte...tell Charlotte. Rachel wasn't sure how to respond to this. It sounded like Grandma Lizzy had been keeping something from her own daughter.

"Uh," Rachel stalled as she tried to come up with something. She cast a glance at Tyler, but he just shrugged his shoulders.

Polly leaned towards her and patted her on the knee. "Don't you worry. Your secret is safe with me."

A s they exited Whispering Waters, Rachel felt a sense of unease.

"What's the matter?" Tyler asked. "You have a weird look on your face. Are you thinking about what Grandma Polly said?"

Rachel nodded, mulling through her thoughts as they got into the truck. Something wasn't sitting right with her. There seemed to be some pieces of the puzzle missing, something that would explain the cryptic message Polly had given her. "What do you think she meant by 'your secret is safe with me'? What secret had been between her and my grandma?"

"Maybe a chronic health issue? Why do you think your grandma didn't tell anyone?" Tyler asked.

"I guess she didn't want us to worry." Rachel stared out the window, watching the snow-laden trees pass by them.

"Well, I wouldn't be too concerned. We don't even know if there really *was* a secret between them. Polly's mind isn't completely intact."

Rachel stared ahead as her brain processed the situation. "There's something I'm realizing about my Scroogyness," she said.

He chuckled. "Your Scroogyness?" He glanced over at her, and his face became serious when he saw she wasn't smiling. After pulling the truck off to the side of the road, he turned and faced her. "What is it? It's okay. You can tell me anything." The look on his face was so comforting, so supportive. He was right. She could tell him anything. A feeling of adoration came over her.

"Remember when I told you about the night with my grandmother at The Curio Shop?"

Tyler nodded.

"I always thought her death was due to being out in the cold that night. Something that could have been prevented if we hadn't gone out. And because of that night, this whole town lost her, not just me. I'd always carried around some guilt because of it. Maybe it's one of the reasons I felt that I needed to move away." Uncertainty filled her to the brim. Her grandmother's death had been such a negative turning point in her life, but she realized there might be more to the story.

Concern drew shadows across Tyler's face. "Listen, Rach, you were just a little girl. I hope you aren't blaming yourself for anything. All the kids wanted to go to that train unveiling. It was a huge deal for us."

"I know, I know." She conceded. "I'd just like to know what Polly meant by that comment. I'll give my mom a call. Maybe she'll know more about it."

Tyler gave her a reassuring smile, then pulled the truck back onto the road and continued towards home.

Their friendship had suddenly elevated to a whole new level. They had shared so much in the past week as if their relationship was on fast forward. She felt a closeness to him she'd never experienced before. With Tyler, there was no judgment, no "helpful" advice that was never asked for. He just listened to her with understanding and acceptance in his eyes.

They were quiet the rest of the drive home, both

lost in thought. Rachel stared out the window at the snow-covered trees. She could feel the rumble of the engine beneath her, and the smell of Tyler's cologne mixed nicely with the earthy smell of the truck. He started humming, "Winter Wonderland," and she looked over at him. Blue jeans, a red plaid coat, and no traces of pretentiousness in him. Something felt right about all this. She felt comfortable in this old truck with Tyler beside her. Planning the festival had brought her to this moment, to this realization. Yet, its purpose was to give her the funds to move away, leaving Tyler behind. Would it be possible to feel the same way in St. Louis? With someone else?

The truck pulled up to her house, and Rachel got out. "Thank you for inviting me today," she said, pausing outside the truck.

"I'm glad you came." He smiled at her. Are you gonna call your mom?"

"I will tonight. Brianna and Chloe are coming over in a little bit to help me choose some pieces for the store in St. Charles, and Chloe wants to make some paper snowflakes to hang in the barn for the festival."

"I hope your mom can shed some light on this for you. I'll be home tonight if you want to call and talk."

"Thanks, Tyler. Thanks for everything." She closed the door then headed up the front steps and into the warmth of her home to find Willow patiently waiting for a belly rub. Looking around her living room, her eyes scanned the glowing Christmas tree, the delicate ornaments, and the angelic face at the top. The joy she felt was because of him. She wanted Tyler to be the one. She wanted him to stay in her life. But she knew that would mean staying in Laurel Valley, and that wasn't a decision she was ready to make.

Chapter Twenty-One

B rianna and Chloe arrived an hour later, and the house suddenly filled with activity. Willow scampered off to the bedroom, and Chloe was close behind, trying to coax her out from under the bed. Brianna came loaded with a bag full of supplies for snowflake decorating.

"Wow! You put up a Christmas tree!" Brianna exclaimed. She went over and held one of the ornaments. "These are beautiful."

"Grandma Lizzy painted them. I have a box of them for you, too." Rachel went to the hall closet, retrieved a box, and handed it to Brianna.

"I love these! I had no idea she painted ornaments."

"I didn't know either. She painted the angel, too," Rachel said, pointing to the top of the tree. "Would it be alright if I kept her this year, and you can put her on your tree next year?"

Brianna smiled at her. "She's lovely on your tree, Rach. You keep her." Brianna said.

Rachel fought the tears forming in her eyes, overwhelmed by her sister's generosity and grateful she wouldn't have to give up the little angel. "Thanks, Bri."

"Where did you find them? Here in the house?" Brianna asked.

"No, Tyler found them in his attic with all the boxes of paperwork from The Silver Belles Club. We discovered that his Grandma Polly and Grandma Lizzy were best friends, not just co-founders of the club."

"Really? That's so sweet." Brianna's face softened at this. "How's the festival planning coming along?"

"So far, it's going well. We received incredible support at the meeting last Friday night."

"You sure did! I saw the lines of people ready to sign the volunteer sheets. It's so wonderful how everyone is coming together to help. What do you have left to do?"

"We've got most of it done already, but we need lots of snowflakes, so I hope Chloe is ready for some fun!" Rachel exclaimed as Chloe emerged from the hall carrying a very grumpy Willow.

"Yes!" Chloe exclaimed. After releasing the cantankerous kitty, she hopped up on a chair.

Brianna pulled a stack of paper snowflakes, glue, a hole punch and tubes of pastel-colored glitter out of her bag. Once Chloe was up and running, she and Rachel went to the kitchen. Rachel pulled out a small pot and added sugar, cocoa, and whole milk. "How is Sam's father doing?" she asked.

"He's still in the hospital. Sam's a mess. He's really close to his parents."

"I'm so sorry he's going through this. How are you getting along with your bookings? Do you need any help?"

The pot was finally boiling, and Rachel pulled it off the burner and added vanilla.

"Yes, fine. Sam asked a friend from school to fill in. And Nick was a lifesaver at Judy's party. It was really sweet of him to jump in and help like that."

"He's a great guy," Rachel agreed. She poured the concoction into three mugs and topped Chloe's with whipped cream.

"Yum!" Chloe exclaimed, then slurped up a mouthful of fluffy cream. Rachel led Brianna out to the porch to show her the items she was considering for the shop in St. Charles.

"I'm so excited about this shop. It's right in the historic district. I spoke to the owner yesterday. He said he wants ten to fifteen items to start with, so I need you to help me choose."

"All of your pieces are beautiful." Brianna examined the items on each shelf. "I think you should bring five of these," she said, pointing to the brilliantly colored mugs. "And five of the white ones. Serving bowls also make great gifts, so include a few of those." Brianna moved to the next set of shelves. "These are adorable," she said, picking up a small trinket dish. "I think they would do well also."

"Perfect!" Rachel beamed. She pulled a stack of tissue paper off a shelf and set it on the worktable. They began wrapping each of the items and placing them in a box. Rachel's thoughts went to her visit with Tyler's grandmother at the nursing home and the mysterious message she received.

"Do you remember anything about the night Grandma

died?" Rachel asked as she wrapped the tissue paper around a mug.

"Like what?" Brianna asked curiously.

"Did you notice if she had been sick before that day or anything?"

"Mmm, I'm not sure. I only remember being at The Curio Shop and seeing the train, not much before that. Why do you ask?"

"Tyler and I visited his grandmother at the nursing home, and she thought I was Grandma Lizzy."

"Wow. That must have been awkward for you," Brianna said with concern in her voice.

"The weirdest part was what she said. She asked me if I had told Charlotte yet."

"Charlotte... you mean mom? Told her what?" Brianna's eyes were full of confusion.

"I don't know. That's the problem. Seemed like it was something to do with her health. I'm going to call Mom tonight and ask her about it, but I thought maybe you might know."

Brianna shook her head. "I can't think of anything. But we were very young. I doubt they would have told us if anything serious had been going on with her. I'm sure mom will be able to tell you more."

The box was finally full of items, and Rachel found some packing tape to secure it shut, then headed to the living room to put it by the door. "You know, Tyler was the one who found this shop in St. Charles for me," Rachel said over her shoulder, her heart beating a little faster with the memory of that day.

A moment of silence followed, then Brianna finally replied, "That was sweet of him. I know it meant a lot to you. Have you heard anything from Grant?" Brianna asked.

Rachel hesitated, sensing Brianna trying to shift the focus off Tyler. She assumed Brianna had been holding out hope of a reconciliation with Grant, so she hadn't planned to tell her about the meeting with him scheduled for Friday night. But since she brought it up, Rachel decided it was best to be honest with her. "Yes. He'll be in town on Friday and wants to drive me by the location for the school." She waited a moment, then added, "We'll probably get some dinner, too."

Brianna's eyes sparkled with interest. "That'll be nice. You'll have to let me know what you think of the space."

Rachel was thankful Brianna didn't dwell on the dinner plans. She'd always had more of a motherly role in Rachel's life, giving her guidance and advice when asked, and sometimes when she didn't ask. But it was time for Rachel to make her own choices, and she longed for Brianna's support, no matter who she spent her life with.

"Mommy, look!" Chloe held up two sparkly snowflakes for them to see. Glitter was everywhere, but it was clear she had a wonderful time making them.

"They are so beautiful!" Brianna said, brushing the glitter from Chloe's cheeks.

"You're an artist, Chloe, just like your Great Grandma Lizzy."

Chloe beamed at the praise. "Can you make some with me?" she asked, sliding a piece of white paper in front of each of them.

"Sure," Rachel replied, pulling up some Christmas music on her phone. They all wiggled to the beat, cutting tiny wedges from the folded paper. Before long, they had made a pile of snowflakes sparkling with light blue, gold, and silver glitter.

"These will be perfect for the barn," Rachel said as she and Brianna tied fishing line to each of them. Her phone buzzed with a call.

"Hello?"

"Hi Rachel, this is Beverly Swain. I'm calling about the property on Windsor."

"Oh, yes, hello Beverly." Rachel's heartbeat quickened. Why was the real estate agent calling?

"I realize you were working out a financing issue, but the property status changed to sold yesterday."

Rachel inhaled sharply as anxiety gripped her, and her temple throbbed. "But I thought a deposit was holding it," she questioned.

"Yes, ma'am, there was, but the acceptance period expired, and another buyer just swooped right in!" She gave a small laugh. "They paid cash, so there was no financing contingency."

Trying to keep the tears at bay, Rachel said, "Okay, I appreciate you letting me know." After setting down her phone, she rushed away from the table to keep Chloe from seeing her tears.

Brianna followed her into the kitchen. "What is it? What happened?"

Rachel grabbed a paper towel and mopped the tears

off her cheeks. "Everything in my life just keeps getting turned upside down." She fought to regain control of her breathing. "Another offer on the space in St. Louis came through, and it's under contract now."

"But I thought Grant had a deposit on it," Brianna said, bewildered.

"When the seller gave him the counteroffer, Grant didn't sign it, hoping to give me more time to raise the money. He was going to help me with a new contract if I could get it together, but someone beat me to it."

Brianna grabbed Rachel's shoulders and pulled her in for a hug. "Rach, I'm so sorry."

Rachel allowed her sister's love to soothe her. It was the second time in just a week a major disappointment crashed through her life like a Tasmanian devil, upending her plans in its path. Her whole world seemed to be spinning towards the edge of a cliff, threatening to topple over like the teetering files she'd ignored on her desk that fateful day she met Tyler.

"Come out here, and let's talk about it," Brianna said, taking her by the hand and leading her to the couch. They settled in as the sun emerged from the clouds, casting a bright glare over the snow-covered front yard. Rachel stared out the window, wondering what she was supposed to do now that St. Louis wasn't in her future any longer.

"I know you don't want to hear this, but maybe you should just start searching for a space here. You'll still have the money from the festival. You could put it towards a local spot."

Rachel didn't answer. She just wasn't ready to throw in

the towel. But it seemed that fate had a different plan for her, and she was having trouble wrapping her head around a new goal.

"What about that space downtown?" Brianna's voice was soft and uplifting, urging Rachel to keep an open mind about the possibilities. "The one next to Patty Cakes. It's a lot bigger than the room at the community center. You'd have enough space to double the number of students you have now."

Brianna's mention of the children tugged at Rachel's heart. They were the ultimate priority, after all. Her original plan after college had been to open a school locally. For the most part, she was very happy here, other than a few underlying grumbles of discontentment, but she hadn't thought about leaving her hometown...until she met Grant. He was full of ideas and ways to advance her dream, and once marriage was a possibility, they naturally focused their search on St. Louis, where he lived and had a business. Over time, Grant's musings about small-town life and the claustrophobic atmosphere seemed to rub off on her. She gradually developed the same outlook and became increasingly enthralled with the idea of life in a big city, away from the spyglass. The freedom was appealing to her.

Brianna studied her face. "And I'd love for you to stay close to me and Chloe."

Rachel felt her rigid stance weakening and realized there were definite pros to staying here. She could live in this house, move the art school next to Patty, and continue to go about life as usual, although it was the complete opposite of what she wanted in St. Louis. She'd hoped for the chance to stretch her wings, be on her own, and experience things that the whole town wasn't privy to. Would she be able to give that up and do an about-face, finally allowing her roots to grow here?

After giving herself time to process the change in direction, the thought of having a space downtown sent her a little trickle of excitement. Finally, her own space!

"Okay, I'll consider it. I guess St. Louis isn't that far away. I could always go for a visit and get my big-city fix!" Her smile found its way back to her lips. "And the spot next to Patty is so charming."

Brianna gave her sister another hug. "What about the dinner with Grant Friday night?"

Rachel hadn't thought about this. She pulled her phone from her back pocket, typed a text to him, and then waited for his response. "He said he just found out today and was going to call me, feels bad, still wants to take me to dinner." She looked up at Brianna. "Do you think I should go?"

"Well, he was so generous to give you that deposit money. It might be rude if you turned him down."

Rachel agreed, and the plan was set. After cleaning up the table and sweeping the glitter from the floor, Brianna and Chloe got into their coats. Chloe ran out into the front yard and laid down on the snow to make a snow angel. Rachel giggled as Brianna sighed, knowing there would be a wet mess to clean up in the car.

"I'm so proud of you, Rach," Brianna said, giving her a warm hug at the door.

"For what?" she asked.

"For your resilience. You aren't letting anything keep you down. It's all going to fall into place. I promise."

Chapter Twenty-Two

T he sun was sinking behind the trees across the lake, and Tyler was at his kitchen sink, watching the sky light up with the colors of a blazing fire. He was hesitant to admit it, but he felt that if the move to St. Louis wasn't possible, they could have a future. The feeling he got when he held her hand at the tree lighting was real. She didn't let go. There had definitely been something passing between them.

An uneasy feeling passed through him as he remembered that Rachel would see Grant on Friday night. Would the old feelings be rekindled? He couldn't shake the sense that a change was imminent. Friday was looming dark and ghostly in the future, just a few days away, and his heart warned him to tread carefully.

Tyler's phone lit up with a call. He smiled, seeing it was from Rachel. "Hey, how are you," he said to her.

"Not so good. Had a wrench thrown in my plans again."

"Oh no! What happened?" Concern welled up inside him.

"I lost the contract on the space in St. Louis."

He could hear the disappointment in her voice, and a feeling of compassion came over him. Her plans were being dashed once again. "Rach, I'm so sorry. That's terrible."

"Thanks." She let out a heavy sigh. "I've had some time to stew about everything." She hesitated before continuing. "I'm thinking about staying here and getting a space downtown for the school."

"Are you serious?" Tyler couldn't believe his ears. His heart was bursting with elation. His feeling was right; a change was imminent. She was staying! And just maybe there was a chance for their relationship to grow into something more. He'd do everything he could to give her all the excitement she could handle...right here in Laurel Valley. Besides, it wasn't just the place you're in. It's the people you're with. "That's incredible! Do you have a location in mind?" He remembered the lack of vacant buildings when his dad tried to find a site for the diner. The only one available was next to Patty. Surely, Rachel wouldn't be talking about that one. He'd told her that Jack was purchasing it...hadn't he?

"Yep. It's next door to Patty Cakes. Used to be the post office years ago. It's a good size, so I think it will work well."

Tyler was stunned. The one spot available was already purchased for the diner. He swallowed hard and tried to think of what to say. "Rach, my dad-"

She cut him off before he could get the words out. "I almost had a total meltdown today when I found out the space in St. Louis was gone. The one thing keeping me sane was Brianna mentioning that space next to the bakery."

"Rach-," he cut in, but she kept talking.

"Honestly, I don't think I could handle another disappointment right now."

Her words caused him to stop short. She couldn't handle another disappointment. He allowed this to sink in. He couldn't break it to her right now. He'd just need to find some way to fix this for her.

Rachel continued, hardly taking a breath. "And you won't believe this. It has the same black and white floors as my grandmother's cottage!" He could hear the uptick in her voice as she grew more and more excited with the new plan. "I know you haven't been in there yet, but I can't wait to show you. It's almost like it was meant to be." Her tone became wistful.

Tyler cringed. Now, she was connecting the space to the happy times she spent with her grandmother. It just couldn't get any worse. His chest tightened, and tiny beads of sweat formed on his brow. He took a deep breath, fighting off his own total meltdown.

"Tyler, are you there?"

"Yes, sorry. I'm glad you're feeling better about things. Did you get a chance to talk to your mom yet?"

"No, I'm going to call her now. I just wanted to tell you my news."

"Ok, call me later if you want. I'm so happy for you, Rach."

"Thanks. And don't forget we are meeting at the bakery Friday morning for cookie duty."

"Got it." They said goodbye, and Tyler headed out the

back door into the chilly night air. The snow crunched under his boots as he made his way down to the lake. Thoughts were swarming in his head like a pack of mosquitos. Rachel was counting on this space. It might be the only thing keeping her here. When she finds out it's gone, will the disappointment become the catalyst for her move to St. Louis or somewhere else? He dreaded telling her, not wanting to lose any ground in the relationship they had gained.

As he reached the shore of the lake, he fought to catch his breath. What were the chances the exact space Rachel wanted happened to be the one Jack purchased? This was just a building to Jack: walls, a roof, nothing more. But the space meant so much more to her. It meant the beginning of a new career, a fresh start with something of her own. For some reason, this space wasn't meant for Rachel. He couldn't understand why it had been dangled in front of her, then cruelly yanked away. There had to be a way to fix this for her. He couldn't let her go. Tyler could only hope that another spot would open up. If not, then maybe their relationship wasn't meant to be either.

Rachel lay on her couch, snuggled under her quilt, staring at her Christmas tree. She regarded each ornament and pictured her grandmother painting every detail. As a child, she'd only seen her grandma paint on canvas and wished she could have seen her create these beautiful pieces.

Her thoughts drifted to her visit with Miss Polly. She realized she had completely forgotten to ask her about the cottage. Rachel had been so thrown with the talk of a secret that it hadn't crossed her mind. She replayed the conversation in her head, trying to make sense of it. Had there really been something wrong with her grandmother even before that night at the Curio Shop?

Picking up her phone, Rachel dialed her mother's number. Charlotte answered on the second ring. "Hi sweetie!" her mother's cheery voice came through, filling Rachel with comfort. It was always good to hear the warmth in her mother's voice.

"Hi Mom! Just calling to see how you're doing. How's business at the B&B?"

"Oh, fine. The house is fully booked for several months. And I invented a new quiche recipe you will love!"

"That's awesome. I can't wait to try it."

"How was your date with Grant last week?"

"Well, not so good. We broke up." She was silent, waiting for the news to sink in.

"Baby, I'm so sorry. I know you must be very disappointed. Do you want to tell me what happened?"

"It wasn't bad. He sold his business to a company in Germany and is moving away. Neither of us wanted to attempt an even longer long-distance relationship. We both knew it was hard enough as it was."

"So, you've had some time for it to settle in. How are you feeling about it now?"

Rachel wasn't sure how to answer this. There were so

many emotions swirling around in her. Things had been changing so rapidly that her brain hadn't had time to fully process the breakup. And now that Tyler had entered the picture, things were even more confusing. He was the complete opposite of Grant, and she wondered how she'd been so attracted to both of them. Before she met Tyler, the breakup and cancellation of her move to St. Louis would have been completely devastating. But Tyler had brought a new light to the town. She saw everything with fresh eyes as if a dull gray filter had been removed. Her motivations, goals, aspirations, and dreams were all changing.

"I'm actually feeling fine about it. Thinking about staying here and moving the art school into a space downtown."

"That's wonderful! Oh, I'm so glad you are staying near your sister. Family is really everything. Sometimes, I regret moving so far away from you two." Her mother's voice cracked slightly.

"Mom, we understand you had a dream to pursue, too. You didn't get to live your own life when we were growing up. You gave us the courage to follow our hearts, and it was time for you to follow yours."

"I appreciated you saying that, baby." She let out a little sniff, then her voice became strong and confident again. "So, tell me what else is going on."

"Judy's nephew moved to town to renovate the old ranch. His name's Tyler."

"Oh, what's he like? Is he your age? Single?"

Rachel laughed at how her mother could bounce right

back into hover mode. "Very nice, same age as me, and yes, he's single."

"That's so wonderful. Have you been able to spend any time together?"

"Yes, a lot. It's been a crazy couple of weeks." Rachel gave her mother a recap of what had been happening since their last phone conversation. "We were planning the potluck together, but after Grant and I broke up, I was trying to purchase the space in St. Louis without him. I needed a way to raise some money, so Tyler had the idea to turn the potluck into a fundraiser. He got the idea from some things he found in his attic. Did you know Grandma was in a club called The Silver Belles?"

"That sounds vaguely familiar, but she passed away so soon after we moved back that I didn't get to learn about everything she did there. I know the town absolutely adored her. She'd been mayor for the previous seven years. Really got the downtown shaped up and running strong."

"She was loved, that's for sure. I miss her a lot."

"Me too, sweetie. She would be so proud of you."

Rachel smiled at that thought. "Mom, had Grandma been sick for a while before she passed away?"

"That's a good question, but I honestly don't know. Why do you ask?"

"I visited one of her old friends today, Polly Harrison. Did you know her?"

"Oh yes. Everyone in town knew Miss Polly. She and your grandma were very close. She must be in her eighties by now. How is Polly doing?"

"I think she has memory issues, but her health seems

good. When I visited her today, she thought I was Grandma Lizzy." Rachel laughed lightly to hide her concern.

"You do look an awful lot like her. Those beautiful cornflower blue eyes, especially," her mother replied wistfully.

"Miss Polly asked me if I'd told you something, I mean if Grandma had told you something. I'm not sure what. Maybe it was some health issue she was keeping from you? But then she said, 'Don't worry, your secret is safe with me.'"

"Hmm, that is strange. Grandma was forever the optimist. She'd never admit to any problems, as if they would disappear if she didn't voice them. If there was a health issue, I wouldn't be surprised if she hid it from me," Charlotte said pensively.

"What do you know about her death? She died of something like pneumonia, right?"

"No, she died of an aneurysm. Maybe that was what Polly meant. Could've been something Grandma knew she had and didn't tell us."

Rachel's face flushed with confusion. "An aneurysm?" Her mind was spinning. "So, it wasn't because she'd gone out with me in the cold weather that night?"

The line was silent for a moment. Rachel heard a small gasp come from the other end. "Sweetheart, is that what you thought all these years?"

Tears streamed down her face as relief washed over her like a warm shower after a day out in the frigid snow, melting away the icy veil that shrouded her Christmas spirit all these years.

"Baby, even if Grandma had been home in her warm bed, she would have passed away that night. I'm so sorry you thought it might have been prevented. I wish I was there to give you a big hug."

"Me too," Rachel said, feeling the miles between them. She dried her face on her sleeve and went to the kitchen to make some hot chamomile tea. "I'm really glad I talked to you, Mom. Any chance you could come spend Christmas with me? The festival is this Saturday."

"I would love to spend Christmas with you! I doubt I can get there in time for the festival, but let me check on some flights, okay?"

"Sure. I can't wait to see you." This one conversation had changed something inside her. Over the past year, she'd started avoiding her mother's phone calls, knowing there would be a subtle interrogation of her relationship with Grant. She hadn't realized the rift it had caused between them. This evening's phone call was an epiphany of sorts.

They said their goodbyes, and Rachel hung up, feeling like a new person. She felt a deepening connection with her mother and a renewed love for Laurel Valley. Grant's persuasions fueled discontent and the desire to leave her hometown. And now the truth was urging her to stay.

Her phone chirped with a text.

I hope you are having a nice evening with Willow by your tree.

It was from Tyler, and he ended it with a smiley face emoji. Her heart soared. Tyler was the reason this was all happening for her. The festival, the Christmas spirit, and the truths she'd learned were all thanks to him. And once she was in her very own space downtown, everything would be just right.

I am. Thank you for all you have done for me. She ended it with a heart, then suddenly wished she hadn't. What if he didn't feel the same? What if he wasn't ready to put his feelings out there?

Seconds passed as she waited for a reply, her unblinking eyes not moving from the screen. Nothing. Feeling incredibly stupid and vulnerable, she laid the phone on the table, refusing to pick it up again until morning. But after just a few moments, she was eaten up with suspense and grabbed the phone back. She watched and waited as three dots bobbed on the screen. Then, a moment later, a little red heart appeared.

Chapter Twenty-Three

A tiny bell chimed as the door to the bakery swung open, and Rachel entered in a swoosh of chilly air. Christmas music gently played throughout the store, mixing nicely with the scent of cinnamon rolls hot out of the oven. The festival was just a day away, and the last task to complete was baking the cookies for the children. She hadn't seen Tyler since last Tuesday when they visited his grandmother at the nursing home, and she was eager to see him again. Spotting him behind the counter in a pink Patty Cakes apron, a twinge of giddiness swept over her.

"Hey, pretty lady!" Patty's cheery voice exclaimed. "Come on back. We're scanning through the ingredient list for Polly's famous sugar cookies." Jack was standing beside her, holding a recipe card, yellowed and tattered with age. Tyler looked up at her, and their eyes locked, sending tingles straight to her cheeks.

The back of Patty's bakery was just as beautiful as the front. Two counter-height, marble-topped worktables formed an L-shape, and an entire wall of antique, oak shelving held an assortment of mixers, cake pans, and bowls. The black and white tile floor gave it a vintage feel. Patty had prepared four commercial-size baking sheets with parchment paper and positioned two per table. Four small bowls of powdered sugar were next to each tray.

"How many cookies are we making today?" Patty asked.

Rachel hadn't even thought of this. "I'm not sure. I have no idea how many people are planning to attend. What do you guys think?" she asked everyone.

"Should we plan on a hundred kids?" Jack offered.

"Let's think big and make two hundred," Patty replied. "If we have any left, I can send them to the veterans hospital with Mr. Merriweather."

Patty multiplied out the ingredients on a pad of paper, then went to the refrigerator to grab the chilled ingredients. She added the measured amount of butter and sugar to the free-standing mixer and set the blades to low speed. Once this was light and fluffy, she added eggs, vanilla and a touch of almond extract. Everyone stood around the mixer as the dry ingredients were added, along with Grandma Polly's secret ingredient, instant vanilla pudding mix.

"I usually refrigerate the dough before using it. Gives the cookies a better texture and flavor. But this will do fine," Patty said.

Once the mixer finished forming the dough, Patty divided it into four bowls, placed one in front of each of them, and then handed them a scoop. They went to work filling their sheets with balls of sweet dough.

"We use parchment paper to line the baking sheets

because we want a chewy, softer texture and even coloring. Foil is good if you want a crispy-bottomed cookie," Patty explained. "The foil radiates the heat upward and keeps the fat in the butter near the bottom."

Rachel loved learning about baking from Patty. She was a master baker, and her creations had won several awards. It was a lot like working with clay, only much tastier!

"What are the glasses for?" Tyler asked, pointing at the small glasses in front of each of them.

"We're going to dip the bottom of the glass in the powdered sugar, then press each cookie. It'll keep the glass from sticking to the dough. Most people use flour, but I prefer powdered sugar," she said.

"I thought they were for your spiked eggnog," Jack quipped.

"I've got a little of that in the fridge once we're done," Patty said, giving him a wink.

"Have a Holly Jolly Christmas," chimed through the speakers, and they all began singing together. The first four trays were filled in no time, and Patty slid them into the large wall oven and then handed them each another tray to fill. Rachel burst into laughter as Tyler bellowed, "OH, BY GOLLY," while twisting to the beat of the music. It felt amazing to finally experience joy at Christmas, much easier than burying her feelings as she had done for so many years.

"Can you believe we are going to pull this off?" she said to Tyler with a glowing smile.

"I never doubted we could do it." Tyler picked up a pinch of powdered sugar and flicked it towards Rachel's face. She let out a squeak, dodging the powdery cloud.

The timer for the last batch chimed, and Patty carefully removed them from the oven, sliding each tray into the cooling cart. "I heard you are entering the fruitcake contest, Jack," Patty said. "Mr. Merriweather is going to be the judge, and he's a tough old goat, so it'd better be good!" she said, laughing.

"Believe it or not, Polly had a recipe for that, too, and it looks delicious!" Jack declared.

They began cleaning up their workstations. The cookies would need time to cool, and Patty and Jack planned to divide them into little bags later that night.

"What are you bringing to the festival?" Rachel asked Jack.

"Bacon Cheddar Cornbread," Jack replied. "I'm planning to have it on the menu at the diner."

"Sounds delicious! I bet you'll have a line of people out the door waiting for seats," she said. "Have you had any luck finding a location?"

"Yep, didn't Tyler tell you?" Jack looked at her with an excited smile. Rachel shook her head and glanced at Tyler, whose face had lost its color. Jack continued. "I bought this building from Mrs. Perry last week. The diner will be right next door." He smiled at Patty. "I should be able to open within a few weeks. Haven't settled on a name yet."

Rachel's stomach dropped, and a burning sensation crept into her throat. She turned towards Tyler, pressing her lips into a thin line. She noticed an anxious crease etched across his forehead. He shifted uncomfortably on his stool, causing her skin to prickle with alarm. She sat for a moment, working through the information as questions burned behind her eyes. Not wanting to believe what Jack had said, she reiterated his words. "This building?" She knew the answer before he even replied, and a jolt of betrayal struck her heart. Tyler must have known. She'd described the space to him. Why hadn't he said anything when she called and told him about her plans?

"Rachel, I..." Tyler stammered, but Jack broke in.

"That's right! It's the perfect location. I love old buildings. They really have a soul to them, you know? Oh, and I'm hosting a free pancake breakfast for all the festival volunteers on Sunday morning as a thank you for their help, so spread the word!" He gave her a wink.

Rachel felt a stab of shock. The rug had been yanked out from beneath her yet again. Her cheeks felt red hot, and she suppressed the urge to run out of the shop. Taking a deep breath to prevent her lips from quivering, she turned and faced Tyler. "Well, I should head out. Grant is picking me up for dinner at five."

"Wait, you're still going to dinner?" he said with confusion.

Rachel ignored his question and turned back to Jack and Patty, attempting to keep the shaking out of her voice. "This was really fun. Sorry, I have to leave. I'll see you guys tomorrow evening." Turning, she quickly headed towards the door with Tyler on her heels.

Once outside, she heard his voice call out to her. "Rachel, stop. I need to explain."

She stood at her car, rummaging through her purse for her keys. She didn't want to hear his explanation. It didn't matter why he kept this from her. All that mattered was that her plans were getting smashed to pieces... again. But this time, Tyler was holding the hammer.

"It's fine, Tyler. Jack bought the space before I was even interested in it. I just don't understand why you didn't tell me." Her eyes brimmed with tears, and she fought to keep them from falling.

"I tried! When you called and told me about the space, I tried to tell you it was already sold. But you were having such a tough time, I just couldn't disappoint you again. It just wasn't the right time."

"That was days ago. You've had lots of other opportunities to tell me."

He gave a sigh of resignation. "You're right. But please, just listen for a second," he pleaded.

She finally got her car unlocked and had the door ajar, ready to get inside, but decided to hear him out. She turned and faced him but kept her eyes on the ground. She knew that if she met his eyes, the tears would fall, and there would be no stopping them.

"These past weeks have been some of the happiest times of my life." He paused, struggling with his words. "Up until two days ago, I didn't think there was any chance of us having a future. You were moving to St. Louis and wanted a life with more excitement. But when things changed, and there was a chance you'd be staying, I worried you'd leave if the space was gone." She glanced up at him and saw him wrestling with his feelings. "I was hoping I could find another spot for you." His voice trailed off with dismay.

Rachel stood quietly, mulling this over. Feeling as if he'd manipulated the situation, she finally looked him square in the eye, her eyes boring straight into his. "I understand that, Tyler, and I appreciate you wanting to help me out." She shook her head in frustration. She was tired of people trying to control her life by hiding behind their good intentions. "But I deserved to know so I could figure out what I wanted to do. You know what I mean? I need to figure it out, not you, not Bri, or anyone in this town." A tear suddenly escaped, and she brushed it harshly from her cheek, punishing it for falling. "If you really wanted what's best for me, you would have told me sooner. The decision to stay or go should be my own."

Tyler cast his eyes downward sheepishly. "I just didn't want to lose you." His voice was low and heavy with regret. She knew he meant well, but she couldn't dismiss the fact that he'd kept the information from her.

With the sting of disappointment still burning in her heart, Rachel let out a heavy sigh of emotional exhaustion. She glanced around the town she dearly loved, but the need to escape was stirring in her once again.

"You can't lose what you don't have," she said curtly, her words biting back at him. Tyler was silent as he stepped away from her car and allowed her to close the door.

Drizzly rain pelted her windshield as she drove down Main Street. Alone in her car, Rachel allowed the tears to stream freely down her cheeks. She knew it was wrong to hold this against him, but she couldn't help feeling betrayed. He could have told her days ago, but instead, the revelation from Jack was like a bucket of ice water thrown in her face, leaving her dripping in disappointment.

It was evident to her that fate was pushing her out of this small town, and if not to St. Louis, then somewhere else. In the back of her mind, she wondered if her grandmother was urging her to follow her dream to St. Louis. The space here was gone. She could wait it out, continue teaching at the community center, and hope another space would materialize. Or she could move forward with her original plan to leave Laurel Valley and find happiness in the face of strangers. All signs seemed to be pointing that way.

Chapter Twenty-Four

The temperature outside had dropped with the sinking sun, and the wind swirled around the farmhouse. The sky was jet black, and clouds masked the stars and moon. Inside, a fire blazed in the fireplace, keeping the room toasty and warm. Tyler stared blankly at the flames; a half-eaten piece of Patty's blackberry pie sat on the coffee table, waiting patiently for his appetite to return to finish it off. He'd been running through the scene at the bakery in his head, and guilt was pressing on his chest. He could see the anger in Rachel's eyes, the tears on the verge of falling down her cheeks, and his heart hurt with the memory.

And what about the dinner with Grant? Why was Rachel still seeing him if the space was gone? Perhaps Grant realized what he'd given up and wanted her back. She would most likely want to move to St. Louis again. There was nothing keeping her here now.

Nick sat next to him on the couch, working to consume every last crumb on his plate while Jack dozed in the armchair. "Patty makes a mean pie," Nick exclaimed as he lifted the last bite into his mouth.

Tyler looked over at him, startled by his voice. "She sure does," Tyler agreed, nodding slowly. His sullen mood must have been coming off him in waves, like the heat emanating from the fire. Nick frowned at the sight of Tyler's down-turned mouth and furrowed brow.

"You okay?" Nick asked. Tyler hadn't relayed the mishap that afternoon, and he wondered if Rachel had said anything to Nick about it. From the perplexed expression on his face, it didn't appear she had.

"You've been quiet all night." Jack perked up at the sound of their voices and reached for his plate to savor the last few bites of the pie. "What are you worrying about over there?"

Tyler shrugged. He didn't particularly want to go into it with either of them, but they were both concerned, and it might be good to get his feelings out in the open. Nick had known Rachel all her life. Maybe he would have some advice.

"I think I screwed up any chance with Rachel today," Tyler finally confessed.

"What happened? Is it the reason she left the bakery so suddenly?" Jack asked.

Tyler nodded. "She'd decided to stay in Laurel Valley and move her art school to a larger space downtown."

"That's great!" Jack said at the news.

Tyler continued. "She thought she'd found the perfect spot because it reminded her of a place her grandmother used to take her to, a cottage where they used to paint together." His mind went back to the phone call he'd received days ago from her. He could hear her excitement and resolute determination as she told him her plans to stay.

"She loved that cottage," Nick said. "It's too bad she hasn't been able to find it."

"So, what happened?" Jack asked.

Tyler's eyes cast downward. "It was the perfect spot for your diner."

Jack shook his head sympathetically. "Oh, no."

"Ouch," Nick winced. "But she can't be mad at you for that," he argued.

"She's upset because I didn't tell her when she called with her news last Tuesday. I just let her keep her hopes up even though I knew the space was taken."

"Why'd you keep it from her?" Jack asked.

Tyler heaved a sigh. "I didn't tell her right away because..." His voice trailed off as he wrestled with the emotions toiling inside his heart. His attempts at suppressing his feelings for her were futile. They'd clouded his judgment, causing him to try and manipulate her choice, the very thing he promised himself he'd never do. "Because I think I'm in love with her." A long breath escaped his lungs, and he felt somewhat elated to finally admit it. Nick and Jack sat silently next to him, and Tyler could feel the weight of his words hanging in the room like a dark fog. "I didn't want her to move away, so I kept it from her, hoping I could find another place for her here." He rested his head on the back of the couch and closed his eyes, waiting for one of them to lecture him about falling so quickly.

"Well, keeping it from her was wrong," Jack conceded, skimming over the profession of love. "But you had good intentions. Give her a little time to cool off. She'll see you were only trying to help."

Nick nodded in agreement. "Rachel's the most forgiving person I know. It was most likely just a shock to her. That's all." He rose from his seat and headed to the kitchen. "By the time she gets to the festival tomorrow, she'll have thought it through, and it'll blow right over," he said back over his shoulder. He appeared in the doorway a moment later. "I'm gonna head out. Jack, dinner was delicious!"

Jack chuckled. "Thanks, Nick. Drive safe."

Tyler followed Nick to the front door. "Hey, Nick, sorry about all this heavy talk tonight."

"Don't worry about it," Nick replied, waving him off. "You've got a heart of gold, my friend. You and Rachel would be perfect together. I'm pullin' for ya!" He gave Tyler a playful punch to the shoulder, then turned and headed down the steps toward his truck. "I'll be back around three tomorrow to see if there's anything left you need help with."

"Thanks, Nick!" Tyler called out, then closed the door on the chilly night air.

Returning to the family room, Tyler felt incredibly grateful to have found a friend in Nick. He swiveled his legs up onto the sofa and laid his head back, staring at the ceiling. The logs in the fire shifted, sending embers floating through the chimney. Golden shadows danced on the ceiling. The men were silent, with only the sound of the wood crackling in the fire. Tyler could hear the wind outside whistling him a lullaby, and his eyes grew heavy with exhaustion.

"I made the mistake of falling for someone who's most likely going to move away because she needs to live in the fast lane," he said softly.

Jack took a deep breath. "You know, I faced some challenges, too, when I met your mother," he said.

"Really? What happened?" Tyler sat up and faced Jack, giving him his full attention.

"We were in high school, and I was working for your grandfather out here at the ranch. There was a building out by the side road, a little country store he owned. He sold honey and apple cider, stuff like that. I brought in boxes of products and stocked the shelves. Then, one day, your mom appeared behind the cash register, and my jaw dropped." A smile spread across his face, and his head tilted back. Tyler could almost see the memories scrolling through his mind.

"She was the prettiest girl I'd ever laid eyes on." Jack continued. "Rose-colored cheeks, gorgeous long eyelashes, and a perfect smile. She'd just turned sixteen, and her dad hired her for the summer. Back then, several small towns were zoned for the high school out on Route 40. It was a big high school with around 2,500 kids, so I'd never met her. For days, we just smiled at each other. I didn't have the nerve to talk to her. I was just a stupid stock boy, and her dad owned the place. It wasn't much, but I came from a lot less, so I thought they were rich and she could do better than me."

Tyler envisioned the scene when his parents met. He had never heard this story before, making him miss his mother terribly. "What did you do?"

"Well, I asked a friend to find out what her situation was, and apparently, she was dating a wealthy guy who drove an expensive car and had nice clothes. But I couldn't get her out of my head. I couldn't stop staring at her when I was in the store. So, I decided to get to know her, and, low and behold, his lifestyle didn't fit who she was. Your mom was the most down-to-earth person I've ever known. She broke it off, we started dating, and the rest is history." He spread out his arms, motioning to their surroundings.

Tyler mulled over the challenge his dad overcame and tried to stitch together the similarities with his predicament. His mother had been on a path that didn't include a new romance, just like Rachel. But after she met his dad, something spoke to her heart, and she came to realize where her true happiness was. Tyler worried that it was too late for Rachel to come around. Disappointments were coming at her one after another, blocking her path at every turn. He knew she must feel like a kite twirling around, directionless in the wind, a single strand keeping her grounded.

His dad smiled adoringly at him. "Son, you don't know what's really in her heart. Rachel thinks she'll be happier in the big city, but it seems to me she's pretty ingrained in this community. Plus, she's had a chance to get to know you. It'll be hard to give all this up."

As Tyler laid back against the cushion, he turned his face towards the window. "Nothing is holding her here now. I think I just need to drop it and move on." His heart ached at the thought of this.

"Can you drop it?" Jack asked skeptically.

His father's words sliced through Tyler's thoughts. As he watched through the window, the clouds parted, and the ghostly white winter moon was suddenly visible. The stars appeared like tiny flecks of paint splattered across an inky black canvas. He studied them as if searching for his answer. So many stars, millions of them.

Tyler envisioned his mother's kind face and tender smile just as a bright light swished across the sky and disappeared. He knew the answer. He wouldn't be able to drop it. Not yet, anyway. Even if Rachel wasn't speaking to him, nothing was preventing him from searching for a new spot for the school. Then maybe she'd consider staying.

Chapter Twenty-Five

R achel sat quietly in her living room with her chin resting on the back of the couch, watching the night sky as if searching it for answers. That beautiful, star-filled sky she'd been gazing at her entire life seemed like the only constant she'd ever known. It never faltered, never changed. She could always rely on it for a brilliant show of hope twinkling down at her. Why had the right path become so obscure? She'd been back and forth so many times her head was dizzy with uncertainty. What was she supposed to do? Where was she supposed to spend her life?

A brilliant shooting star raced across the ebony sky, and a tiny smile drew across her face. She was filled with the sense that her grandmother's hand had just caressed her cheek, and the weight of the world seemed a little lighter now.

Headlights streamed into the room, and she rose to gather her purse from the bedroom. Checking her watch, she noticed Grant was on time for a change. The doorbell rang as she came down the hall, and a swarm of butterflies filled her chest. It had been just shy of two weeks since he'd been here, and she wondered how it would feel to see him again. As she opened the door, his familiar grin peered around a bouquet, reminding her of the last night they spent as a couple. So much had changed in her life since then. Two weeks ago, she didn't think she'd ever see him again, and seeing him now felt a little surreal.

"Hey Rach, it's so good to see you. You look beautiful!" Grant's tall stature loomed over her as he stood on the porch.

"Thanks!" she said, noting he was as handsome as ever. As he passed by, he leaned down and gave her a brief kiss on the cheek. "The flowers are beautiful," she said, walking to the kitchen. It was strange having him here. As he moved about the room, he just seemed out of place. Even Willow found his presence unusual. She glared at him from the back of the couch, swishing her tail in annoyance.

"Nice Christmas tree. What made you decide to put one up this year?" his voice called from the living room.

Rachel paused as she reached for a vase over the refrigerator. Tyler's face flashed through her mind, causing her throat to constrict. Why had she gotten so angry at him when he was just trying to help? "Just felt like it, I guess. The town seems more Christmassy this year for some reason. Got me into the spirit." After placing the vase of flowers on the dining room table, she walked through the living room and saw Grant eyeing the caricature portrait of her and Tyler from the office party. She had meant to take it down from the mantle before he arrived and wondered what he was thinking about it. He had no right to be jealous, yet she could tell by the way his back stiffened that something didn't sit right with him.

"That's really cute," he said humorlessly. "Who's the guy?"

"That's Judy's nephew, Tyler. He was at the office party last week." She grabbed her coat from the closet and handed it to him for assistance. He held the coat open, allowing her to slide her arms into the sleeves, and she noticed a hint of his cologne. It was sharp and citrusy, very different from the warm campfire feel of Tyler's scent. So reflective of their personalities. Thankfully, he didn't pry any further, and they headed outside. It was really none of his business, anyway.

Grant started the car, and the dashboard glowed with illuminated high-tech knobs and buttons. Rachel thought they were very festive and remembered standing in her living room with Tyler after they had decorated her tree. She squinted her eyes and watched as the lights on the dashboard blurred.

"What are you doing?" Grant asked, noticing the strange look on her face.

"A quality check," Rachel said, giggling. "Don't worry, all the lights on your dashboard are evenly spaced." Grant shook his head slightly with confusion, then backed the car down the driveway.

They passed the old post office building on the way out of town. She mourned the loss of the space, feeling it had been fate. Surprisingly, she had quickly warmed to the idea of staying in Laurel Valley, and now she wasn't sure where she would end up. But down in her heart, she had a feeling there was something even better coming her way.

The car continued down Main Street as a light snow began to fall. Rachel watched out the window as shoppers bustled in and out of the stores, gathering essentials for their holiday festivities. She smiled at the beautiful decorations. Every storefront was dressed for Christmas, and lights were on in all the shops. Snowflakes sparkled like falling glitter through the twinkle lights in the trees. Rachel recalled her first conversation with Tyler as they walked around town. Some of his best memories were taking in the brightly colored displays with his mother, and she could see why. This was the Christmas magic Tyler remembered sharing with her.

The buildings gradually became further apart, and the road opened up as they headed towards St. Louis. The moon emerged from the clouds to light their way, casting sparkles across the snow-cloaked hills. She'd made this drive with Grant so many times before, and it was reminiscent of a knight whisking the princess away from a repressive kingdom. She used to love this feeling of breaking free, even if it was just for an evening. It was an escape from...something. But in that moment, she realized there hadn't really been anything to escape from. The confusion surrounding her grandmother's passing had been resolved, and Rachel no longer connected her death to the tender moment she spent with her that Christmas.

Rachel's eyes cast around the car at its luxury appointments then landed on Grant's profile. As he prattled on about his trip to Germany and details of the buyout, Rachel wondered what was going through his mind. They'd spoken by phone yesterday and discussed the sale of the building, yet he still wanted to take her to dinner. With no hard feelings between them, she didn't see the harm in going. But something hovered in the back of her mind like there was a purpose for the brief reunion. There was no mention by him that the breakup had been a mistake, and there was nothing in his body language to give her the impression that he'd missed her that much, although he had never been very expressive of his feelings, anyway. The small kiss at her door was hardly noticeable, and she definitely didn't feel any lightning bolts of passion coming from him.

She tried hard to listen and appear interested, but the more he talked, the more she felt the evening would end with a permanent goodbye, so keeping her mind in the conversation was difficult. At this point, she just wanted to get the dinner over with. Judy had called it "going through the motions," and that's precisely how Rachel felt. They would have a pleasant dinner, promise to keep in touch, and that would be it. Grant would move to Germany, and she would move on with finding a space for the school.

She was eager to have things normalized in her life and found relief in the thought that tomorrow would come, and she would figure out a fresh new path. There were options, and she knew she'd find contentment somewhere.

"You seem a little quiet. Is everything okay?" Grant's voice pulled her away from her thoughts.

She shrugged. "Well, after I found out the spot in St. Louis was sold, I decided to stay in Laurel Valley a little longer. I thought I'd found a space for the school on Main

Street, but turns out it was already sold. I'm just a little disappointed to be back at square one. Not sure I will find another spot as perfect."

"I'm sorry to hear that. But just be patient. There's probably a better place on the horizon for you." He smiled warmly at her, and she appreciated his kind words of encouragement.

Soft jazz music played on the radio as the Gateway Arch appeared. The city lights were beautiful and reminded her of the Christmas tree by the gazebo in town. "Can we listen to some Christmas music?" she asked.

Grant looked at her, stunned. "Really? I didn't think you liked Christmas music," he said as he changed the station. Bing Crosby's "Silver Bells" began playing through the speakers, and Rachel couldn't help smiling at this perfect timing.

"I thought about you a lot while I was in Germany... about our relationship," he said as he reached over and took her hand. "I realized how prioritizing my work over you must have made you feel unappreciated. And I'm so sorry for that."

Something inside Rachel stirred as she felt her hand in his, but she wasn't sure what it was, and the confusion caused her heart to jump into her throat. He'd always held her hand during their drives to St. Louis, and it felt warm and soft, just the way she remembered. As she listened to him speak, she tried to predict where he was going with this.

"I know there've been some changes in your life since I left. I can see them in you. You really stepped up your game when push came to shove. I'm really proud of how you organized the festival so quickly. That type of thinking will bring you a lot of success in the business world."

His kind words of praise felt good after the last few days of heartache. "Thanks, but really, the whole town came together for me. All of us worked hard to make it happen. It was a great experience and should be fun for everyone."

"I always knew you had a sharp business mind. You're a go-getter, like me."

Rachel had never thought of herself as a go-getter. Sure, she was passionate about her career, but her goals had always included giving back something to the community. She felt compelled to make a difference in other people's lives. She'd rather be thought of as a go-giver than a go-getter.

She felt the car slow as Grant pulled into a parking spot in front of a two-story white brick building, and she recognized it from the photos he'd sent her of the space for the school.

"Isn't this the building I was trying to buy?" she asked. "Why are we here?"

"Come on, I want to show you something," he said. They exited the car, and she stood beside him in front of the arched doors of the building. It was difficult to stand here, looking up at a dream lost. She'd spent hours here in her imagination, placing the furniture, redirecting the lighting, working with the children. She felt as if the building could feel the loss, too, as it stood in the cold, windows dark and lonely. It was more beautiful in person than in the photos. The stained wood front door was arched at the top, and a matching arched window was on each side.

A jingling noise caught her attention, and she watched him pull a key from his pocket and unlock the door, then stood aside, urging her to enter. She didn't understand why Grant wanted to bring her here, walking around a building she couldn't have. It seemed like a waste of time.

Rachel took in the vast space as Grant flipped a switch on the wall, and the room came to life. The walls were a very soft beige and tracts of spotlights broke up the black ceiling, pointing towards empty spots on the walls. The sound of her heels against the wood floor echoed off the bare walls.

"What do you think?" he asked.

She wasn't sure what he meant. She spun back to face him. "About what?" she said.

"About this space for the art school." He was smiling so broadly she thought she could see every tooth in his mouth.

"What do you mean? I thought someone else bought it." She struggled to wrap her head around what was happening.

He nodded, waiting for the realization to sink in with her. "Meet Someone Else." His arms raised outward, and his hands pointed back towards his face. "I wanted to surprise you."

Rachel's chest tightened as a shock wave stormed through her. She could hardly breathe, feeling lightheaded and disoriented. She was standing right here, in the building she'd envisioned for the school. This was the original plan all along, and he was serving it to her on a silver platter.

Her heart began beating wildly in her chest while her eyes darted between Grant and the room as he continued talking. "I own it now. You can run the art school here rent-free." Grant beamed with excitement, proud of what he'd done for her.

Rachel stared at him, trying to keep up with all the information he was throwing at her. Her pulse was throbbing in her ears. She knew she needed to say something to him, thank him for what he'd done, but she couldn't get the words to form on her lips. "I don't..." Her voice trailed off as she saw him lower down to one knee and produce a tiny box from his pocket. Her mouth hung open in shock.

"Rachel, these past two weeks have made me realize how much I love you." He opened the box to display a large princess-cut diamond in a platinum setting. Rachel gasped, and tears filled her eyes. She had dreamed of this very moment only eleven days ago, and it was exactly how she envisioned it. But after their breakup, she had filed away this dream and had steered her life in a different direction, one that didn't include Grant.

Dizziness clouded her vision, and she felt as if her legs would give out. She had no idea Grant was going to propose tonight. Yet here he was, down on one knee, offering her the perfect life. "But what about your company? I can't ask you to give all that up."

"I asked if I could remain in St. Louis, and they agreed. Once I got the okay, I went ahead and finalized the contract here. And I won't be working the long hours I used to put in. It's really just a consultant position. I'll need to travel to Germany every few months, and you can come with me. We'll be able to spend more time together."

The only thing she felt had been missing from their relationship was time spent together. And he'd solved it. "Grant, I'm.... I'm shocked! I don't know what to say." Nervous tears streamed down her face as Grant stared at her wide-eyed, waiting for her answer.

He stood and hugged her, then kissed her softly. "I know it seems out of the blue, but I also know that I love you, and I want to spend the rest of my life with you. I want you to have the wedding of your dreams, anything you want! And guess what? My apartment is in the building right around the corner. You could walk to work every day. You're going to love living here, Rach!"

Less than two weeks ago, she would have thrown her arms around him and accepted without the slightest hesitation. Grant had everything going for him. And the generosity he showed by following through on the contract was more than she could ever imagine. Was this the space she was meant for? Had the spot next to the bakery fallen through because this was where she was meant to be?

He removed the ring from the box and said, "You don't have to give me an answer now. I know this must be overwhelming for you. But will you wear the ring while you think it over for a few days?"

Confusion tore through her. She'd been sure the evening was going to end with a permanent goodbye and had prepared her brain for that conclusion. But the complete opposite was happening. Her eyes fell toward the ring, sparkling in the overhead lights. She recognized it. It was the one she'd been eyeing at Glitter & Gold. And now Grant wanted to give her the perfect wedding and the perfect life to go along with it.

"Will you wear the ring while you think about it?" he asked again, taking her hand.

She looked deep into his eyes and finally saw the love and adoration he felt for her. All she had to do was say one word, and every dream she'd ever had would come true in an instant. All she had to do was say yes.

Chapter Twenty-Six

T he renewal of the Silver Belles Christmas Festival had caused quite a stir in the sleepy little town of Laurel Valley, and everyone was eager to rekindle old friendships, enjoy delicious food, and support a local resident. The festivalgoers arrived at Lake Haven Ranch with spirited anticipation, marveling at the magical atmosphere. A light dusting of snow had fallen overnight and blanketed the grounds. Small, brown paper sacs illuminated with candles lined the driveway, leading past the farmhouse and down to the lakefront, where the Christmas fanfare was underway. The house glowed brightly against the dark sky. Evergreen wreaths with large red bows hung in each window, and a tuft of gray smoke lazily escaped from the chimney.

Around back, the local bluegrass band had assembled underneath the sprawling branches of a 200-year-old oak tree. Its majestic limbs were wrapped in twinkle lights that flashed against the glassy finish of the instruments. A country rendition of "Frosty the Snowman" played as the audience sang along, and spirited music traveled across the icy surface of the lake, reaching all the way to the other side.

Volunteers were plentiful, running this way and that to ensure a joyous experience for everyone. Jack was manning the entrance, accepting donations in a small, colorfully decorated box. Those who could give were giving generously, and before long, he was running up to the house to find another box.

Two long picnic tables had been pushed together to form the cookie decorating station. Children tugged at their parent's hands, dragging them to where Patty stood holding a basket of cookie bundles. Bowls of colorful sprinkles, crushed peppermints, and chocolate chips lined the center of the table, and tubes of gooey red and green frosting oozed onto the checkerboard tablecloth. Tiny fingers joyfully worked to carefully create their masterpieces.

Aside from the band, the blazing campfire was the main outdoor attraction. People gathered around in folding chairs, soaking up the cozy warmth from the flames. Children waited patiently while their marshmallows impaled on long sticks tanned in the heat, then squealed in delight when the little white puffs caught on fire, their smiling faces reflecting the amber glow.

Mr. Merriweather had been overjoyed at the chance to help with the festival. He was seated on a wooden bench outside the barn, dressed head to toe in authentic Santa attire. A beautiful backdrop of greenery, twinkle lights, and red bows formed a picture-perfect scene. Children were taking turns hopping up on his lap to trust him with their Christmas wishes, and Nick was ready to snap a keepsake photo, capturing their delight.

The barn had also received a holiday makeover. Lighted garland was tacked into place around the sliding doors, and a large wreath with a big red bow hung above them. Twinkle lights were tacked across the entire roof line, and strands of lighted garland lined every doorway and window. Inside, the main beams were wrapped in twinkle lights, and Chloe's delicate paper snowflakes dangled from the rafters, fluttering in the breeze. Long buffet tables filled with delectable dishes lined the far wall, and there wasn't an empty spot on any of them. Warming lanterns were scattered about, creating the perfect setting for the Christmas feast.

The silent auction was well underway in a feed storage area off the main barn. Handmade magnolia wreaths with black and white buffalo plaid bows, birdhouses crafted to resemble tiny Victorian doll houses and even a weekend getaway to the Laurel Valley Inn were among the available items. Festival goers wielding #2 pencils lined up at each item, eager to put in their winning bids.

Patty had donated multiple scrumptious items for the bake sale, including three of Polly's famous apple cakes, which were the first to go. Pre-bagged lemon scones and boxes of gooey cinnamon buns were also favorites. At the center of the table was the grand prize for the winner of the fruit cake contest: a towering layer cake smothered with heavenly buttercream frosting, garnished with ripe raspberries and delicate chocolate shavings.

As Tyler had predicted, the star of the show was a

ten-foot balsam fir tree standing majestically in the corner, proudly displaying handmade ornaments crafted by the elementary school children. Ignoring fears that something would happen, Rachel insisted on Grandma Lizzy's angel being placed at the top of the tree. Her porcelain face was aglow from the twinkle lights, smiling down upon everyone, spreading hope and good cheer.

Tyler bent towards the fire, adding logs to feed the flames, sending glowing embers rising toward the stars.

"You are an expert at making campfires, Tyler!" Brianna kidded him. She was relaxing in a chair with her legs stretched out, while Chloe carefully constructed a s'mores tower.

"I didn't get much practice in Manhattan, so that's a great compliment!" He smiled warmly at them both. Staring into the flames, he wondered if Rachel had arrived. It was possible that she'd been there for a while but chose to avoid him. Tyler knew she had kept her dinner date with Grant after she left the bakery, and he struggled to fend off the possibility of their reconciliation. His frantic call to a local real estate company this morning hadn't produced any leads on a location for the school, but he wasn't giving up.

He gave the burning logs a fierce jab just as he felt a light tap on his shoulder. As he stood, he saw Rachel's beautiful face. She was bundled in a black coat with a red and white plaid scarf encircling her neck. The bright flames reflected in her eyes, and the warmth gave her cheeks a rosy glow. Her genuine smile filled him with relief.

"Hey, I was wondering if you were here yet," he said hesitantly, worried she was still angry. His eyes darted around, noticing Grant wasn't with her. A spark of hope flickered inside him.

"I got stuck on a phone call with my mom." She took in their surroundings and smiled at the crowd, enjoying the merriments. "Everything is just beautiful!" she exclaimed.

"Yeah, I can't believe what a great turnout we're having."

She nodded in agreement. "Listen, I wanted to apologize for running out of the bakery yesterday."

Tyler raised a hand to quiet her. "You have nothing to apologize for. I am the one that is so very sorry I didn't tell you right away. And I've already been putting the feelers out for a new spot."

"That's really sweet of you." Her angelic eyes sparkled in the light of the fire. He wanted to tell her everything he felt inside, how he looked forward to the moment he set eyes on her each day, how he craved the sound of her laugh, how she brought a light to his heart he hadn't known in years, making the move to Laurel Valley even more worthwhile. "Rachel, I really need to tell you how I'm feeling. Spending these past couple of weeks with you has been so amazing, and I..."

A firm pat on the back interrupted his confession. "You must be Tyler!" Grant was suddenly behind him. How long had he been there? How much had he heard? "I recognize you from the caricature drawing, although your body's bigger than I'd imagined." Grant gave a dry laugh and winked at him, then draped his arm across Rachel's shoulders. "Judy's asking everyone to head inside," he said, ushering her towards the barn.

Rachel glanced back at Tyler, and he searched her face for answers, unable to read the look in her eyes. Was it confusion? Or was it pity? As her figure moved farther away, he felt the light inside him grow dimmer. Reluctantly, he forced his body to move and follow their path.

As he approached the barn, he saw the couple pass by Nick, who gave Rachel a questioning glance. "I thought they broke up," Nick said to Tyler once they were out of earshot. Nick had seen the chemistry between Tyler and Rachel but had warned him to give her space while she settled her feelings about Grant. It seemed like good advice, but neither knew what to think after witnessing Grant escorting her into the barn. Maybe Tyler should have made his feelings clear.

"Can I have everyone's attention?!" Judy shouted across the room. She stood on a hay bale wearing black knee-high boots over her blue jeans, with a burgundy pashmina draped over a cream cashmere sweater. "We have a winner for the fruitcake contest!" Applause rang through the barn as Judy turned and waited for Patty to hop up next to her, holding a large cake box containing the grand prize.

"Mr. Merriweather loved each and every one of the entries," Patty shouted. "It was an incredibly tough decision, but he's made up his mind. The winner of this quadruple chocolate raspberry cake goes to..." she paused for dramatic effect. "Jack Patterson, who used Miss Polly's delicious fruitcake recipe!"

The crowd cheered as Jack approached her, his face blushing from the attention. She handed him the box, and he helped her down from the hay. Judy raised both hands to quiet the crowd.

"I just want to thank everyone for attending our Silver Belles Christmas Festival." Hoots and cheers popped out among the crowd. "This tradition was started many years ago by my mother, Polly Harrison, and her best friend, Liz Parsons, one of our town's most beloved mayors. In years past, our festival benefited the families struggling on the outskirts of our community, but this year, we have the privilege of helping one of our very own town residents, Miss Rachel Noelle." The crowd cheered as Rachel waved a gloved hand in the air.

"And now she'd like to come up and say a few words." Judy stepped down from the hay as Rachel climbed on.

Rachel waved her hand again in greeting. "Good evening, everyone! I just want to say how much I appreciate your support to encourage visual art instruction to children." Tyler saw her eyes move toward Grant on the other side of the room as she spoke, standing with his hands in his pockets. His smile seemed to clash with his stiff posture, and his GQ-Magazine attire matched the reserved personality Rachel had described.

Tyler watched Rachel's eyes fan out across the room, then finally meet his gaze. He leaned casually against a wooden pillar, but the lack of a smile on his face must have flustered her, causing her voice to shake.

"There is nothing I enjoy more than introducing a child to their artistic imagination and seeing the glow on their face as their hands create their first masterpiece." She moved on to detail the programs she planned to offer full-time, as well as the scholarships she could award with the town's donations. Tyler listened, watching her face fill with passion as she spoke of the children, but all he could think about was the abrupt change to their relationship. He knew there was always the chance she would leave, and it was good to find it out now instead of further down the road. "I appreciate all of you coming together tonight to raise money for this project. Your support means the world to me...and I love all of you." Her smile had faltered, and tears were forming in her eyes. He knew the decision to leave her hometown wasn't easy. But Grant must have found a way to make her dream a reality. "Grandma Lizzy may be gone," she said, swallowing back a sob. "But her kind and generous spirit is alive and well here in Laurel Valley."

Whoops and whistles echoed off the rafters as Judy returned to the makeshift stage, and Rachel made her way back towards Grant. "Please join me in thanking Tyler Patterson and Rachel Noelle for having the courage to put this evening together in such a short amount of time. They were a great team!" The room again cheered for the duo. Tyler felt the rumble of unease inside him. The previous notion that he and Rachel were a team was lost now that it appeared Grant had returned to her life. They were simply friends who put together a fundraiser, nothing more. He knew his life needed to go on, with or without Rachel Noelle in the picture.

Judy cast a glance down at Tyler. Although public speaking evoked waves of nausea, Tyler wanted to personally thank the people of the town. "And now, Tyler Patterson has something to say to all of you.

Tyler stood in the front, facing the crowd, and shoved his hands into his pockets. "Uh, thank you everyone for coming out tonight. I want to tell you all what a pleasure it was to host the Christmas Festival here and see the joy this place brought to all of you. I'm thankful for your generosity and support of my transplant to Lake Haven Ranch, and I can't wait to bring it back to its glory days." The clapping of the crowd gave him one last shove of encouragement. "I was recently informed of a monthly potluck tradition you all had here at the ranch, and I'm happy to announce that the tradition will continue!" The crowd gave a collective hooray! "I hope to see you all back here the first Sunday in January for the next family potluck."

The heartfelt applause continued, then Grant's voice suddenly interrupted the celebration. "As long as we're making announcements," he said as the noise died down. "I am thrilled to tell all of you that Rachel and I are engaged!"

Everyone turned towards them, and a hush fell over the crowd. Tyler's gleeful smile slid from his face. His eyes locked on Rachel's, and an instant later, she was being hugged and congratulated on all sides.

"Let's see the ring!" shouted Mrs. Perry, and the crowd cheered in agreement. Tyler held a steady gaze on Rachel, hoping she would refute Grant's claim, but a strange look of being caught off guard was plastered on her face. She seemed surprised at the announcement, but as Grant thrust her hand up for everyone to see, Tyler's heart shrunk to the size of a cranberry. The enormous diamond sparkled all the way across the room.

Wishes of congratulations were sprinkled over the couple like powdered sugar. Tyler headed for the door and faintly heard Grant's excited voice tear through him like a dagger to the back. "I've just purchased the building for the new school. It'll be perfect for her!"

It was the final blow. Rachel had been given everything she ever dreamed of, and soon, she would head to St. Louis to start her new life. He ran outside, hoping the chilly air would cool his heartache.

Chapter Twenty-Seven

As the crowd began to die down, the cleanup effort was underway. Tables were folded, and chairs were stacked. The baked goodies and auction winnings were distributed, and the plastic containers found their way to their owners. The barn was quickly transformed back to its original splendor.

Rachel had been holding back her anger for over an hour and was eager to get to the car. "Could you take me home now, please?" she asked Grant as they finished folding the last of the tablecloths. She had tried her best to keep a smile on her face at the festival, not wanting to spoil everyone's fun with a scene.

"Sure. You know I don't like this kind of thing, anyway." His words were like water on the campfire, dousing out the fun. Yes, she knew Grant did not like this kind of thing. He didn't like Christmas trees because they dropped needles, and he didn't want to decorate cookies because it was too messy. He didn't enjoy hanging up stockings, and he didn't like campfires because they made his clothes smell smokey. These characteristics had never bothered her before. But her grandmother had cherished Christmas and all its silly traditions, and now Rachel did too.

As they walked towards the field of parked cars, Grant attempted small talk. "You know, you guys did a great job with what you had to work with. But wait till you see Christmas in St. Louis next year!" He rambled on, seemingly oblivious to Rachel's growing irritation. "There is a huge festival at Kiener Plaza. Live reindeer, light projection show, and fireworks...it's spectacular."

"We weren't really aiming for 'spectacular' here in Laurel Valley," she countered with a resentful edge to her voice. Grant looked at her, startled by her discontented tone. Without another word, she got in the front seat of his car and stared out the window. Her cheeks burned with anger.

Grant finally broke the silence as they headed back towards town. "Listen, I'm sorry I announced our engagement. I was just really excited."

Her face shot towards him. "Grant, I haven't even said yes yet!" Her voice shook with fury. "How dare you make an announcement like that! I only agreed to wear the ring while I thought things over for a few days."

"I know, I'm sorry," he pleaded. "But to be honest, I assumed you were going to say yes... so I didn't see the harm." She could see the hurt brimming in his eyes.

Her temper lowered a few degrees, and a feeling of self-reproach settled in. Of course, he thought she would say yes. Before he left, it was all she wanted; she'd even hinted at it a few times. She shouldn't blame him for assuming her answer would be yes.

"There's just a lot of things I'm trying to work through right now," she reasoned. "I've discovered a whole new side of my grandmother that I didn't know existed, and it made me feel even closer to her, closer to these people. This town was important to her. She left a big void when she died. A void that no one else could fill. They basically gave up on having a big Christmas celebration because of her. And tonight, I was able to give that back to them. It felt fantastic."

Grant stared at the road ahead, and she knew how confusing this must be for him. It confused her as well. As long as they had been together, she'd looked forward to shedding her life here. She hadn't shown any interest in Christmas celebrations or any of the town's other traditions. But in just two weeks, her priorities had changed, and she was struggling to fit them into one mold or the other.

Tyler crouched by the fire, watching it burn down to just a small pile of glowing embers. A part of him was happy for Rachel. Her dream of the perfect space for the art school had come true, and she'd be able to leave behind Laurel Valley, just like she wanted.

"Hey, Tyler." Brianna's voice came from behind him. "Everything was perfect. Thanks for having the festival here. I know it was a lot of work."

He stood up to face her and plastered a smile on his face.

"It was my pleasure," he replied. She didn't move, staring straight into his eyes.

"What are you going to do about Rachel?" she finally asked.

His face tingled, but he wasn't sure if it was from the cold or from her direct question. His mind raced as he wondered what Rachel had said to her. Did Brianna know he was falling for Rachel and didn't want him messing things up for her? "Nothing...I don't know what you mean." He tried to brush it off.

"I can tell you have feelings for her." It seemed like an accusation, one that he couldn't deny. He turned his face toward the fire to hide the pain in his eyes. "And I think she has feelings for you, too."

Tyler wasn't sure how to respond. "What difference does it make? She's engaged now."

"Actually, she hasn't said yes to him. Grant overstepped when he made that announcement."

"But she was wearing the ring," he argued.

"She only agreed to wear the ring while she thought it over. Both the proposal and the announcement were a complete shock to her." Tyler couldn't allow the hope inside him to take over. It was too soon. How could he trust what Brianna was saying? Rachel didn't deny the engagement, and she left the festival with Grant. "I think if you told her how you felt," she continued. "It might make a difference. Honestly, I don't think she has been happy with Grant for a while, and I'm partly to blame. Whenever she came to me with an issue, I just blew her off and made her feel bad for complaining. I should have listened to her. But I've known her all her life, and I can tell when she puts on a happy face to cover a sad heart."

Tyler worked through this new information in his head. "You really think I should tell her? What if I do, and she marries him anyway?" He ran his fingers through his hair, fighting with uncertainty.

"You should at least try. If you don't, you might always wonder what could have been. And that's worse, don't you think?"

Tyler hesitated, not sure what to do. The last thing he wanted was to confuse Rachel more. What if she didn't feel the same way about him? Sure, she may have second thoughts about Grant, but that didn't mean she was ready to give him up. Straightening his back, he contemplated his next move.

"You should go after her." Brianna said. 'Everything is pretty much done here."

He gave her a sideways glance, and she responded with an encouraging smile. His face brightened, and he knew what he needed to do. "Thanks," he said to her, then ran up the hill toward the house.

Tyler jumped into the old pickup and gave the key a turn. The engine sputtered out a long screech and refused to come to life. "Not now!" he thought in frustration. He gave it a few more tries without success. He sat for a moment in the quiet of the truck to collect his thoughts. What was he doing? He can't just charge over there in front of Grant. It wasn't right. Grant hadn't done anything wrong, and Rachel didn't deserve to witness a confrontation. If he was going to do this, he needed to get her alone. Rachel would be at the pancake breakfast in the morning, so maybe he could pull her aside. And if not, he'd find another way to confess his feelings. He wasn't going to let her leave without a fight.

After a long talk, Rachel promised to think things through overnight and meet Grant at the coffeehouse in the morning.

"I'll see you tomorrow," he said, stepping out onto her front porch. He turned back to kiss her lightly, and her heart ached with confusion.

Rachel watched his taillights head out of sight toward the inn and was left to work through her feelings. She stared down at the ring on her finger. It was incredible. When she met Grant, he seemed to be everything this town wasn't, and he was offering her everything she'd dreamed of. There had been a void inside her, a light that had gone out many years ago, and Grant had opened a whole new world to her, full of bright lights and excitement. There wasn't anyone here that could offer her that feeling.

But was this feeling, this pursuit of excitement, so important to her now? Something changed inside her when she met Tyler. He was so down-to-earth and allowed her to be herself. She didn't have to downplay any of the town's quirkiness to him. He loved it just as much as she did. Or just as much as she used to.

Brianna's warning crept through her mind. Stability is everything. She'd only known Tyler for two weeks. Was she crazy to throw all this away for him? She wasn't even sure if his plans for the ranch were going to work out. What if she turned Grant down and gave up everything, only to find out Tyler couldn't handle the country, and he moved back to Manhattan? Besides that, there were rarely any vacancies downtown, so there was no telling when she'd find a spot for the school. Maybe it was best if she accepted Grant's proposal and moved to St. Louis. She'd have a larger space there, and it was an incredible location. Plus, she'd never lived anywhere but Laurel Valley. Could this be the shove she needed to get out into the world?

She padded off to bed with Willow at her heels, ready to snuggle under the covers. There were more questions than answers running circles in her head. If her grandmother were here, what would she think of all this? Would she want Rachel to choose the sure path to success or to follow her heart down a road that may be riddled with problems to solve?

Chapter Twenty-Eight

As the ghosts of the Silver Belles Christmas Festival evaporated with the morning fog, Lake Haven Ranch readied itself for a new day. A lazy trail of smoke escaped the charred logs in the fire pit, but thanks to the work of the volunteer clean-up crew, there weren't many remnants left of the evening, although the twinkle lights in the branches of the oak tree and interior of the barn were left in place, ready for another evening of magic in the near future.

Tyler smiled out at the scene through the kitchen window. He woke with a heavy heart this morning, but last night's festivities renewed the Christmas spirit in his beloved hometown, easing his pain and reminding him why he moved here in the first place.

He'd promised to meet Jack at the diner early this morning to help with the pancake breakfast, and after a fifteen-minute drive, Tyler found a parking spot near the diner and headed inside. The smell of hot coffee and maple syrup surrounded him like a warm hug. He scanned the crowd, hoping to spot Rachel. It was just before eight o'clock, and the tables were already filled with the festival volunteers. Laughter and happy chatter hummed through the room. It thrilled Tyler to see these old friends coming together again and hoped this would be a new beginning for the whole town.

Patti was weaving her way between tables, setting down piles of golden flapjacks in front of each patron, then hurrying back to the kitchen for more. Tyler spotted Nick clearing dishes from a table and headed towards him.

"Hey, Tyler. How are you holding up?" Nick asked, his inquiry filled with condolence.

"I'm okay," Tyler answered, his eyes darting around the room. "Have you seen Rachel come through this morning?" he asked in a hushed tone.

"Not yet." Nick stopped collecting the plates and looked up at his friend. "Why? Are you going to ask her about the engagement?" he asked warily.

The foreboding inflection in Nick's question drove a spike through Tyler's bravery. "Well," Tyler hesitated. "I need to tell her how I feel." He saw Nick's eyes widen but wasn't sure what he was thinking. "Do you think I should?" He searched Nick's face for the answer, knowing Nick would do anything to protect her. But Tyler knew he couldn't live with himself if he kept silent about his feelings.

Nick gave a sigh, then put both hands on Tyler's shoulders. Tyler braced for the words that would crush his soul. "Dude," Nick said, looking squarely at him. "Absolutely. I know you love her." His eyes closed, and his head slowly shook back and forth. "And I can't imagine anything better than seeing you two together." The harsh lines that had formed on his brow softened, and a bright smile lit up his face. Tyler beamed as he felt sparks of adrenaline course through his limbs. "Now go get a tub and help me out here. You can deal with your love life later!" Nick teased.

Tyler pushed through the swinging door and saw Jack pouring batter on the griddle. "Hey, Dad! How's it going in here?" Tyler asked, surveying the room. The once-tidy kitchen was now in complete disarray. Mixing bowls dripping with batter were piled in the sink, broken eggs oozed in their carton, and the worktable was covered in flour.

"Busy!" Jack replied. Grabbing a spatula, he quickly flipped several bubbly pancakes over and steam escaped from the edges. "I love to cook, but once this place opens, I think I'll stick to greeting the guests and leave this to a professional." Jack stole a quick glance at his son. "You doing okay this morning?" He pointed his spatula at a stack of clean plates, motioning for Tyler to bring them to him.

Tyler turned away from him to grab an apron off a hook behind the door. "Yeah, pretty good, actually." He placed the top of the apron over his head, tied the strings around his waist, then grabbed the plates and placed them on the counter next to the stove.

"That was quite an announcement from Grant last night," Jack said, as he placed three pancakes on the top plate, and Tyler moved it to the prep table for Patty. They continued with several more plates, then started the process all over again with fresh, gooey batter.

"I know. Really threw me for a loop. But I talked to her sister after Rachel left. Turns out she didn't say yes to him yet."

"Oh, really?"

"She wanted to think about it. And I can't blame her for that. It's everything she wanted all tied up in a neat little package."

"What are you going to do?" Jack faced his son with sympathetic eyes and gave him his full attention, ignoring the pancakes.

Patty pushed through the kitchen door, and the noisy chatter from the dining room temporarily filled the kitchen. Her face brightened when she saw Tyler. "Hey, Tyler! How's everything going?" Her voice was upbeat as usual. She glanced up at him as she rested a large, brown serving tray on the worktable, then arranged the plates of piping hot flapjacks, topping each stack with a tiny butter ball.

"I'm good," he smiled reassuringly at her. "Thanks for asking, Patty." He smiled, having just received his first taste of small-town smothering and loving it. "Can I help you with that tray?"

"I'd rather you help me clear some tables if you don't mind," she replied, hoisting the tray onto her shoulder.

"You got it!" Tyler grabbed a bussing tub then glanced back at his dad. "It's gonna burn," he warned, pointing to the smoke billowing up from the griddle.

"Yikes!" he heard Jack exclaim as he headed into the dining room.

The bell over the door jingled, and Judy entered, bringing a gust of frosty air that quickly dispersed into the warmth of the diner. Under her arm, she had a folded-up newspaper and carried a small wooden box. "Hey, Tyler!" she said, giving him a quick hug. "I've got something for your dad. Is he in the back?"

"Sure is."

"Great!" she replied. "Did you see the write-up of the festival in The Post?" she asked, handing him the paper. He watched as she made her way towards the back, stopping at several tables to chat along the way. Tyler unfolded the paper and read the column.

The Laurel Valley Post
Sunday, December 24

'Tis the season for holiday events, and last night's festival did not disappoint! It was a night to remember for the residents of Laurel Valley. The newly resurrected Silver Belles Christmas Festival was brimming with holiday magic, bringing a sense of community and love to adults and children alike.

The town went almost 20 years without a community Christmas celebration. But thanks to the efforts of two residents, Rachel Noelle and Tyler Patterson, Laurel Valley had a night of excitement and holiday joy.

With the help of local volunteers, Noelle and Patterson transformed the town's ho-hum annual potluck dinner into a winter wonderland.

But the celebration didn't go off without a hitch. The original venue suffered damage from a flash snowstorm, and the organizers had to scramble for a new locale. Luckily,

273

Patterson himself, offered to host the event at his family's ranch.

"We couldn't have the event without a venue, and I just knew my old hay barn would work perfectly!" said Patterson.

And that wasn't the only obstacle they had to overcome. Putting together an entire festival in less than two weeks was nothing less than miraculous. "Laurel Valley is a special place full of kind-hearted people. Once they heard a Christmas Festival was being considered, they sprang to action," said Mayor Jeb Oldwick. "Seems they just needed a little fire set under them, and Rachel Noelle was just the one to light it. Their vision became a community effort, and the event was a huge success."

Festivalgoers enjoyed singing along with a local country band, visits with Santa, cookie decorating, a silent auction, s'mores by a campfire, and, of course, lots and lots of delicious food!

"The festival is a wonderful tradition started by two special ladies, my grandmother Liz Parsons, and Tyler's grandmother Polly Harrison," Noelle said. "We are privileged to be entrusted with this tradition and carry on the spirit of hope and giving."

Proceeds from the event will go towards a new children's art school headed by Rachel Noelle. The location is yet to be determined. Patterson plans to host more celebrations at Lake Haven Ranch, so keep an eye on the society page for announcements.

A broad smile spread across Tyler's face, and he scanned the room, noticing a charge of energy. Smiles were on every face, and vibrant conversations were at every table. They had really done it. The festival had revived the spirit of the town. He could see the difference in everyone here and a calming warmth spread within him. After clearing some tables, he headed towards the back to drop them in the sink. Nick was standing at the sink rinsing some plates as Judy held the small wooden box out to Jack.

"Please," she said. "I want you to have them. I hate to cook, and it would thrill her to see her recipes enjoyed."

Jack hesitantly grasped the box, and Tyler saw tears prick at the corners of his eyes. He walked over to see what was happening. "Looks like I'll have plenty of recipes for the menu," Jack said to him, his voice quivering slightly with emotion. Tyler's eyes went to Judy, who was wiping a tear from her cheek.

"You will be able to keep Mama's recipes alive. And the people in town love them. So, they are yours now." Judy patted the top of the box and then left the kitchen. Jack followed, with Nick and Tyler trailing after them.

As they entered the dining room, Jack held up a hand to quiet the crowd. "Hey everyone, I just want to say a few words." The noise level dimmed, and all eyes went towards him. "We want to thank all of you for helping with the festival last night. I know I, for one, had a lot of fun doing it, and I'm looking forward to next year already." Clapping rose from the tables. "On a side note, I've thought of a name for this place." All eyes were on him as he paused for dramatic effect. "Welcome to Polly's Diner!" Jack shouted, smiling from ear to ear. Judy rushed over and gave him a big hug as the crowd cheered.

Chapter Twenty-Nine

R achel sat in a back corner of the coffeehouse next to the window, cupping her hands around a warm mug. As she watched the steam rise and dissipate, a thought occurred to her. This was the same table she had sat at with Tyler recently. So much had changed since then. Overnight, she'd made up her mind about the proposal, and her entire outlook on life was different. The scene beyond the window seemed brighter, too... sweeter, more inviting. Snow had fallen again overnight and covered the tops of bushes and tree limbs. The shopkeepers were bustling in and out of their stores, setting up sidewalk displays and encouraging patrons to come in out of the cold.

She checked her watch and noted that Grant would arrive soon to discuss their plans. She twisted the diamond ring that encircled her finger. A clang came from the doorbell, and she saw Grant enter and wave to her. Her posture stiffened as she watched him pay, then wait to the side for his coffee.

Rachel thought back to Friday night when he'd picked

her up for their date. The light kiss on the cheek hadn't made her heartbeat quicken. But if she were to be honest with herself, she had never felt much at all from his kisses. Grant was a straightforward, no-fluff guy. There had been no long evenings snuggling on the couch or romantic walks under the fall leaves. His visits had a strict agenda, and he always seemed to be running out of time and needing to move on to the next task. It was the fast-paced lifestyle she had become familiar with since knowing him. Such a different vibe than the go-with-the-flow attitude she grew up with here. And she wondered if he'd really be able to slow down.

Grant turned from the counter and headed towards her. As she watched him approach the table, a strange feeling crept over her, as if a camera lens was being adjusted and things were sharpening in her mind. Warming relief spread through her, and she knew she was making the right decision. He smiled as he took the seat across from her.

"You look pretty this morning," he said. The compliment took her off guard, and her heart ached for the disappointment she was about to deal him.

Rachel filled her lungs with a deep breath of courage. "Thanks, especially since I didn't sleep much last night." She looked into his stealthy gray eyes and missed the warm caramel circles she'd grown to love in Tyler's. Grant returned the stare, then a frown darkened his face as he realized what she was going to say.

"You've come to a decision about the engagement." He hesitated before continuing. "And I'm thinking it's not in my favor." He placed a hand over hers.

Rachel nodded. "Grant, two weeks ago, the night you came to my house with the news of the buyout, I saw a fiery passion in your eyes. You were so excited to move to Germany and experience a new culture." She watched his expression, hoping to see him acknowledge the truth in what she was saying. "You assumed I wouldn't want to move there with you, and you were willing to break up with me to pursue your passion." She saw the regret in his eyes, and he opened his mouth to speak. Rachel raised her hand to quiet him. She needed to say everything that was in her heart without any interruptions. "And that's okay. Everyone needs to..." She searched for the right words and remembered what Tyler said. "You need to live the life you dream of, and not let anybody hold you back." As she spoke the words, she thought maybe Grant had actually been holding her back in some way. His constant jabs at this quaint little town made her feel as if there was something better out there. But what she realized is that St. Louis isn't better, it's just different.

Grant sat quietly, staring at her for a moment. "Does this have anything to do with that guy? Judy's nephew?" he said in a low voice, a hint of accusation in his tone.

Rachel hadn't been expecting the question and wasn't sure how to answer it. Had she not met Tyler, things may have been different. She would most likely be sitting here right now, discussing wedding plans with Grant. But it wasn't just her feelings for Tyler that made her reject the proposal. It was everything she'd discovered about herself. She realized she didn't need the chaos of a big city to feel fulfilled. She needed to hear Mr. Merriweather's imaginary war stories. She needed to see the tiny Christmas village in Mrs. Perry's window. And she definitely needed Ben's famous peppermint mocha lattes and Patty's baking lessons. Besides, who would continue the work of the Silver Belles and organize the next Christmas Festival? These things made her feel alive and connected to these people. She'd taken for granted the community she grew up in, the people who'd watched her grow up, and the bonds they all shared.

Ignoring his question, she said, "Your dream is in Germany, and mine is in Laurel Valley." Never in a million years had she thought she would say that. But it was the truth.

Grant's brow wrinkled with worry as he grasped at one last attempt to win her back. "Rachel, I know you have found a new love for this town, which I don't really understand, but what about your dream of opening your own school? I bought the perfect space for you."

Through gritted teeth, she said, "I know you thought you were doing a really nice thing for me, and it was so kind and generous. I'm truly grateful. But, Grant, we were broken up when you decided to buy the space. It was wrong of you to assume I would just fall back into step behind you." She didn't like someone making a major decision in her life without consulting her, and the fear of a life full of these types of "helpful" deeds was something she couldn't ignore. She looked down at her hand, then quickly pulled the ring off her finger and placed it on the table in front of him. It represented a bond to him she wanted no part of. "I'm really sorry, but my priorities have changed, and I want to stay here in Laurel Valley."

Grant took the ring in his hand, the weight of disappointment and regret causing a slump to his shoulders. "I just wanted you to be happy," he said. "And I thought you would be happy with me."

Her wrinkled brow softened a little. She knew, on some level, he saw the error of his ways. She believed he loved her, but not in the way she wanted to be loved. They were both meant to be with other people, and she knew exactly who she was meant to be with. He didn't have millions in the bank or drive a fancy car. He was simple, kind, and generous. He was here in Laurel Valley, and she couldn't imagine spending the rest of her life with anyone else. A twinge of excitement festered inside her. The urge to rush out the doors to find her true love was overwhelming. And the old blue pickup parked across the street pointed her to his exact location.

Grant stood to leave and gathered his coat. Their eyes met for the last time as he bent down and gently kissed her cheek. "You deserve anything you can dream," he said, then turned and walked toward the door, giving Ben a wave goodbye as he exited the coffeehouse, and her life, for good.

Rachel turned towards the window and saw dozens of people heading into the diner for the pancake breakfast. The space wasn't meant to be hers, and she was okay with that. The town had two new residents and would prosper because of them. She had faith she would find another location, and it would be even better.

Stepping out onto the sidewalk, Rachel drew in a deep,

invigorating breath of crisp December air. The scent of a distant cracking fire tickled her nose, and she could hear soft Christmas music coming from The Curio Shop. She strode towards the diner, an air of confidence giving her an encouraging push. She needed to find Tyler and profess her feelings to him.

As she crossed the street, she saw Mr. Merriweather heading towards her. His snow-white beard was floating around his chin in all directions with the breeze. To her relief, he was dressed warmly in a bright red sweater with green suspenders holding up his blue jeans, and his pant legs were tucked into furry-topped, black rubber boots. He seemed to have embraced his likeness to Santa even more today. "Good morning, Mr. Merriweather. Are you heading to the diner?" she asked, falling into step beside him.

"I sure am. I want to see if those flapjacks are as good as Miss Polly's," he said, giving her a wink. "So when will you be heading to St. Louis?"

"Well," Rachel said, grinning from ear to ear. "I've decided to stay in Laurel Valley."

Mr. Merriweather stopped short and faced her. "Is that so?" he replied, giving his beard a few strokes. "That's a bit of good news! So, you'll be needing a spot here for your art school, am I right?"

"That's right! Might take a while, but it'll be worth the wait."

"Well then, I've got a proposition I want to run by you."

A week ago, Rachel would have dreaded being

approached by him, knowing there would be some strange request involved, like taking inventory of his empty hangers or helping him arrange the display of vintage hand grenades in his front window. But she didn't have that feeling of dread today. She was happy he felt comfortable enough to ask for her help like a family member would. And he'd done so much for the Silver Belles festival. There was no way she would turn down his request, no matter how silly it seemed.

"Of course. What can I do for you?"

"The roof of the VFW building will be fixed right after Christmas. I got to thinking about what the space is used for. Besides, the VFW office, it's mostly storage for my collections until someone needs to use it for an event. But I talked to Tyler last night, and the barn worked so well for the festival that he's considering turning it into a permanent venue."

"Really?" Surprise rose in Rachel's voice. She had no idea Tyler would consider this. But it made perfect sense. The hay barn was the farthest from the house and had access to a side road for visitors. There was a large field for outdoor gatherings or parking. And she remembered him mentioning adding small cabins around that side of the lake. They would be great for families visiting from out of town.

"That's what he said." Mr. Merriweather continued. "So, I think I'm going to sell the building."

Rachel waited for him to continue, wondering what this had to do with her. "I could help you find a real estate agent. I bet Judy would know..."

"I don't need an agent. I'm pretty sure I've already found a buyer." His silvery blue eyes twinkled, and a smile spread across his face.

Her eyes opened wide in realization, excitement brimming within her. She could hardly speak the words for fear her assumption was wrong. "You'll sell me your building?" Her hands trembled slightly with nervousness.

"Sure. Isn't doing me much good sitting there empty," he said. Rachel nodded as he spoke, unable to form words. Mr. Merriweather continued. "And I love what you're doing with those kiddos at the community center. You need a bigger space, and I want to unload that building. It's a win-win!" He crossed his arms over his protruding belly.

The most she'd ever hoped for was a space large enough to fit half a dozen tables. This building would be large enough for two classrooms, one for general art and one dedicated to ceramics. It was more than she ever dreamed possible, even better than the building Grant had purchased in St. Louis.

"But I don't think I have enough of a down payment to get the loan," she said, suddenly snapping back to the grim reality of money. The value of his building would surely be several hundred thousand dollars, and she knew a down payment of twenty percent was the minimum the bank required. The paltry amount she had saved, in addition to the festival earnings, wouldn't even be close to what was needed.

Mr. Merriweather shrugged his shoulders. "Well, how much ya' got?"

Rachel's eyes cast down along with her spirits. "Only about ten thousand." She shook her head.

Rachel felt his hand under her chin as she raised her eyes to meet his. Staring back at her was the same love she remembered in her grandmother's face. "You're in luck," he said softly. "The Bank of Merriweather only requires half that. You use the other half to get your supplies."

A flood of emotions ran through her. Relief, hope, a sense of belonging...she felt them all. This incredible community of kind and generous people was the best Christmas gift she could have ever asked for.

Rachel wrapped her arms around Mr. Merriweather in a joyful hug, and his bear-like arms gave her a hearty squeeze. As the tension lifted from her shoulders, tears began trickling down her cheeks, whisking away her sadness as they were absorbed into his wooly sweater.

"Since you're just getting started, we can delay your payments till you've had a chance to get going," he said, pulling away, then offering her his elbow. "I'll have Judy draw up the contract right after the holidays."

She nodded as she swiped her cheeks dry with her gloves, then weaved her arm through, and they walked into the diner together.

Brianna was right. No matter what life had thrown at her, things seemed to be working out. The pieces of her life that had been tossed into the wind were fluttering down around her and falling right into place.

A s Tyler headed back to the kitchen with a tub full of dishes, he heard the door to the diner swing open, and Rachel entered with Mr. Merriweather. Tyler's heart began pounding in his chest. He watched as they made their way to Judy's table and took a seat. Rachel's hands moved gracefully as she spoke to Judy, and her eyes lit up excitedly. After a few moments, Judy gave her a hug, and Tyler assumed she'd said yes to Grant's proposal. He approached their table, his heart threatening to beat right out of his chest.

"Well, hello there, Tyler!" Mr. Merriweather said.

"Hi everyone," he replied timidly.

"Hi, Tyler," Rachel said, beaming. She appeared to be oblivious to the pain and confusion he was feeling. There was now a chasm between them, with Grant in the middle.

"Can I get you some pancakes or coffee?" he said awkwardly.

"I'd love some," Mr. Merriweather replied.

"Just some coffee for me, Tyler," said Judy.

"Nothing for me, thanks," said Rachel. "I just came from the coffeehouse, so I'm fully caffeinated." She had a vibrancy about her, an intensity he hadn't seen before.

"And she has some news!" Judy beamed.

Tyler focused on Rachel's face and noticed the excitement illuminating her eyes. His confidence slowly drained out of him. Not wanting to hear that she was moving away, he took a step back from the table. "Um, I'd love to hear about it, but I'm pretty busy. I'll be right back with coffee and pancakes." He turned abruptly and headed towards the back. Once in the kitchen, he slammed the tub full of dishes on the counter, angry at himself for not following through with his plan.

Jack turned from the griddle and gave him a questioning look. "Everything okay?"

Tyler avoided his eyes. "Yeah, everything's fine." He blew out a breath and loaded the dishes into the sink. What just happened out there? He considered himself a friend to her, yet he completely blew Rachel off when she had something to share with him. It shouldn't matter what the news was. He should have listened to her. He needed to march himself back out there and be supportive. If he still felt compelled to share his feelings, then so be it. But he needed to allow her to share her plans, no matter where they led her.

After grabbing a plate of pancakes, he pushed through the swinging door and started towards her table, but stopped abruptly. Rachel had left, leaving Judy and Mr. Merriweather casually chatting about real estate contracts. His phone gave a buzz in his back pocket. It was a text from Rachel.

I know you're busy, but I need to talk to you.

His heart fluttered just at the sight of her name on his screen. He quickly tapped out his response. *Sure, I'm finishing up here around 11. Do you want to meet at the coffeehouse?*

I can't. I'm on my way to the airport. My mom is flying in today. Can you stop by my house tomorrow afternoon? I want to share my news with you in person.

Tomorrow was Christmas Day. He wondered what

could be so important that she'd interrupt her time with her family.

Chapter Thirty

Renovations to the ranch had been on the back burner while Tyler focused all his energies on the festival for Rachel, but it was time to regroup and figure out a plan for his future. Rachel wasn't expecting him for a couple of hours, so after enjoying a scrumptious Christmas brunch with Jack, Frank, and Judy, Tyler bundled up and headed out towards the orchard, hoping to get a look at the building once used by his grandfather as a country store.

As the sun rose over the hill and began shedding light on his path, Tyler made his way through the sparse rows of trees until he came into a small clearing with three buildings, a large one flanked by a smaller one on each side. He stood in the clearing, assessing the exterior of the buildings and calculating renovation costs. The structures were made of brick that had been painted white many years ago. Rusty tin roofs topped each building and would most likely need to be replaced. Vines covered most of the exterior, devouring the walls and crawling around the windows. The larger building was about 1,800 square feet, a good size for the store. The other two were about half that.

With a hearty shove, he pushed open the rotting wooden door of the central building and stepped inside. The vines had grown through the cracks around the windows, and dirt covered the floor. The walls were natural colored shiplap, and beadboard covered the ceiling like in the farmhouse. Shelves stretched across one wall, holding a few dusty jars and small boxes. An old cash register sat on a wooden counter at the other end of the room. Tyler went to it and touched the keys, envisioning his mother standing right there. His eyes went to the wall of shelves, and he imagined his father stealing glances at her. Their love blossomed right here in this room, and the ghosts of those days lingered all around him.

Despite the disappointments of the previous evening, Tyler felt a warmth spread through him as he envisioned the ranch's future. It was going to be perfect. The space was large enough to be divided into sections, and he quickly fleshed out a new floor plan in his mind. One side of the store would be dedicated to perishables made on-site. He could see bottles of crisp cider wine and jars of preserves, flower-infused honey, and apple butter lining the shelves. Small vignettes displaying handmade soaps and candles would fill the other side of the space.

After jotting down some notes on his phone, he headed back outside and entered the smaller building to the left, thinking it might be suitable for storing inventory. Right away, he noticed some differences between this room and the larger building.

Instead of bead board, the ceiling had an intricate pattern. He stood on tiptoes to run his fingers over its surface. It was cold to the touch and felt like tin that had been painted white. The walls were whitewashed, but years of fading revealed some of the beautiful wood grain beneath. He glanced around the room, taking in the contents. A long table stood under the windows, with two wooden stools slid underneath. Cobwebs covered the legs, and some of the crossbars were broken. As he approached the table, he saw several old jars, yellowed papers, and a wooden box covered in dust. He slid his fingers over the top to brush away the dust, then carefully tilted open the lid. Tiny compartments held dried chunks of old paint. On the underside of the cover was a label that read "Osborne's Superfine American Water Colours." What was an old paintbox doing in here? His brow furrowed in thought. There was something familiar about all of this. The hair prickled on the back of his neck.

Turning around, he gave the space a good look, then his gaze was drawn downward toward the floor. Using his foot, he brushed away the dust, revealing octagon-shaped black and white tile floors. His heart raced. The black and white tile floors, the old paint box... could this really be the cottage Rachel's grandma used to bring her to, right here on his property the whole time? His hands shook with nervousness, feeling the weight of the discovery and what it could mean for Rachel.

The wheels in his mind were on overdrive, working through the details. The room wasn't big enough for a classroom, but it would make a lovely gallery for her ceramic pieces. Thoughts raced through his head at lightning speed. The school was most important to her. If he followed through on his plan to create a venue in the barn, he could build on a small store and sell the products there, then Rachel could use the larger building for a classroom.

Tyler charged through the door and back towards the house in a feverish sprint. He wasn't sure if it would sway her decision, but optimism flooded through his heart. As his pace slowed coming up on the farmhouse, he grabbed his cell phone from his back pocket and dialed her number. His breath was heavy and labored as he waited impatiently for her to answer, but after four rings, her voicemail picked up. Trying to steady his pulse, he tapped out a text message to her.

Good morning, and Merry Christmas! I know we planned to talk at your house this afternoon. But I've discovered something on my property I'd like to show you. Can you drive out here instead?

A feeling of hope burned in his heart as he waited for her reply.

Rachel and her mother sat curled up on the couch before a blazing fire. "I love how you've decorated," Charlotte said, casting her eyes around the room. "You've really given it your own personal touch."

Rachel's heart warmed at the compliment. "These walls are full of love and happy memories.

Charlotte stroked the quilt on the back of the couch, running her finger along the delicate pattern. "This is the one Grandma made when you were born."

"It's held up good all these years," Rachel noticed. "I used to drag it around everywhere with me."

"I know! I remember finding it out in the backyard after you dried the dog with it. It was so muddy; I thought the stains would never come out."

Rachel giggled. Their little Maltese dog, Heidi, had been filthy after digging under the fence. Afraid her mother would be angry, Rachel decided to rinse Heidi off with the hose, then attempted to dry her with the afghan. Unfortunately, the four-legged lightning bolt ran into the house through the doggie door, leaving a trail of muddy footprints on the floor, the couch, and her mother's bedspread. Rachel thought for sure she'd get punished when her mother found the mess, but she didn't. Instead, Charlotte taught her how to get mud stains out of fabrics with vinegar and baking soda.

It was a good lesson, one that she still used for removing clay from a blouse. Her mother was notorious for turning a catastrophe into an opportunity. When Rachel was ten, she spilled fruit punch on the dining room chair after her mother warned her to stay in the kitchen with it. But instead of grounding her, her mother drove her to the fabric store and allowed her to choose a new fabric for the seat cushions. Rachel paid for the material with her own money, and when they returned home, Charlotte taught her how to recover the seats, good as new. The hard work and money it took to recover the chairs were punishment enough.

Rachel placed her hand on Charlotte's and felt her soft skin. These hands had dried tears, fixed boo-boos, mended doll clothes, and gave the tightest hugs. She was sad they'd spent so much time apart these past several years. Living without her mother close hadn't seemed like a big deal until now. A renewed sense of family and togetherness had bloomed in her, and Rachel felt she was getting to know her mother again.

The timer buzzed, and Rachel headed to the kitchen to remove the bubbly breakfast casserole from the oven. Old-fashioned Christmas music played from her phone, and she bobbed around to the beat. Once she filled a large ceramic bowl with fresh fruit, she headed to the dining room and set it in the center of the table. The doorbell rang, and Chloe burst through the door.

"Merry Christmas, Grammy!" she shouted happily as she bounded into Charlotte's arms. Willow scampered off to the bedroom to hide.

"It's so wonderful to see you, Mom." Brianna set down an armload of gifts and then gave her mother a warm embrace.

They enjoyed a delicious breakfast together, and the girls described the festival and all that had been happening around town.

"I can't believe you haven't talked to Tyler yet. Are you going to see him today?" Brianna asked. Rachel had filled in both of them on the breakup with Grant and her feelings for Tyler, and she loved the change of attitude Brianna showed towards him.

"He's coming over this afternoon. I wanted a chance to spend the morning with you guys first."

"I can't wait to meet him," Charlotte said. "Brianna, how is Sam's father doing?"

Brianna frowned. "Not good. They think he had a stroke. Sam's going to stay and help his mom a while longer."

"Oh, I'm so sorry to hear that," Charlotte replied with compassion filling her voice. "Are you going to be okay handling things until he returns?" She placed a hand over Brianna's.

"Yes, I've got a friend of his helping me. I'll be fine." She gave a reassuring smile to her mother.

After breakfast, Chloe begged to open presents, so they settled on the floor in front of the tree. The room came to life with laughter as they recounted happy times spent together. The backdrop of the overcast sky made the lights on the tree appear even more dazzling. They enjoyed watching Chloe tear into the gifts, sending wrapping paper and bows flying in all directions.

"I think it's time for hot cocoa," Rachel said, heading to the kitchen. She returned with a tray of steaming mugs and set it on the coffee table. A bowl of mini marshmallows was in the center, and Chloe dove in for a fistful and added them to a cup.

"We should be using your Grandma Lizzy's beautiful teacups for our hot chocolate," her mother said, sipping her cup.

Rachel stared at her, excitement rising inside her. "Do you know what happened to them?"

"Of course. They're in a box on the top shelf of the hall closet." She pointed down the hallway. "I thought you'd have found them by now."

Rachel sprinted to the closet and retrieved the box from the top shelf. She brought it to the Christmas tree and set it on the floor. The box was filled with items wrapped in plain white tissue paper. Rachel unwrapped the first little cup and held it in her hand, admiring the beautiful floral design, then handed it to Brianna.

"I remember these," Brianna said. "Grandma used to put apple juice in them, and we would pretend it was tea, remember Rach?"

The sisters sat together, unwrapping the rest of them. There were 12 cups in all, and each had a matching saucer. When the box was empty, they divided them up, then re-wrapped the cups Brianna would take home.

"Mom, where did Grandma get these teacups?" Rachel asked as she cleared some knick-knacks from the mantle. Her eyes met Tyler's caricature face, and she giggled to herself.

"Grandpa Lou got them for her. He used to drive a truck and was always on the road at Christmas. But whatever town he was in, he would search until he found the perfect little teacup to bring back to her for her gift."

"I didn't know Grandpa drove a truck," Brianna said. "I thought he worked at the hardware store."

"He drove a truck when they were first married. But he didn't like being away from his family, so he found a local job."

Rachel was only four years old when her grandfather

passed away, but she had several vivid memories of him here in the house. He bought this little bungalow for her grandmother, their first year married, and her mother grew up here. The house was full of generations of happy memories. Rachel could see her grandparents in this very room. Her grandpa loved taking naps on this couch, and Grandma Lizzy was always bustling about in the kitchen, preparing some type of goodie.

Rachel's phone buzzed with a text message, and a slight tingle went up her back as she read the message from Tyler. She tapped a response, then set the phone back in her purse, happy to be seeing the man of her dreams in just a few hours. She glanced down at her mother, sister, and little Chloe. There was nothing more important than being with family. Everything she could ever want was right here. And she realized she never lost her Christmas spirit. It was here all along in Laurel Valley, tucked away, waiting to be found, just like Grandma Lizzy's teacups.

Chapter Thirty-One

Christmas music blared over the radio as Rachel pulled her car down the snowy driveway to the farmhouse. Although she was eager to confess her feelings for him, she was curious to find out what Tyler had been so anxious to show her and tempered her excitement. He was standing on the porch, waiting for her as she pulled the car to a halt. Their eyes met, and elation swept over her. If there'd been any speck of doubt left within her, it completely vanished in that moment. There was no question in her mind about her feelings, but after seeing her with Grant at the festival, she was sure he'd been badly hurt, and his feelings might have changed. She decided it might be best to let him speak first and see where things led.

As she approached the house, Rachel's heart struck the walls of her chest, forcing a warm sensation into her cheeks. The tip of her nose remained cold, and she imagined it was probably a bright shade of red. She watched his face as a broad smile spread, the same smile she'd swooned over in the restaurant when they first met.

It was a good sign.

Tyler hopped down the porch steps and approached her with his hands burrowed deep into his coat pockets. He stood close but held a reserved stance. It was understandable, considering he most likely knew nothing about her break from Grant.

"Thanks for meeting me out here," he said casually, leading her around to the back of the house. "How was the visit with your mom?"

They walked side by side past the house and towards the orchard. "It was really nice. It's good to have her here for Christmas," she replied.

"That's great. I hope I'll have the chance to meet her while she's here." He didn't say anything else for a moment, and she wondered if she could contain her emotions much longer. The tension was overwhelming, and she wanted so badly to throw her arms around him and feel the warmth of his presence.

"I went for a walk out past the orchard this morning," he said, finally breaking the silence. There are some buildings back along the side road, and my grandfather had a little country store in one of them."

"Really? How sweet." Rachel wondered why Tyler felt compelled to bring her all the way out here to show it to her. She knew he wanted to open a store, and he could have easily told her about his plans or the condition of the buildings over the phone. Nonetheless, she was happy to be here with him and contemplated the best way to break her news.

They made their way between rows of trees that jutted

towards the bright blue sky. Brittle twigs snapped with the weight of their steps. "When will the trees blossom?" she asked, attempting small talk as they walked.

"Usually in May. Judy said they are Braeburn apple trees. They're perfect for baking and have a great flavor for cider." After a few minutes, they came upon a clearing, and she saw the three buildings, all in a row by the road. "This is what I wanted to show you," Tyler said, leading her to the smaller building on the left.

Rachel wondered why he wanted to show her this run-down shack but kept an interested smile on her face. After opening the door, he stepped aside to allow her to pass. As her eyes swept the room, a feeling of déjà vu crept up her spine, and her brow wrinkled with confusion. She'd been here before. She glanced up at the ceiling, then down to the floor, and spotted the place in the center that had been cleared of dust.

As if moving in a dream, she glided towards the table by the windows, unsure if her feet were even touching the ground. She stood quietly, looking down at the paintbox, then gently stroked the worn edges. She could feel the closeness of Tyler behind her, and the intensity of the moment caused tears to form. In a hushed tone, he said, "Do you recognize it? I thought you might like to come out here sometime and...watch for fairies through the windows."

She felt a smile spread across her face, and tears dripped down her cheeks. He knew what this place was. She slowly turned to face him, struggling to keep her emotions from exploding. At the sight of her tears, he moved closer to her and put his hands on her arms.

"Rachel, I didn't mean to upset you," he said, panic rising in his voice. "I'm so sorry."

Her sniffles blossomed into laughter, and she threw her arms around him, releasing the weight of the past two weeks into his arms. "You found my grandmother's studio! I can't believe it!" She felt his arms pull her in for an embrace, and he rocked her gently from side to side. "It was right here all this time," she sobbed.

She felt his warm breath on her neck. "I wanted you to know about all your options so you could make your own decision." She felt his arms grow tighter around her. "But I was hoping you would stay now that you have your grandma's place to come to." She let go of him and stood back, happiness beaming from her eyes. He continued. "The building next door is big enough for a classroom, and Jack wants you to supply all the plates and bowls for the diner. And I thought you could turn this room into a gallery for your ceramic pieces." Rachel just listened to him rambling on, nodding her head, and laughing.

Wiping the tears from her face, she said, "Can I tell you my news now?"

Tyler's smile dimmed and the muscles in his jaw tightened.

"I'm buying Mr. Merriweather's building." She watched as the magnitude of her words sunk in.

"Are you serious? That's great!" Tyler said, his eyes wide with excitement. He pulled her in again for a congratulatory hug.

"I know! I really can't believe it. He's going to hold the

mortgage for me, so I don't have to come up with a gigantic down payment." She finally pulled away from him, their eyes locking on each other. She saw a shadow pass over his eyes, dimming the joy that had been there.

"What about Grant? Will he move to Laurel Valley?" he asked timidly.

His statement hit her in the gut as it dawned on her that Tyler still expected her to marry Grant. In an act of selflessness, he'd brought her here, offering this cottage to her, thinking she was in love with another man. She pulled the glove off her left hand and held it up for him to see. Delight filled her as she saw the realization crash over him like an avalanche.

Rachel placed her arms around his waist and pulled him in towards her. As she gazed up at him, finally ready to surrender her heart, she saw the faintest hint of tears in his eyes. She struggled to get her words out, her voice catching in her throat. "When I first saw you in the restaurant two weeks ago," she whispered. "I had no idea what an impact you'd have on my life. I thought I had everything figured out, thought I was on the right path." She felt him pull her a little closer. "But as the days passed, you created this whirlwind of new information about my family, about this town. I started questioning everything I'd built my dream around." She took a sharp inhale of breath. "And at first, it scared me." Her lips began to tremble, and Tyler's hand rose to her cheek. "I'd always seen myself leaving Laurel Valley for something more, something bigger. But I realized there is so much here in my hometown that I haven't even discovered yet. And now, I can't imagine spending my life anywhere but here with you."

Tyler's hands rose to her cheeks as he lowered his face towards hers, leaning down to meet her lips. She sunk deep into him this time, finally allowing herself to bask in the warmth of his love. The volatile roller coaster her life had been on for the past two weeks was finally over, and her heart was filled with peace, knowing where her future was. Tyler was her knight in shining armor, rescuing her from a lonely life in a big city, and a life with no Christmas spirit.

THE END

Epilogue

It was early July, and Tyler's idea to open a store in the main building had taken off. Within a few weeks of The Laurel Valley Mercantile opening its doors, the parking lot was full of customers eager to get their hands on a bottle of Polly's Cider Wine. Tyler had initially struggled to keep it in stock, but as more and more trees bore fruit, his supply could finally keep up with the demand. He now had two employees to help with the cash register and assist the customers with their purchases.

Restoring the store had taken over three months. He'd hoped to keep the original beadboard ceiling, but a prior leak in the tin roof had damaged too much of it, and he was forced to replace it all with new panels. Recessed lights were added to the ceiling, giving the interior a modern rustic feel. The floors were refinished and sealed with a clear coat, showing off their natural age and imperfections.

Delectable food items filled the front of the store, all made with apples from the Lake Haven orchard. In addition to the cider wine, bottles of vinegar, hot sauce, and syrups filled the shelves. Jars of apple butter, spicy apple relish, apple-infused honey, and apple sauce were also among the selections. Patty kept a pie safe in a corner filled with turnovers, strudels, and Polly's Cinnamon Apple Cake, all made fresh daily.

Towards the back, Tyler created a home and spa area. He'd found an antique clawfoot tub on the side of the farmhouse a few months back and had it refinished, then placed in a corner of the store. A custom-fitted shelf was inside the tub and held bins filled with handmade soaps made by a local artisan. Adjacent to the tub were shelves filled with bottles of lotions, bath bombs, and stacks of luxurious white hand towels tied with black ribbon. A large antique armoire he'd found in the attic was on the opposite wall. The doors had been removed, revealing shelves filled with vintage tablecloths, dishtowels, and handmade quilts.

Breezeways connected the two smaller buildings to the main store, providing access to an office and storeroom on one side and Rachel's gallery on the other. The gallery's interior walls had been stripped down and given another coat of whitewash. The black and white tile floors were polished to a high shine and sparkled beneath the small spotlights scattered throughout the ceiling. Display shelves were built along all the walls, with cabinets for stock storage underneath. Rachel had arranged the gallery by color, giving the room a soothing feel. The shelves held an assortment of items in white, light blue, and natural taupe, with the copper matte raku pieces displayed on a round, antique table in the center of the room. Customers were amazed at the beautiful pieces, and word spread quickly about the Noelle Gallery.

The Laurel Valley Children's Art Center was up and running as well, hosting thirty-five children during each of its summer programs. Once school resumed in August, Rachel planned to offer classes for home-schooled children, an after-school program, and continue the weekend workshops. With the overwhelming interest in the school, she hired two staff members and accepted an intern from the local art college. The newly renovated building included two large classrooms, a reception area, and an office. The make-shift ceramics studio that once occupied Rachel's back porch had a new home in the back of the building. Sales from her pottery had skyrocketed. Rachel was already fulfilling out-of-state shipments to online customers, and her pieces were featured in thirteen stores around St. Louis County. It seemed to her that life couldn't get any better.

Rachel turned off the main road and down the side street towards the ranch with a backseat full of inventory for her gallery. The evening summer heat billowed into the store as she headed towards the breezeway carrying a large box, waving to a staff member as she passed through. It was almost closing, and the last customers were settling up at the cash wrap. Standing at the threshold of the Noelle Gallery, she stood for a moment, taking in the beautiful displays of her work before unloading the items from the box. As she kneeled to arrange a few items on a low shelf, Tyler appeared beside her.

"How's it going in here?" he asked. "Almost finished?

I've got some ideas for the barn I want to run by you."

She smiled up at him, then stood for a quick kiss. "Yep. You can carry this empty box out for me."

After setting the box on the porch at the house, Tyler grabbed Rachel's hand and led her down the hill toward the barn. The sun was setting over the lake, casting shades of pink and purple across the sky. The air was warm and thick with sweet scents from the orchard. She spotted Nick out in the paddock, leading two rescue horses towards the stable. "Rita and Ginger are filling out nicely," Rachel said, noting their slim, rigid physiques were becoming round and muscular.

"I agree. Nick's done a great job with them. Might be time to get them some fellas."

As they reached the barn, Tyler grabbed the handle and slid open the barn door. Rachel's eyes widened at the sight. The interior was illuminated with more than a dozen candles. Strips of silky white fabric cascaded down from the rafters, and green ivy wrapped around all the posts. The twinkle lights had become a permanent addition after the festival, and the tiny lights gave a warm glow to the room. Tyler led the way inside, describing the changes he planned.

"I'm having three chandeliers installed in the main ceiling beam." He pointed upwards. "Also thinking about adding a kitchen to the back for the caterers. This space was perfect for the festival, but I want to spruce it up a bit for weddings. What do you think?"

Rachel's eyes scanned the room, taking in the romantic ambiance. "It's perfect! I love it," she beamed. He went over to her and put his arms around her waist, and she reached up to bring his face close to hers. The warmth of his kiss made her knees wobbly, and they melted into each other.

He held her hands, and she was surprised to feel them shaking slightly. "For now," he said a little breathlessly. "It makes a great place to ask you to be my wife."

He pulled away from her, and her mouth dropped open as she suddenly realized what was happening. Reaching into his front pocket, Tyler produced a small gray box. Rachel clutched a hand to her chest. Tears formed in her eyes as he opened the box, revealing an oval aquamarine ring with a halo of tiny diamonds. They sparkled like the glimmers of sunlight on the surface of the lake.

"The stone matches your eyes," he whispered. "It was my mother's, and I know she'd be so happy if she could see it on your hand."

Rachel couldn't speak. She could only stare at the ring as it sparkled in the glow of the candlelight. Her eyes met his, and tears streamed down her face. Nodding her head slowly, she held out her left hand and allowed him to slip this precious gift onto her finger.

Tyler's arms wrapped around her as her chest shuddered with each whimper. She'd never dreamed of being asked to spend the rest of her life with Tyler. Dreaming carried too many risks; she learned that with Grant. But had she dared to envision the perfect proposal, it would be here at this dusty ranch, an old rickety truck outside, from this incredible man. Her grandmother's words passed through Rachel's mind as if they were being whispered in her ear. *What's meant to be will be.*

Incredibly, her life had worked out exactly how it was supposed to. She was happier than she could ever imagine, surrounded by the love of Tyler, her family, and the town of Laurel Valley.

Grandma Polly's Apple Cinnamon Cake

2 eggs

1 ¼ cup oil

1 teaspoon salt

1 teaspoon vanilla

½ cup chopped nuts

1 teaspoon cinnamon

1 teaspoon baking soda

½ cup sweetened coconut

3 cups peeled diced apples

2 cups sugar

3 cups flour

Preheat the oven to 350ᶠ. In a large bowl, mix
together the wet ingredients. Stir in the salt,
baking soda and cinnamon, then add the
remaining ingredients one at a time, mixing
after each. Place in a 13 x 9" pan
and bake for 50 minutes.
Best enjoyed when it's warm with a scoop of
vanilla ice cream!

Thank you so much for reading
"A Silver Belles Christmas."
Please consider leaving a review by scanning this code:

You can also join my mailing list and be notified of future
books by visiting RebeccaSamsWillis.com
or by scanning this code: